PREY

WOLVES OF WINTER CREEK

BOOK ONE

INTERNATIONAL BESTSELLING AUTHOR

SARAH SPADE

FOREWORD

Thanks for checking out *Prey*!

This is the first of three books that will feature Fallon Witt as an unsuspecting human woman navigating her way through the secretive world of supes. Up until this series, all of my paranormal romances in this overarching universe featured wolf shifters and vampires as the two types of supernatural creatures. In **Wolves of Winter Creek**, there will be wolves (obviously), but I'm also introducing witches!

In this world, supes are an open secret. In Fallon's case, she has no clue what she's dealing with until she arrives in Winter Creek... and, even then, she still doesn't quite understand. Not yet, at least, but by the time her trilogy is done... she will.

While this series is a standalone, the books in the trilogy are not. Each one will be an important arc in

Fallon's story, set directly after the one before it. There will be cliffhangers, a brooding, secretive hero you'll want to throttle (even as you desire to drag him out into the woods—though maybe not to do what Fallon wants to do to him), a chaotic bisexual heroine who is blissfully unaware of who she is, what she wants, and who she'll happily spend forever with until she *isn't,* and a found family to replace that one that would happily tie her up to a tree to sacrifice her to the beast of Winter Creek...

CWs: mentions of a parent's death due to illness (five years prior to the start of the book) as well as being an adoptee, bloodshed & hemophobia, an open door sex scene, plenty of cursing, a primal chase, and a cliffhanger ending that is resolved in book two.

And if all that hasn't warned you off, please enjoy!

xoxo,
Sarah

My estranged grandmother first made contact with me through a telegram of all things.

The fact that it was a telegram was weird enough. Who does that? An email, yeah. Text? Sure. Even a letter would've made more sense, but given how often I check my mailbox these days, it probably would've been weeks before I got it.

A telegram, though? To be honest, I didn't even know they still *had* them anymore.

It was hand-delivered, too, one evening after a long day at the office. Brought right to my door on the fourth floor of my building by a hunched old man who smelled vaguely like the fresh mulch laid out in front in the spring, and who looked like he might have been around the last time telegrams were the fashionable way to send off a missive.

But there he was, holding out the yellow bulletin with a solemn, "Message for you, miss."

Raising my eyebrows, I jokingly asked if he was going to sing it.

In a mournful voice, he murmured for me to go on and give him a key.

That took all the fun out of it. With a more serious expression befitting his bright red messenger outfit—complete with an honest-to-God bellboy cap—I took the telegram. I even thanked him.

He didn't leave. Instead, he just stared at me with a pair of watery brown eyes as if waiting for something.

The messenger whistled as he breathed. It was a little freaky.

Thinking he was hanging around for a tip, I handed him a five and slowly shut the door in his face. After hesitating for only a moment, I locked it. Another moment and I slid the deadbolt across.

I watched him through the peephole. He stayed there for almost five minutes; I know because I kept anxiously checking the time on my phone. I was beginning to wonder if I was going to have to text my landlord for a little help when he finally shuffled off and I exhaled in relief.

My back against the door, I held onto the telegram for a few more seconds after he finally disappeared if only because it took me that long to figure out how to open the stupid thing.

Fold the sides, fold the bottom, gently ease open, don't tear—

Oops.

I just about ripped the telegram in half, and when I finished reading the message printed inside, I wished that my hand had slipped further.

Like all the way.

My whole life, my mother never hid the fact that I was adopted as a newborn; as an adult, I appreciate that. I've never once felt unwanted, and I rarely thought about what led me to live with my mom. I'm only glad that I did. No one could have loved me more.

Mine was an open adoption so technically the telegram was *possible*, just not likely. At twenty-five, I had long ago given up wondering if I'd ever hear from my bio family. My parents had died, leaving me in the state's care because no one could find any other family. I just figured I didn't have any.

So to have received a telegram from a woman claiming to be my maternal grandmother... I had to read her message three times before I got the gist of what she was saying:

I've been searching for you... would love to meet you... take the train... you have a home here...

Just in case, I looked at the name typed at the top of the telegram in the hope that maybe it was meant for someone else. Nope. It had my name—Fallon Witt—printed on it, plus my address. It was definitely mine.

Did that change anything?

That was another nope.

All these years after my adoption and suddenly some stranger wanted me to come meet her in some small town I'd never heard of? Was she serious?

No.

No, thank you.

Uh-uh.

Nope again.

Moving away from the door, I started to head for the kitchen with the express intent to throw the telegram away. To pretend I never received it, forget the old man who delivered it, and go on my merry way.

But I didn't.

Though I'm still not really sure why, I shoved it to the bottom of the tote bag I lug to work even as I found myself thinking about the six weeks of vacation time I had hoarded.

I'm coming up on my sixth anniversary at the office where I work as a glorified pencil pusher. I spend more than forty hours a week filling out forms, filing memos, and entering pointless data into an ancient computer I share with two other girls just like me. It pays well enough for me to break even at the end of the month, but it was all I could land even with my college degree. So it's boring. If that's all I have to complain about, I should be glad. It can always be worse.

With as much vacation time as I have piled up, I could've gone to visit my so-called grandmother if I wanted to. Jeremy would have approved it, and I certainly don't have anyone or anything going on in my life that would keep me from dropping everything and traveling to meet this stranger.

My mom's gone, my closest friends all live out of state, and I haven't been in a committed relationship since things with Danny went south shortly before graduation. I've had a few flings and one-night stands when I got lonely, but I'm in the middle of a dry spell and have been for months.

So, yeah, I might've entertained the idea of going once or twice when I returned home to an empty apartment *again*.

Family... I could've gone.

Rather than putting in a request for time off, I offered to cover for Sandra and Kelly instead. And that was that, until—suddenly—it wasn't.

CHAPTER 1
BLOOD

I'm on my way home after another gruelingly dull twelve-hour shift when, for about the hundredth time since I received it, I think again of the crumpled yellow bulletin still folded up at the bottom of my tote bag.

Even after three months of obsessing over it, I'd be lying if I said I'm not a tiny bit tempted to look into this. Of course, whenever I start to reach for the telegram, I'd remember that I haven't had any family since my mom died when I was twenty. What would I do with a grandmother *now*?

Nothing, that's what. Yearning for a grandmother who's been absent my whole life just seems like a slap in the face to Mom's memory.

Besides, can I really believe this Marie woman?

How do I know this isn't just some kind of a scam? Not like I have anything a scam artist would want, but still. Jeannie once told me that my picture took the place of the word 'gullible' in the dictionary—it didn't, I checked, and I embarrassingly didn't understand the irony of that until much, much later in the semester—but I'm not *that* trusting.

So why didn't I just throw the damn telegram away? I'm not really sure, but I've read the message so many times, I have it memorized.

I'm once again running the printed words through my mind when an unexpected shove comes from out of nowhere, knocking me almost completely off balance. Honestly, it's probably my fault I was so distracted. There's always a ton of people on this street after I get out of work and, eager to get back to my apartment, I'm usually better at bobbing and weaving through the crowd.

Not tonight.

An ingrained apology is halfway to my lips before I trade a muttered 'sorry' for a hiss between my teeth. My elbow suddenly *hurts*, a burst of heat blooming along the crook of it, a lingering pain shocking me enough to go silent as I stop short.

What the—?

Cursing under my breath, I step out of the flow of traffic and look down at my sleeve. And then I look some more as if that'll change what I *am* seeing.

It takes me a long, terrible second to understand: there's a new slice in my sleeve, a tear right through the thin fabric.

Oh, I think calmly. *Too* calmly.

I've been cut.

Hm.

I poke my finger through the hole, stretching the material out, marveling that someone could have done that so quickly. It doesn't even occur to me to wonder *why* because, when I pull my finger back, the tip is slicked with red. And... yeah. There goes my calm.

Blood.

I'm *bleeding*.

Uh-oh.

I gulp, swallowing roughly as I fight the urge to flap my hand in a vain attempt to loosen my blood-covered finger and send it flying far, far away from me. My stomach immediately heaves, and I clamp my jaw together with enough force that my teeth rattle. It's better than the alternative. I'd really rather not hurl when the rush hour crowd is bustling down the busy street.

Then again, considering the way my head is spinning, passing out is definitely another possibility.

"You alright, miss?"

Someone has stopped in front of me. From the deep rumble of a voice and the shape of the shadow that falls at my feet, it's a dude. A tall dude. He sounds concerned, too.

Can't say I blame him. I can only imagine how spooked I look. If I'm not green right now, that's only because I've gone as white as a sheet once I saw that I was bleeding.

"What?" I know better than to keep staring at the blood. It wouldn't be so bad if I don't see it. Still, I can't look away even as I mumble, "Oh. Yeah." My voice is hoarse, my breath coming too quickly. "I'm fine."

I'm *so* not fine.

"Are you sure? Because you don't look—ooh, watch it, dearie."

And... there go my wobbly knees. I'm surprised they held my weight as long as they did.

I hate it. The whole "damsel in distress" thing isn't me—except for when I see blood. Even my own.

Especially my own.

It's ridiculous. I'd gone sky-diving when I turned eighteen. I watch psychological thrillers with glee. I'll walk to the corner store at three in the morning with only my wallet and my mace and never think twice about it. Snakes? No problem. Spiders? I'd shrug and capture them to release outside while Jeannie and Lorelei shrieked on the other side of our dorm room.

But a single drop of blood? I lose any and all sense, and it's been like that for as long as I can remember.

Pitiful.

From the time I was a little girl, my mom constantly worried about the extent of my phobia but, three shrinks later, she eventually conceded that I'd have to get over it on my own. We considered it a success when I stopped fainting at the sight of my period, but that's as good as I ever got.

In her intensely logical way, Lorelei tried to reason away my fears. That didn't work; all her incessant droning on ever did was help me with any occasional bouts of insomnia I might have.

Lorelei's twin liked to prick her fingers on purpose and watch me flip out whenever she was bored.

That's Jeannie for you. Great help there, right?

I do have to admit that this male stranger standing nearby actually is kind of helpful since he reacts quickly, catching me when I stumble. In the back of my mind, part of me expects him to take advantage and cop a feel, but he's a perfect gentleman.

Good. I'm in no state to go rooting around my bag for my mace right about now.

Once I'm steady enough, I pull away from him, willing my weak knees to hold my weight again.

"Sorry about that," I mumble. "I must've tripped."

Glancing up, I finally get a good look at the man. Well. A good look at *most* of him. Like I thought, he's pretty tall—he's got at least a head and a half on me and I'm not on the short side or anything. He's built like a house, solid and sturdy. His salt-and-pepper hair is shaggy and his skin is like soft brown leather. I'd put him at about forty, maybe forty-five. He's wearing a pair of dark denim jeans, a long coat, and a small crooked smile that says he knows I hadn't tripped at all.

He bows his head over my left side, his eyes on my ripped sleeve.

"You're cut," he says needlessly. "Bleeding."

Don't look, don't look—

Too late.

Crap. The edge of the fabric's tear is already stained a brilliant red. The cut may be shallow for all I know, but it definitely hasn't stopped bleeding yet.

My stomach clenches as my body gives an involuntary jerk. The autumn wind blowing a strangely floral scent right into my face doesn't help my queasiness.

His hand shoots out, taking my uninjured arm. He just manages to keep me from dropping down to the sidewalk into a Fallon-sized puddle.

Once I can forgive. Twice is absolutely humiliating. Embarrassment chases away the fear as I pointedly look anywhere but at my stupid bloody elbow.

Realizing he's still holding onto me, I give him a firm but gentle shove. "Thanks, but I think I got it now."

He lets go. The sickly sweet flowery stink fades a little as he backs away, though my stomach is still as wobbly as my poor legs.

When there are about three feet between us, he

rumbles softly, "Just making sure. I saw someone bump into you and I heard you cry out. Then you paled..."

Yup. That would've been when I first saw the blood. Jeannie used to say that I made Casper look like he had a tan whenever I was around the red stuff.

"It looks like you've been hurt." The man pulls a phone out of his coat pocket. "Do you want me to call for help? 911, maybe? I can get an ambulance here if you want to get that checked out."

Ah, hell. I must look really freaking awful. 911? An ambulance? Who'd consider an inch-long scrape and a couple of drops of blood an emergency? Especially with my shit insurance, there's no way I'm going to the hospital for a scratch.

"No, no. I can't." They'd think I was ridiculous. Forget the ER, they'd probably put me in the nuthouse *and* the poorhouse. "It's just a little—"

I close my eyes, gulp again, then try to pretend that I hadn't done either. My grin is shaky. I'm being silly and not only do I know it, now this good samaritan does, too.

I mean, look at me. I can't even *say* the b-word out loud.

"Just a little cut," I say at last. "An accident. Sometimes I lose my head over seeing the"—I gulp and spit it out between clenched teeth—"blood. Stupid, I know, but I'm gonna be fine."

For the first time, I finally meet his eyes. They're dark, so dark they're almost black. He doesn't blink. The small smile tugging on his lips doesn't quite reach his eyes, either.

And I think to myself: this is a predator's gaze.

I shiver, quickly drawing away from him. My pounding heart—which had finally begun to slow—starts up again with a vengeance.

Okay, then. Time for me to get out of here.

I offer him another grin, shakier than the first. "I should be going anyway."

"At least let me help you—"

"It's okay. You've already done enough—"

I don't know where the hell he pulled that handkerchief he's holding from. It's suddenly there as if he's had the piece of white fabric in his hand all along.

Before I can stop him, he presses it against the crook of my elbow. I jerk away from him again, but I'm too late. A small streak of my blood stains the cloth now.

The urge to hurl from before returns with a vengeance. I don't know what's worse, either: that he touched my cut without permission, or that he doesn't seem to care that he's getting my blood all over his handkerchief.

Oblivious to my horrified expression, he tucks the bloody cloth back into his coat pocket.

"There," he says, pleased with himself, "all better."

"What the hell is *wrong* with you?"

Okay. Probably not the best way to show my gratitude for his earlier help, but I couldn't stop myself. Maybe my reaction to blood is a bit extreme. Still, I'm pretty sure it isn't normal to be so happy to sop up a stranger's bodily fluids like that. I don't think my snapped question is too far off base. There's gotta be something seriously wrong with this guy.

And, silly me, my mace is still stowed all the way at the bottom of my bag.

The dark stranger opens his mouth to reply, only pausing when the phone in his other hand suddenly rings. It's a weird ringtone, too, a cacophony of cymbals clanging loudly with no rhyme or reason. Pure noise. It was enough to rouse the dead.

He glances down at the screen, tilting it toward him. It's awkward in his hand, as though he's unfamiliar with the type of phone it is, and he hesitates with one finger poised over the screen.

"Ah... I've been waiting for this," he says, an apology in his voice. Those eerie dark eyes of his rake me over one last time as he puts off answering for a second. "Tell me, dearie: you sure you'll be okay?"

So we're back to 'dearie' again, huh?

I'm so close to telling him that I'll be better when he and his bloodied hanky are gone. And if he hadn't stopped to help me in the first place, I might have.

Since he did, I decide to settle on something a little less rude to show my gratitude.

"Uh. Yeah. Thanks for—"

Hmmm... would *'giving me nightmares about wackos running around with my blood on a hanky in their pocket'* be too harsh?

I try to summon a friendly smile. It's probably more like a grimace. "Thanks for everything."

He doesn't seem to notice my less-than-enthusiastic response. Offering me a quick, crooked grin of his own, he finally jabs the screen with his thumb, answering his phone. He greets the caller in English before switching over to a language I've never heard before.

Without another look back at me, he moves into the flow of foot traffic, rejoining the crowd.

I wait for the dark stranger to reach the corner at the end of the street before I tuck my elbows in close and start to speed-walk the rest of my way toward my apartment building.

I need some peroxide, stat.

At first, I thought the knocking was part of my dream.

It was a good dream too, one that I've had more than a couple of times in the last few years. Mom was in it; instead of passing from a sudden illness while I was twenty, she was *alive.*

We were in my childhood home, me curled up on the couch, Mom sitting on her favored recliner while doing the crossword. She was nibbling on the cap of her pen, absently running her fingers through her short red hair—even if she had never hidden the fact that I was adopted, no way would anyone look at the two of us and think I was her biological daughter—when the knocking began.

Telling Mom I'll get it, I'm about to open the front door when I jolt awake and realize that I had been fast asleep all along.

Operative word being *had,* of course.

Groggy and annoyed, I roll over onto my back. I refuse to open my eyes just in case I was imagining the noise. Mom's waiting for me. I want to fall back into my dream if I can.

I cozy up against my pillow.

Knock, knock.

I scowl.

And then—

"Telegram."

Even from my bed on the other side of my studio apartment, I was able to make out that one word in a somber male voice.

Shit. *Really?*

Cracking one eye open, I turn my head to the right.

The bright red digits on my alarm clock cheerfully announce that it's currently 5:57 am.

Normally, nothing gets me out of bed a single minute before eight, even on a work day. This is unforgivable.

Maybe if I close my eyes again and stubbornly pretend I can't hear him, the messenger will go away.

It's a sound plan, I decide, and it might have worked if I didn't suddenly remember that I live in an apartment building that shares a hall with at least four neighbors. Neighbors who would know that the early morning wake-up call was *my* fault.

Mr. Laurence would know it was my fault.

A divorced man of about thirty-five, Mr. Laurence is the perfect neighbor for five days out of the week— and then there are his weekend visitation rights. The ex-Mrs. Laurence drops off their two young boys— Ryan, two, and Kevin, six—every Friday afternoon. Mr. Laurence turns into an overprotective papa bear whenever they're staying over. And if anyone pisses him off? His roar is the least of our worries.

It's Saturday. If the knocking wakes up either of them before eight, no one on our floor will get sleep for a week in retaliation. When the frat boys in 4C threw a party last 4th of July, we all learned *that* the hard way.

You don't mess with Mr. Laurence.

At just the thought of his name, I begrudgingly

kick my blankets away from my feet. 5:58 in the morning and I'm getting out of bed. Someone is gonna regret this, but at least it won't be me.

"I'm coming," I grumble.

There's no way anyone could have possibly heard me. I don't care.

I start to lift my hands, figuring I should probably try taming my bedhead, but then I purposely don't. If someone is knocking at my door this early, the least they deserve is an eyeful of me at my worst: messy hair, morning breath, and all.

Navigating my way through my cramped studio apartment, I step over a pile of dirty clothes and the tennis shoes I kicked off last night before detouring around my second-hand coffee table. I'm almost to the door when the knocking sounds again.

It seems so much louder than it did back when I was still in bed. Mr. Laurence's red face flashing through my memory, I close the gap between me and the door. Fingers fumbling, I slide the deadbolt over as I squint one eye closed and peek out through the peephole.

"Telegram."

With a frown—and certainly against my better judgment—I swing the door open. The same little old man from three months ago is standing there. The same silly outfit. The same strange mulchy stink clinging to his uniform.

He has another yellow bulletin in his wrinkled hand.

Seriously?

Because I can't think of a good enough reason not to, I take it. No tip this time; I don't have pockets in my sleep pants and my bag is who knows where. So, with a quick 'thanks' I don't really mean and that's all, I nod at the messenger and shut the door in his solemn face.

Hey. He should have known better than to deliver a telegram at six o'clock in the freaking morning.

Once I turn the lock, I glance down at the telegram he brought for me. Feeling bitter and annoyed, I come very close to actually throwing this one way. I know who had to have sent it, even if I can't imagine why she would when I so obviously ignored the first one.

Just in case, I read the return address in the hope that there might've been someone else who thought it was a brilliant idea to send me a telegram. Who knows? Maybe telegrams are popular again and I'm simply the last one to find out.

Nope. Same address—well, it's *almost* the same address. Huh. I'm pretty sure it's the same house number I memorized off of the first telegram. Same town name, too. But, for some strange reason, it has a different state printed on it. Instead of Connecticut, it says Pennsylvania.

Okay. That's kinda weird.

With a shrug, I rip off the sides, then the bottom,

just like I did with the last one. I don't manage to tear this one—I guess practice makes perfect—and I get it opened quickly.

And that's when I see that there are only four words printed in that strange old-fashioned type-writer-style font:

My invitation still stands.

CHAPTER 2
WINTER CREEK

"**A**ttention passengers. We are now approaching our next stop: Winter Creek. Last three cars, please walk forward."

Winter Creek.

Finally.

I've lost track of how long I've been on this train. Long enough that, as I stand up and reach for my luggage on the rack over my head, there's a notable crick in my neck and my poor butt is super sore. I'd been sitting for too long.

And this is my *third* train.

Considering how close this place was supposed to be to New York, I was beginning to think they were sending me back and forth on purpose before I finally found a track that would come this way.

Winter Creek, Connecticut—or is it Pennsylvania?

I haven't figured that out quite yet, blaming it on the size of the small town as well as its proximity to the border between states.

Honestly, I'm pretty lucky to have found it all. According to Google, it doesn't exist. If an app can laugh, the maps one on my phone would've cackled at my feeble attempts there, and knowing how well it keeps track of the countless Starbucks and McDonalds standing on every freaking corner, that made me just a little bit suspicious.

Especially since all I had to go on was a questionable address and the simple instruction my grandmother left me in the first telegram: *take the train.*

It cost me two days, about eight different phone calls, and half a paycheck, but I eventually had three different trains booked back to back, and a very sweet woman named Sheila's promise that she would get me to my grandma.

When I'm home again, I'll have to buy her a fruit basket or something.

No one was sitting in the same car as me. I thought that was strange when I transferred to this final train, but maybe it isn't. Not really. I mean, if even Google doesn't know about Winter Creek, it can't be a tourist's top destination. Honestly, I should probably be counting my blessings that this train stops there at all.

When it coasts into the station, I disembark from the train, rolling my overstuffed suitcase behind me.

Far from being pissed at my sudden vacation request, Jeremy had actually warned me about coming back to the office before my two weeks are up. I don't know how long I'll be staying in Winter Creek—or what kind of clothes I would need when October on the East Coast can be hot as balls one second, and freeze your tits off-chilly the next—and I admit that I might have overpacked.

Oops. Oh, well.

No one else climbs off the train with me. Somehow I'm not surprised.

What does surprise me, though, is the platform I exit out onto. After three train rides and countless stops since early this morning, I thought I was a pro at recognizing a train platform. But this? This is some-thing new.

The platform itself is just a platform: a place for passengers to gather together, waiting for the train. Cement floor and wooden beams. Maybe five feet wide, it spans the length of the railroad tracks behind me, disappearing into the distance. But where most of the other train platforms I've seen have stairs that lead the passenger either up or down and out of the station, I don't see any in front of me.

Nope. I only see the bridge connected to the platform.

The *rope* bridge.

My eyebrows shoot sky-high.

I've never seen a rope bridge like this outside of an Indiana Jones movie: wooden slats at my feet and a rope as thick as my wrist knotted all over to keep the bridge sturdy and strong. It looks as if it's been here for a hundred years or more—and that it'll still be standing even after I'm dead and gone.

But *why*?

Walking over to the edge of the platform, I glance over the side. And I understand. I mean, I don't get why they can't have, I don't know, a real steel bridge or something like that, but it totally makes sense why the town has some sort of bridge since they'd built the train tracks on the far side of a raging river.

Because that's what is below the bridge. A river that has to be about thirty feet across, with white rapids and a current that warns against anyone trying to swim in its depths.

If this is the Winter Creek the town is named for, someone has a real twisted sense of humor.

The bridge itself is swaying softly in the slight breeze. I'm not so worried about that. Sure, I'm about three stories above the ground, but the height isn't anything to me. The churning water below doesn't frighten me at all.

Nope. My only kryptonite is blood.

Grasping my suitcase by the handle, rolling it behind me, I step out and onto the bridge. I grab the rope railing with my other hand as I heft the suitcase up as high as I can, carefully making my way across.

I might not be afraid of heights, but I'm also not an idiot. One quick gust, one wrong step, and I'll be in the water—and, silly me, I left my swimsuit back in my apartment.

Despite the wind picking up, I make it across the bridge easily. I only stumbled once, about halfway to the other side. I'm not sure what exactly happened. One second I was lowering my foot when I felt a shock, a harsh buzz that made the hair on my arms stand up on end, and I fell against the rope railing, panting as my heart began to pound. Putting it down to one hell of a case of static electricity, I shook it off and finished my trip without any other missteps.

I don't know what I was expecting when I got to the next platform, but I'm glad to finally see a set of stairs that should lead down to the actual train station. At least, I hope so. My suitcase is starting to get heavy, and I really don't want to lug it that much further.

Except, as soon as I finish dragging the rolling luggage down the last step, I discover there isn't any train station down there.

There isn't much of *anything*.

Dirt. I see dirt. A dirt path that winds away from me in both directions as far as I can see.

And trees. On both sides of the narrow path, dense swaths of forest block out most of the sunlight. Even though it's only about four o'clock, it seems so much later. The air is colder, too.

I shiver inside of my jacket.

October trees are usually empty, or on their way there. While most of the leaves I see are a variety of crisp autumn shades—red, orange, yellow—each tree is lush and full. A soft breeze whistles through the branches, making the trees sway. It's mesmerizing.

After a few seconds of watching the hypnotic motion, I shake my head. The wind had started out when I was on the rickety rope bridge, but it's really whipping now, leaving me both battered and chilly. Long strands of my loose hair are flying in my face, stinging my eyes and getting trapped in my lip gloss. My jacket is too thin for Winter Creek. I'm pretty sure I'm beginning to go a little numb. I've got to get out of the cold and into a warm house as soon as possible.

And... that's when I realize the flaw in my plan to visit my grandmother: I have absolutely no idea where to go next.

Sure, I have an address, but the people of Winter Creek weren't considerate enough to post a directory in the middle of an empty dirt road. During my train rides, I figured there would be a taxi stand or something like that when I arrived; that's the New Yorker in me, I guess. Eyeing the dirt road, I'm not really holding out hope that this place is a big 'taxi' town. Uber's probably out, too.

Since living in a nonexistent train station isn't an option, I glance left, then right. Either way will work, but I'm not about to go any nearer to the trees than I have to. They grow so close together that all I can see are thick tree trunks and a sliver of fading sunlight.

One thing for sure: if I ever make good on my promise to kill Jeannie, I found a perfect site to dump the body...

Who knows what goes on in there? Or what lurks inside?

Wolves, I decide. Or maybe bears. They have bears here, right?

Ah, crap. I'm totally going to get eaten by a bear—and that's if I don't freeze to death first. My fingers are definitely numb now, and the only reason my teeth aren't chattering is because I already clamped my jaw down in pure determination.

I've got to start moving.

I still don't know exactly where I'll be moving to. My grandmother hadn't left a phone number for me to call so that's not any help, and it's not like she's actually expecting me, either.

Hmm...

Figuring it's as good a way to choose as any, I reach into my back pocket and take out one of the coins I used for the vending machine at one of the train stations I stopped at earlier.

Heads, I'll go left. Tails, right.

I toss the quarter high in the air but before it starts its descent, the sound of something moving toward me has me jerking my head that way.

The coin falls to the dirt. I leave it there.

My senses are on high alert. I can hear the beat of my heart as it thuds inside of my chest, pick up the whistle of the wind as it whips through the trees. Then there's the undeniable crackling of the underbrush as something comes closer... closer.

Squinting my eyes, I peer into the spooky trees. Too bad my vision isn't as good as my hearing. I can't see shit.

That realization only makes my sudden nerves *worse*. What the hell is out there?

If I hear a howl or some big grizzly bear comes out of the trees to eat me, I think I might just curl up and let it. Maybe. Is it possible to outrun a bear?

I'd have to try. I don't know where my brain has been the last few days because it suddenly dawns on me that, if I die here in Winter Creek, no one will ever know. Jeremy and my co-workers are fully aware that I'm on vacation—but that's all. Stupidly, it never occurred to me to at least call Lorelei before I left. She would care if I went missing.

My best friend would, but she'd also tell her twin sister. Yeah... I can't let that happen.

A small, shaky, nervous laugh escapes me as I realize that I'd rather try to take on a wild animal than give Jeannie Lipton the satisfaction of dying in some backwater town without anyone here to mourn me.

Gripping my suitcase by the handle again, I heft it a foot off the ground, gauging its weight. If I have to, it would make a pretty passable weapon.

Okay, quiet stalker in the woods. Bring it on.

I don't know why I immediately assumed the noise belonged to an animal. Probably because I didn't think anybody with half a brain would be out traipsing through the woods. Needless to say, I'm more than a little taken aback when a person slips out from between two trees.

He sees me. Stops. *Stares.*

That's okay.

I think I'm staring, too.

He's gorgeous, and I don't mean that lightly. Like, he's timeless movie star-handsome, model-perfect, jaw-dropping, *I can't believe what I'm seeing* gorgeous.

I put him in his mid-to-late twenties, perfect for me. He's just the right height, too, maybe about four or five inches taller than me—maybe 5'11' or so—and he has the sort of toned, lean muscular body that usually belongs to a professional athlete; swimmer, maybe. Though we're on the East Coast, this guy has what I think of as California coloring: his skin glows with a healthy tan, his dark blonde hair is cut short with a small wave curving the longish part in the front, and his eyes...

Wow.

I've seen some pretty cool eyes in my time. My own peepers are a strange shade, more gold than anything else. But this guy's eyes... they're the main reason I can't look away.

His irises are blue. Not dark and stormy, but pure, unadulterated icy blue. They also seem to reflect the sun because, suddenly, a whitish sheen rolls over his gaze, there and gone again as if I'd imagined it.

I blink to be sure. When I open my own eyes again, the odd effect is gone. And his eyes are still amazing.

Of the two of us, Blondie recovers first.

"Why, hello," he says, greeting me with a sly smile. His voice is silky smooth. Hello, indeed. "Come from the train, have you?"

Good guess. Of course, my big suitcase probably gave it away, but it's probably too much to ask for looks like that and a brain.

When I don't answer, he makes another poignant observation.

"We don't usually get many visitors here. I wasn't expecting anyone arriving just now, but I thought, what the hell. Let me check." His handsome face blossoms with a grin that has me going just about slack-jawed. He gestures to himself by patting his chest. Oh, do I suddenly envy his hand... "I guess you can think of me as the welcoming committee."

Considering I had such a hard time finding my way

to Winter Creek, I instantly believe him when it comes to a lack of visitors. I've got a solution for him. Slap that pretty face of his on a tourism flier and wham! Folks would be lining up to take the train into town.

I just manage to refrain from saying that out loud. Instead, I raise my eyebrows. "Really? No train station, no taxi stand... no rental cars, I'm betting... but there's a welcoming committee?"

"Mm-hm. That's precisely why I'm here. It's tough to figure out Winter Creek if you're new. I can help. If you want me to."

He starts to prowl. There's no other word for it. With both of his hands stuck securely in the back pockets of his jeans, he leans in toward me and begins to circle me as if getting my measure.

He never takes his startling eyes off me. I doubt he even blinks.

Blondie moves with a lazy grace that I can't match. I try anyway. As he circles me, I move with him, warily tugging my suitcase behind me.

For some reason, it doesn't seem like a good idea to leave him at my back while he's prowling around me. My grip on my case tightens as I lock my elbow. If he gives me a reason to, I'll totally swing it right at his perfect face.

It would be a shame, but I'd do it.

He must pick up on my intent because he lets out a laugh; it's a real nice laugh, like he's had a lot of practice with it. Blondie stops stalking me at once, resting back on his heels in a deceptively casual pose as though he hadn't moved at all.

"I just want to help," he says, his lips quirking just so. "Won't you let me?"

Following my gut, I keep moving away until there's a good three or four feet between us. I don't know why, but he seems a bit too eager all of a sudden.

I want to slap myself. You'd think I would've learned from my past mistakes by now. I know what he sees when he looks at me. A blonde chick in her mid-twenties who can pass for younger, wearing the wrong clothes for today's weather, dragging a suitcase half her size. I'm the perfect mark, even before I basically drooled when I saw how gorgeous he was.

But *gorgeous* doesn't mean *safe*, and I'm an idiot. Because where is my freaking mace? Buried so deep in the bottom of my suitcase that Blondie could take me out before I even have the chance to yank on the zipper.

Yeah... time to go.

"You know, it's so nice of you to offer," I tell him with a slightly uneasy smile of my own, "but I think I can figure it out myself. Thanks, though."

Whether he notices how nervous he's making me or not, at least he keeps his distance.

"You sure?" he asks. "Gotta say, it's not a good idea to be out in the woods at night." His unnaturally pale blue eyes gleam. "I wouldn't like to think of a pretty girl like you getting lost."

Oh. He thinks I'm pretty?

My stomach flutters. Nerves—or something else? I don't know, and I'm not sure I want to find out.

Does that stop me from continuing the conversation?

Yeah, that would be a *no*.

Taking one step closer to him, I bolster my grin. "Who says I'll get lost?"

Blondie laughs again, holding up his hands in a warding-off gesture. "No offense meant, but it's a pretty safe bet. Since I know just about everyone in Winter Creek—and I would've remembered your face, trust me—you must be new. Only locals can get around here. But, if you have a destination in mind, I can take you where you need to go. And," he adds, with another smile that I can't quite decide is teasing or not, "if you're not going anywhere special, well, I don't have any plans tonight, either."

I tighten my hold on my suitcase. This time I'm not so much afraid as I'm kind of stunned.

Is he... is this Adonis really hitting on *me*?

Narrowing my gaze on him, I search his face and find only a friendly invitation waiting there. Unless he's one hell of an actor, he's probably not a creep—or a serial killer sizing me up.

Woof. I must be bone-tired. I tend to get a bit snappish and overreact when I'm short on sleep and it has been a long couple of days. Maybe Blondie's coming onto me for some reason, or maybe he really is the self-proclaimed welcoming committee for Winter Creek. Either way, I do need help, and I shouldn't always assume the worst about other people.

So, tucking a strand of hair behind my ear, I pull an expression that I hope is as open and friendly as I mean it to be. "You know what? You're right. Sorry. I shouldn't have been so rude. Long day."

"I gotcha. And you weren't rude. We don't often get visitors, but some of the others... now, *they* were rude."

He's trying to make me feel better—and it works.

The smile feels more natural. I glance up at him, looking away when I see that he's watching me closely.

Letting go of my suitcase handle, I yank my grandmother's first telegram out from my jacket pocket. I point at the address. "This is where I'm supposed to go. If you could point me in the right direction, that would be a really big help."

His gaze flits across the page, but I pull it away before he can see anything besides the address. From the way he frowns, he's either annoyed by that—or he recognizes where I want to go.

And then he says, "The Coven House? You've gotta be pulling my leg," and I know which one it is.

Shoving the telegram back inside of my pocket, I tell him, "My grandmother invited me."

"Your *grandmother*?" He sticks his leg out. "Go on. Pull it. I dare ya."

Oh, don't tempt me, Blondie. I almost want to.

Shame that I don't.

"What's wrong with the, uh..." What did he call it? "The Coven House?"

"I didn't say there's anything wrong with it. It's just—"

As if his ears caught something mine didn't, Blondie suddenly tenses and stops talking before he's told me anything else about my grandmother's address. Glancing over his shoulder at the trees behind him, he subtly shifts his stance and his weight so that he can still look at me without presenting his back to the woods.

Honestly, I think that reaction is even weirder than our little dance from before. And then, coming from just past the line of trees, I hear it, too.

"I'll take her." The voice is slick yet commanding, a rich male voice that precedes the newcomer. "The girl... she's mine."

The girl... me?

My back goes right up.

She's mine.

Oh, no the hell she isn't.

CHAPTER 3
REMY

Even before he emerges from the trees, I decide to dislike the second guy on principle—and then I get my first glimpse of him and I totally understand why he thinks he can just claim me like that.

With looks like his, he must find it as easy as Blondie to crook a finger and have women falling at his feet. Good thing I'm leaning against my rolling suitcase for support or I might've been one of them.

Whoa.

While Blondie shines bright like the sun, this new arrival is dark. Everything about him reminds me of shadows. His hair is the color of inky tar, the straight strands pulled back into a ponytail that barely clears his shoulders. He has a deep, deep tan, but the sort of tan you get from working long hours in the sun rather than laying out on a beach or in a tanning bed. His features are overwhelmingly strong: a long nose, wide-set eyes—black, naturally—and a jaw with an edge as sharp as a knife.

No one could call him pretty, but that's what makes him so enticing. The dark and striking thing he has going on totally works for him. And yet... I still can't help but think that Blondie with his Ken doll looks and his easy-going, flirtatious nature is the more dangerous of the two.

Ponytail has a pair of golden hoops in his ears and a surprisingly friendly expression on his face as he turns his dark gaze my way. He nods once in greeting before turning back to Blondie.

His friendliness disappears instantly. Their eyes lock, both of them a little wary and neither surprised to find the other standing there.

"You heard her," Ponytail murmurs. While his voice has a harsh edge to it, he speaks a lot softer now that he's standing with us. I have to work to hear him. "She's going to the Coven House. I live at the Coven House, too, since I work for her grandmother. I'll escort our young visitor over." His smile twitches, then widens. "You shouldn't leave your post, after all."

"And you don't get to tell me what to do," argues Blondie. "You might work for Marie, but I certainly don't."

There isn't any real heat in his voice, though I get the feeling this is an ongoing argument between them.

Ponytail leans into Blondie with a wicked grin. "But I am coven," he says again as if that means something.

Or maybe *everything*.

It must have. Though the two men stare at each other with an intensity that has me wondering if they even remember that I'm still standing here, Blondie eventually inclines his head. With an exaggerated sigh, he steps back.

"Lucas will hear about this," is all he says, the friendly warmth gone. Blondie is suddenly all business.

"I don't doubt it," Ponytail agrees.

Turning to me, he offers his elbow. When I hesitate, he quirks his eyebrow. "Come, come," he says, sounding cheery and light all of a sudden. "You can trust me. *I* won't bite."

Out of the corner of my eye, a fiercely dark expression flits across Blondie's gorgeous face as he looks from Ponytail's extended elbow to me, frozen in place. His pale eyes seem to shine again—but then he blinks, relaxes, and that open, inviting expression is back at home on his face.

He nods at me. "Until we meet again."

And then he's gone. With only one last daring glare over at Ponytail, Blondie lopes off, jogging easily down a path leading straight into the woods that I only just notice now.

I can't help myself. My gaze follows him until the trees swallow him up and he's out of my sight.

Once he is, the words slip free without me even realizing it: "Who *was* he?"

Ponytail stiffens for a heartbeat before he lets his arm fall back to his side.

"He's no one. Just one of the local mutts who likes to step out of bounds sometimes." He gives me a small secretive smirk and chuckles, as if he had made a joke. "If you're lucky, you won't cross paths with him again. I'll do my best to make sure of it."

"Thanks." I guess. Sure, Blondie might have seemed dangerous for a minute there when he was circling me, but who's to say that Ponytail isn't worse? I clear my throat. "Um. I'm sorry—who are *you*?"

"Of course. Let me introduce myself. My name is Remy. Your grandmother sent me to find you, Fallon."

"You know my name," I say before the rest of what he said registers. Hang on... "My grandmother?"

He'd mentioned before that he worked for her, but I'd glossed over it. Him telling me that my mysterious grandmother sent him to find me?

Now *that's* got my attention.

"How?" I ask. "I never told her I was coming."

"You didn't have to. She already knew you'd visit. It was just a matter of when."

Remy offers his elbow to me again. I don't know why, but something tells me that I won't get another word out of him unless I take it. Which, with the lightest grip on the underside of his arm, I reluctantly do.

He's not wearing a coat. As though the cold doesn't bother him, he's got on a snug t-shirt—surprising absolutely no one, it's black—and matching jeans, but no coat. My fingers land on his heated skin. I'd expected a little chill, and the warmth surprises me. I breathe in and nearly choke when I get a lungful of... *roses?*

As crazy as that sounds, this close, the dark stranger smells like roses. Not the fake, over-whelming scent—like floral perfume—but some-thing fresh and alluring, with just a hint of spice. Cloves, I think.

Unaware that I'm dissecting his unique scent like a weirdo, he reaches past me with his free hand and easily lifts my luggage up as though the rolling case isn't close to fifty pounds. "Here, let me take your suit-case for you."

I let him do that without any hesitation at all. I'm done with lugging that thing around.

Once he has it, he says, "It's not that far of a walk to the Coven House. Only two miles. It'll be easier for you if I'm responsible for its weight."

Oof. We have to work on his definition of far. Two

miles? A long stretch of dirt road with no visible street signs that I can see?

And without Blondie around to act like a buffer between me and Remy, I'm supposed to rely on a complete stranger who already seems to know way too much about me?

Not that I should trust another guy I just met, but it didn't seem like they were fans of each other. At the very least, I doubt they're working together to lure poor unsuspecting city girls to their doom.

Unless they are...

I can just see it now. On the off chance that they do track my poor murdered body to Winter's Creek, Lorelei will shake her head and Jeannie will snort when they discover I willingly walked off with a darkly handsome stranger.

But what else can I do?

I glance behind me. The train station looms past the length of the rope bridge, empty yet inviting. There's no station, so no workers and nowhere to wait for another train except for the platform, but maybe that's a better idea.

Until Remy shoots it to hell with a casual comment that has my head jerking over my shoulder again to peer up at him.

"The train to Winter Creek runs on a very reliable schedule. On the days it stops here, we can expect it to roll in at exactly four o'clock." He pauses. "*Only* four o'clock."

On the days...? Ah. I get it. It must have a weekday-only schedule. But, still... one train that arrives at exactly four and that's all? That sounds kinda weird.

My phone is in the back pocket of my jeans. With the hand not still holding loosely to his arm, I tug it out, flipping it toward me so that I can see the time.

The first thing I notice? Remy is right on the money. It's ten after four. If both he and Blondie knew that the train would be rolling in at that time, it makes a lot more sense that they both came to "welcome" any arrivals.

But the second thing I notice? The top bar on my phone is full of dashes. No wi-fi signal—which isn't surprising—but the LTE symbol? It's gone. So is the name of my provider.

"No service," I mutter.

Are you shitting me? I can't tell you the last time I had *no* service.

I frown. Remy chuckles.

"Service is spotty at best here," he tells me. "Sorry."

Funny, that. Courtesy of his chuckle, he doesn't sound the least bit apologetic at all. In fact, as his dark eyes seem to glitter in amusement, I'm sure he finds my frustration and confusion funny.

I blame the woods and the raging river behind me. If the Coven House is two miles out from the train station, maybe these are the rural outskirts of the rest of Winter Creek.

Service is spotty, huh? It might be better closer to town. So long as I survive the walk over with Remy, I can swallow my pride and give Lorelei a call about what kind of mess I've gotten myself into this time.

For now, unless I want to sleep on the platform and wait until four tomorrow to hitch a ride home, tagging along with Remy to finally meet my grandmother is the only other choice I have.

Nodding at him, I shrug just enough to make his arm move with the gesture. "Which way to meet my grandma?"

With another quick grin, Remy begins to lead me down the dirt path; toward the left, I notice, tucking that little nugget aside, just in case.

As he does, he rewards my "lamb naively heading to her slaughter" attitude with a bit of a welcome explanation:

"I'm sure you've already noticed, but visitors are pretty rare around here. Your grandmother sent me to check to see if anyone got off the train whenever it stopped at our quaint little town. She's been waiting for months now, Fallon. I'd just about given up hope on you, but she was certain you'd come eventually."

I blink. Huh. Now, that's a good trick considering I hadn't been quite sure I'd take her up on her offer until I impulsively did a few days ago. So while my mysterious grandmother might have been expecting me, there's no way she knew for sure *when* I'd arrive.

Or, for that matter, what I looked like so that Remy would be able to recognize me.

Both guys might've pointed out that Winter Creek doesn't get too many visitors. Was it just a guess that I'd be Fallon—or did Remy somehow know who I was?

"I've never met her before," I say, suspicion lacing every word. I wonder if he would let me have my suitcase back so that I can get my mace. "She doesn't know what I look like. So how did you know I was me?"

Remy looks surprised that I even had to ask. "You're Marie's granddaughter. You might've been gone for years, but you're still one of us. Trust me. I know these things. You stay with her long enough, you might, too."

Trust me? No, thanks.

Long enough? Yeah, right.

At this point, I'm just hoping she'll stand by her offer and let me visit for a few days when I finally show up unannounced on her front porch.

But what about *one of us*?

"One of us," I echo. "You said you lived with my grandmother, right?" At his nod, I ask, "So, does that make us related?" I came here looking for a grandmother I've never known. Could I wind up with an even bigger family than I could've imagined? "Are you my cousin or something?"

"You're Marie's granddaughter, so you're definitely coven like me—"

He referred to her house as the Coven House. I just thought it was a name. But when he says 'coven' like that?

A shiver dances down my spine.

"Coven?" I interrupt. "What do you mean, *coven*?"

Remy's light-hearted expression turns thoughtful. "What do you think it means?"

I can't say it. The idea of a coven makes me think of witches standing around a cauldron, chanting and waving their hands, green plumes of smoke drifting over a brewing potion. And though Halloween is my favorite holiday, that doesn't mean I actually believe that witches are real or anything.

I shrug again. "I don't know. That's why I asked."

His lips twitch just enough that I'm convinced he knows *exactly* where my thoughts had led.

"When I say it? I mean 'family'. That's all."

Right. And that leads me back to the question I had before. "So we're related?"

Remy shifts his stance just enough so that he can peer down at me, his dark eyes burning with something I've only ever seen when watching Lorelei getting ready to devour her favorite pumpkin cheesecake: *hunger*.

I gulp.

"No," he says, his voice little more than a purr.

"We're not blood. And I couldn't be happier about that."

———————

"This is it?"

"The Coven House? Yes."

"This?"

"Mm-hmm."

Oh. Okay. "It's so..."

I don't have the words to explain so I stop right there and, basically, just gape at the structure in front of me.

Remy laughs. Not gonna lie, I like the sound of it. "Not what you were expecting?"

He could say that.

For some reason, when I heard that the locals call my grandmother's home the Coven House, I imagined it would be more like a fairytale witch's cottage; despite refusing to answer Remy before, I couldn't get the 'witch' idea that he obviously planted out of my head.

But this? This is a *castle*.

You'd think the two-mile walk with Remy would have prepared me for this. Not even a little. We'd passed enough houses once we got away from the train platform and the raging Winter Creek—because, yes, the river I crossed really is the namesake for the town —to make me feel like I've left the city behind and walked right into Stepford. Up until I arrived at the Coven House with Remy, all the houses looked the same: two-story townhouses with manicured lawns, no driveways at all, and neighbors who gave me a curious stare until they noticed Remy and simply called out a greeting.

Everyone we passed seemed to know him. When I mentioned that, all he said was that their neighbors knew—and respected—my grandmother. Once they realize I'm 'coven', they'll be friendly to me, too.

Considering the reception I already received from Remy and Blondie, I wouldn't be surprised. It doesn't seem like they get new meat in town all that often, and while I'm no supermodel, I'd be lying if I said I had a hard time attracting dates.

That had never been a problem for me. Getting one to stick around after sex? That was a little harder.

And, no, I'm not bitter that every relationship, one-night stand, and fling I've ever had has been the type to nail and bail, why do you ask? Even Danny, who I spent a year and a half with during junior and senior year at Rutgers, eventually left when our relationship fizzled out.

I say 'left'. What really happened was Danny decided that he was done, and he wanted to move on with Jeannie of all people. Despite how often I butted heads with Lorelei's twin, she was offended that Danny thought she'd help him cheat on me with her. She popped him in the nose, then told me everything as he tried to stop the bleeding that she thoughtfully blocked me from seeing.

That was the last real relationship I had, and when Remy slyly asked if I was single, I couldn't deny that I was. I can't say I'm looking for a new one while I visit my grandmother, but it's been a few months since I've gotten laid and, hey, I could do a lot worse than the darkly attractive Remy.

Especially since he lives in this freaking castle, too. From the outside, it appears huge, but if I could navigate the dorms at Rutgers before I settled down with Danny, I'm sure I can find my way around the Coven House to see Remy again.

I glance up at it, then silently amend that to: *maybe*.

The Coven House looks like someone took four massive homes and squeezed them all together so that they formed one huge structure. The front entrance wouldn't be out of place on a museum, it's that fancy with its high arches, double doors, and a winding walkway leading up to the stairs in front of it. I see balconies up top. Turrets even higher. Everything is made of this whitish-grey stone that pops against the forested backdrop that butts up to the rear side of the 'house'.

It's quiet. With a building this ginormous, I'd expect some noise to leak out—but it doesn't. Not only that, but no one is milling around outside, either.

Remy mentioned that, at any time, up to twenty family members live in the Coven House. Some are related by blood, others by history, and every single one looks to my grandmother as their matriarch.

Faced with her home, I start to have second... third... *fourth* thoughts about springing myself on her. On the plus side, at least I won't have to worry about her squeezing me in somewhere. With as many rooms as there are inside, she can shove me in one corner if she wants to avoid me.

No service means that it never even occurred to Remy to give my grandmother a heads up that I'm here. When I offered him my phone, inviting him to call if we ever find a spot along the walk where the stupid thing would work, he shook his head. So distracted by his ponytail's sway, I shoved my useless phone back in my pocket and resigned myself to being a surprise.

Only... I think Remy was right before. When he said that my grandmother knew I would take her up on her invitation... he was right. Because, as though she'd been milling around the bottom floor of the Coven House waiting for my arrival, as I gape at the building, suddenly the front doors swing in.

A woman in a champagne-colored dress that hits midway down her upper calves steps out onto the porch set in front of the house. Her stiletto heels clack as she strides toward the stairs, the skirt fluttering past her knees with every purposeful step forward.

I'm twenty-five. I have no idea how old my bio parents were when they had me, but whether it's the distance or something else, the woman I'm looking at is barely sixty. Her lovely face is unlined, brilliant hazel eyes—the same color as mine, more gold than green—sharpening her features. Her hair is a lighter shade of blonde, styled in a chignon that matches her easy elegance.

For a moment, I'm stunned. All this time I had a vague idea of what a grandmother would look like. Maybe a grey-haired, plump woman with rosy cheeks and cookies on a tray. Only too late do I realize that, without actually having a grandmother of my own until now, I've been picturing Mrs. Claus.

Yeah… not even close.

I don't have to ask if that's her, or if this is just another one of the people who live in the big house. Recognition singing in my blood, I just know that's my grandmother.

Remy confirms it for me anyway.

"Marie Bordeaux." His voice drops, a tone of reverence slipping into it as he says her name. "The head of the Coven House."

As my grandmother approaches, I stand there awkwardly, not sure what I'm supposed to do.

Do I introduce myself? Remy murmured her name, but do I wait for her to introduce herself to me? Do I throw out my arms and say "Grandma"?

No. Probably not that last one…

Lucky for me, she takes the decision out of my hands. Once she's within arms' reach of me, she lays her palms on my shoulders, pressing a kiss to one cheek, then the next before releasing me.

She smells like flowers, too, I notice. Not as dark as Remy's rose-and-clove scent, but lighter. Honeysuckle maybe? And here I am, after a full day of travel, wearing my thin jacket, a nervous smile, and probably not smelling my best.

Out of habit, I reach for my necklace. A good luck talisman if nothing else, I keep it tucked beneath my shirt whenever I'm out in public. It's the priciest piece of jewelry I own—worth a couple hundred bucks—but its sentimental value is priceless.

Just tugging on the chain, feeling the weight of the stone as it settles back in place over my shirt, is enough to ease some of my nerves.

Marie's gaze lands on my chest. "Oh. What a lovely necklace."

As if her name didn't give it away, her gentle voice has a hint of a French accent. It suits her.

"Um. Thanks." I pat the opal hanging off the chain. I didn't mean to draw her attention to it, but I obviously did. "My mom gave it to me when I graduated high school."

"Your mother? But I thought..." She purses her lips. "Pas grave. Never mind. Forgive me."

Ah. I understand. "My adopted mom," I clarify.

Her first telegram made it clear that she knew that I was adopted out as a newborn, and that she spent the first ten years of my life believing that I'd perished in the same car crash that killed my birth parents. When the state couldn't find any relatives willing to take a three-week-old baby, I was almost immediately adopted by Adrienne Witt. As far as I'm concerned, she's the only mother I've ever had.

This woman is my bio father's mother. From my

understanding of the situation, they were estranged when he died, and Marie was under the impression that my bio mother hadn't given birth to me yet. By the time she learned the truth, I was already ten, and she didn't know where to start to find me.

But she finally did, and maybe it's a good thing that she was so persistent. It never occurred to me to search for any family on my own. If I'd never received the telegram in the first place, I wouldn't have known I had any.

Marie cocks her head slightly. "And she... she did not want to come with you, no? I would love to meet the family that loved you when I could not."

My stomach goes tight. I thought she knew. "Mom passed. Five years ago, actually. It's just me now."

Next to me, Remy murmurs an apology. I nod. It doesn't matter how long she's been gone, talking about her death never gets any easier, or accepting platitudes from well-meaning friends and strangers.

"Ah, jolie. I'm sorry to hear that. But at least I've finally found you. Now you have une grand-mère."

I try to mimic the word, but my New York accent mangles the lovely French. It comes out more like "grandmere" than anything else. And that's even after a couple of years of French.

She laughs softly. "Grandmere it is, then. And you, of course, are Fallon."

"I am."

"Please. Come inside. I have a room prepared especially for you."

I wasn't expecting that. I wasn't expecting her greeting to be a kiss, either, but a room? When I only just showed up here unannounced? "Really?"

"Oh, oui. Of course. It's been yours long before I thought I'd ever see you return to Winter Creek."

A lump lodges in my throat. "So you're not mad that I just showed up on your doorstep like this? I got your invitation."

"And, like I told you in my last message, it still stands. You're always welcome here, jolie. For as long as you want to stay, consider the Coven House your home as well as ours." Marie turns toward the shadow beside me. "Remy?"

"Yes, Madame?"

She says something to him in French, so quickly that the only word I recognize is *jolie*, and only because she said that before when she was talking to me. The little bit of French I remember from high school isn't enough to translate a fluent speaker, but I do remember what that word means.

Pretty.

That's a little bit funny to me, too, because hearing Blondie call me 'pretty' before gave me butterflies. When my grandmother—when Grandmere—does it so casually in her lilted voice, I want to preen.

I'm sure they're just being nice. I need a long

shower, a good night's sleep, and my blow dryer before I can be halfway presentable, but I'll take their compliments gladly. I'm vain enough to know that my looks are probably the one weapon I have, apart from my mace and a super heavy suitcase. At least I know how to use them to my advantage.

With that thought, I turn a beaming smile on Remy as he agrees to whatever it is my grandmother told him. I'm assuming it has to do with him bringing my rolling luggage inside for me because he took one step toward the house with it before catching sight of my smile for him.

He nearly trips before he recovers and, throwing me a smoldering look of his own, starts up the stairs.

It's a good smolder. Dark and lascivious. I'll give Ponytail that.

But I didn't stumble.

Ha. Looks like Fallon's still got it.

MY ROOM IS TUCKED ON THE SECOND FLOOR, TOWARD the back of the house. To get there, Marie sweeps through the first floor, giving me a quick tour. It's a whirlwind. Starting with the great hall, she points out an honest-to-God ballroom, a kitchen, a solar room, three bathrooms, and a stuffed pantry that's bigger than one of the bodegas back home.

And then, before we reach a spiral staircase located at the far end, she shows off her sewing room. Sorry—no. It's one of *six* that are scattered around the house. Full of bolts of fabrics, a row of sewing machines, and comfy-looking chairs, Marie explains that this is basically her office. She tells me she's a seamstress, but after a few pointed questions, I learn the truth.

She's a one-woman-led fashion empire, creating dresses by hand with the help of those who live in the Coven House and work under her. The head of Bordeaux Designs, Marie employs nearly half of Winter Creek. That's why everyone loves and respects her. Without her, there wouldn't *be* a Winter Creek.

As she leads me up the spiral staircase, she brushes aside my awe at all she's accomplished. I'm not really big into fashion myself—I'm a jeans and sweater kind of girl—but when she mentions shipping a dress out for a queen's coronation, it's pretty impressive.

You know what else is impressive? My so-called guest room.

It's bigger than my entire apartment back in the city. I'm not even sure the bed would squeeze into my space in New York. It's at least a king-sized, when I'm used to curling up on a twin, and it has a canopy with pale pink gauzy fabric wrapped around the bedposts. The dresser and nightstand match the dark wood of the bed frame. The carpet is a cream color that makes me realize I'm still wearing my sneakers.

My suitcase is parked at the foot of the huge bed. And though we passed countless others in the halls during my tour of the house, it's almost like Remy has disappeared. He must have gone straight to my room, dropped off the luggage, and headed off on his own while I was busy downstairs.

That's fine. He knows where to find me if he wants to, and it isn't like I'm not dying to sit down and kick off my shoes after all the walking I did from the train platform. Throwing myself in the middle of the gigantic bed and going starfish on it seems like a brilliant plan, too.

And food. The last thing I ate was a vending machine snack I got between my first and second train, and while I'm thinking ordering food is out of the question, Marie made sure to let me know that I was free to request a meal from the chef manning her kitchen whenever I wanted to.

Then, when I must've made a face at disturbing her employee, she graciously suggested I raid the pantry should I get peckish.

Sneaking down to the pantry and finding a snack from in there? Yes, please. That's definitely more my style, especially since the smiles and nods and the knowing looks passing between my grandmother and the others in the house make it pretty damn clear that they all know exactly who I am.

The prodigal granddaughter has returned, right?

I'm going to have to get used to it; at least, for the next few days, I'll have to deal. But tonight? I'm going to settle in and hope for the best.

Turning slightly, a 'thank you for everything' on my lips, I hesitate when I notice that Marie has paused in the entryway, one arm wrapped around her slender waist, the other bent. Her fingers are pressed lightly to her bottom lip as she watches me closely.

"I... Marie?"

"Grand-mère," she corrects gently.

Grandmere. Right. "Is everything okay?"

Taking them away from her mouth, she flutters her fingers at me. "You look just like... Forgive me. I didn't realize how much the resemblance would carry on."

I want to ask. The way she's looking at me right now... I want to know who she sees. Do I look like her son? I have the same eyes she does. Maybe he had them, too. Or my birth mother? What did she look like?

What was her name?

I have so many questions, but I can't bring myself to ask them. Not yet, at least.

Not while my grandmother is coming to grips with meeting me for the first time, the same as I am with her.

So, swallowing back what I really want to say, I simply tell her, "Thank you for everything," like I had wanted to.

Marie nods. "Of course. Think nothing of it. Now, if you need me, there are two bells attached to the wall."

She points with one delicate finger, showing off the polish on her perfectly shaped nail. It matches her dress proving, again, that my father's mother is way more put together than I'll ever be. Maybe by the time I'm sixty instead of twenty-five, I will be, but I'm not holding out much hope.

Because she's still pointing, I look at the part of the wall near the headboard. Like she said, there are two bells, each complete with a pull string.

"The one on the left," she explains, "leads right to my room. The one on the right will summon one of the maids. Feel free to use either."

I smile and nod, knowing damn well that this room could be on fire and I probably would try to hop out of the second-floor window myself than bother my grandmother or one of her employees.

"Breakfast is at seven before I start work for the day. I'd love for you to join me, then the rest of the day is yours. Dinner, of course, will be at six, but I'm sure you'll want to freshen up and relax. I'll have Belinda bring up a plate for you tonight."

I have to work to hide my grimace. Not because Marie is being so thoughtful as to arrange for me to eat dinner without me having to sneak around first, but because she obviously expects me to join her at her table at seven.

No wonder she didn't seem to think twice about sending a messenger to my apartment at six o'clock in the morning. To my absolute horror, I'm related to a *morning person.* Worse, she expects me to be one, too.

And I will be. Vacation or not, I want to make a good impression on Marie, even if that means I'm up and dressed before seven a.m.

DINNER IS DELICIOUS, AND I'M NOT JUST SAYING THAT because all I ate today was the small snack between trains, and a Dunkin' bagel before I hopped on the first one.

Marie's chef prepared me a plate of steak—medium rare—plus roasted broccoli, a side of au gratin potatoes, seasoned wild rice, and a slice of strawberry cheesecake. Fresh from my shower, and wearing the fluffiest robe I've ever felt in my life that I found in the bathroom, I remind myself that I *am* on vacation and—like any good adult who left her responsibilities back at home—I grab a fork and dive into the cheesecake first.

No surprise, then, that I'm partially stuffed by the time I turn my attention to the rest of the meal. I get down half the steak, all of the potatoes, some of the rice, and a single piece of broccoli before I move the plates and cutlery over to the tray on my nightstand.

Belinda, a sweet-faced woman in her forties wearing a vintage-style housewife dress, is the maid who brought me up my dinner. To go with the food, she had a pitcher of ice water and a glass on the tray. I drink some after I'm done eating, leaving that within reach in case I get thirsty later on.

I know I should bring the tray down. Belinda seemed very friendly and she told me to ring the bell when I was done, but I can't bring myself to do it. Instead, pretending like I'll wake up in the middle of the night and want some broccoli as a midnight snack, I leave it where it is.

Then I completely pass out.

I didn't mean to. My grandmother invited me to explore the Coven House after I was done with dinner, and since part of me was interested in continuing the conversation I'd been having with Remy on our walk, I thought about seeing if I could track him down. Nope. I sat down on the bed, marveling at how comfy it was, and before I knew it, I was fast asleep.

I wish I could say I made it through the night without stirring. I needed the rest, especially since I knew I had to be up by six-thirty at the latest if I wanted to be ready for breakfast at seven. No matter how many times I peeked at my screen, I had to accept that there was absolutely no service at all in this part of Winter Creek. My phone still worked perfectly well as an alarm clock. It was set for six, six-fifteen, and six-thirty—but when I wake up to see that I conked out with the lights still on, my phone tells me that it's only a few minutes after midnight.

My first instinct is to roll over and go back to sleep. Only, now that I know the lights are on, I can't in good conscience do that. I might not be paying the electricity bill here, but if I wouldn't do that in my studio, it's messed up to take advantage of my grandmother's generosity.

It takes me a few minutes to find the light switch. Instead of the normal one I'm used to, the one in the Coven House is old-fashioned. It kinda reminds me of a doorbell, a circle with a button in the center, and it's dumb luck that I found it. I just started poking random things, hoping one would turn off the lights.

When I finally do, I'm surprised at how much light is still filling the room. That's when I notice that there's a break in the curtains covering the massive window to the side of the big bed. Thanks to the split in the fabric, moonlight is streaming into the center of the room.

That'll annoy me. I'm a back sleeper, mostly, but I sometimes roll to my side. If I do, I'll be staring right at the moonlight. The moon is a good three-quarters of the way full tonight. It's pretty freaking bright.

No, thanks.

Besides, it's my fault that the moonlight is seeping into the room. Earlier, when I was looking around the room, I tugged open the shuttered curtains so I could see what the backyard of the Coven House looked like. I don't know what I was expecting, but it was a surprise to find another dense swath of forest almost directly butting up to the back of the house.

It shouldn't have been. During my walk, Remy explained that the train platform was built on the other side of the Winter Creek for a reason. This small town was mostly wooded terrain, bordered by hills on one side, the river on another, and trees forming a natural border between this hamlet and its neighbor.

So, yeah. From where I'm standing, all I see is a line of trees beneath the moonlight—until, suddenly, something flashes low to the ground and I realize that I just caught a glimpse of an animal's eyes reflecting the moonlight.

Blame it on being half-asleep—even though I've been stumbling around the room for a good five minutes already, searching for the light switch—but midnight-Fallon thinks it's a great idea to muscle the window open so she can get a better look at whatever that animal can be.

If it's a bear like I thought before, I might wake up the entire house with my screams.

It's not a bear.

It's a *dog.*

That's what it looks like to me, at least. As soon as the window creaks open and I stick my head out into the chilly October night, the movement catches the animal's attention. Stepping out of the shadows of the trees, I make out a pair of pointed ears, eyes that seem to glow as it pads closer to the house, and a sleek body that makes me think of a husky, only with black fur.

If it wasn't for the eyes, I never would've seen the dog. But now that I have, my heart breaks for it. It must be a stray, trying to survive in the woods.

I'm from New York. Dogs belong at dog parks with their owners, not walking around off-leash, scavenging for food. I've never been to the suburbs before, let alone a small town like Winter Creek, but if they let their dogs loose to roam the forest at night, it's definitely not my kind of place.

Poor thing. Stopping midway between the edge of the trees and my window, the big dog rests on its haunches. Its ears twitch, hearing who knows what, but its gaze is pointed straight at me.

Dogs have amazing night vision, don't they? I'm not sure, but unless I'm totally imagining it, it's watching me the same way I'm watching the dog.

Then, as if to prove it, it opens its muzzle and lets out a soft whine.

It must be hungry. Considering it sees a human and its first thought is to make such a pitiful sound, it had to belong to someone once upon a time if not now.

I can't have a dog. My apartment has a no-pets policy, and I've always been more of a cat person anyway.

But just because I'm not trying to claim this dog, that doesn't mean I can't do something to help it tonight. Knowing me, if I don't, I won't be able to fall asleep, too busy obsessing over a stray dog going hungry.

Showing it my finger to indicate that it should stay right there—and only realizing how ridiculous that was when I turned away from the window—I scurry over to the nightstand where I left my meal.

The little bit of au gratin potatoes left on my plate is a congealed mess. I don't even know if a dog can eat rice, and if I avoided touching the broccoli, I'm not about to offer it to the stray.

Good thing I still have half a steak left.

Grabbing the meat between two fingers, I move back to the window. The dog doesn't look like it's moved a muscle—until I toss the steak as near enough as I can get from my post at the window. Then, rising up to all four legs, it starts toward my offering.

Once I see that the big dog has found the steak, I lower the window. Then, yawning yet undeniably pleased that the dog won't be hungry tonight, I close the curtains and shuffle back to bed.

And if I end up dreaming of wolves chasing after me for the rest of the night, I only have myself to blame.

I probably shouldn't have scarfed down all that cheesecake so quickly.

Getting up so early for breakfast wasn't so bad, mainly because I was able to slink back to my room afterward to go back to sleep. Well, no. That wasn't true.

I made a quick pitstop out the back entrance to the house, inching out onto the dewy grass so my sneakers don't slip. I'd forgotten all about last night's stray, only remembering halfway through breakfast with Marie—and about seven of her fellow seamstresses—when my grandmother asked me if I enjoyed my dinner.

After telling her that it was delicious, I purposely added an extra helping of bacon to my plate. Wrapping it in a napkin when the table was distracted, I tucked it in my lap until I could bring it outside.

There was no sign of the dog when breakfast broke up. Glancing around, making sure no one could see what I was doing, I dashed across the grass until I hit the entrance to the woods where I first saw the dog last night.

It was still gone, though it left something behind. There, in the dirt, was a pair of preserved paw prints that looked like they belong to something way bigger than a husky.

Unwrapping the napkin, I left the bacon next to the paw prints. If the dog from last night doesn't find it, one of the creatures in these woods would.

Then, my good deed for the day done, I crumpled the napkin up, shoved it in my back pocket, and decided it was time for a small nap.

When I wake up again much later, I unpack my luggage. Over breakfast, I gave a tentative date for when I'd be heading back to New York. My grand-mother invited me to stay for as long as I want to, so I decide on sticking around for at least a week. Since I don't want to live out of my suitcase, I move everything into the empty dresser before putting all of my toiletries into the attached bathroom.

After that, I run out of things to do. There's no internet in the Coven House to go along with no service, so my phone is basically useless as a distrac-tion. If Marie has any televisions, I haven't seen one yet. Lucky for me, I have a couple of books I packed for just such a scenario, but I want to save them if I can.

Something tells me that the long hours while Marie is busy at work won't get any easier.

Just a little before dinner is scheduled, I go looking for Remy. He wasn't at breakfast this morning, and I'd expected Ponytail to stop by before now. I'd be lying if I said that I didn't notice there was a hint of a spark passing between us during our walk and... well, a girl's got eyes. If my grandmother is too busy with work to keep me company, I'm okay with spending some of my vacation with Remy.

Too bad I have no idea where to start looking for him.

After wandering around for a while, peeking into open doors and tiptoeing quickly past closed ones, I nearly bump into a young woman in a long black dress as I turn another corner. About my age, she has her rich brown hair pulled back in a low bun and is holding a basket of rose petals of all things. When she sees me, she tightens her grip on the handle.

Weird.

I smile over at her. "Excuse me. Hi. I'm—"

"Yes, miss. I know who you are." Her gaze dips to my chest. No. To my *opal*. "Are you looking for Madame? She's in a meeting, but I can bring you to her."

"Oh, no. No. That's okay. Actually, there was a guy I met yesterday I was looking for. Black hair. Ponytail."

"Remy Gauthier?"

Sure. "Yeah. Remy. Have you seen him around?"

"Madame sent Remy and two other couriers to the town square to make deliveries. If he doesn't eat there, he'll be back for dinner."

Bummer. "Thanks. I appreciate it."

She ducks her head, then continues past me and down the hall.

No Remy. I should've known better. If my grandmother is busy with work, why wouldn't one of her employees be? The woman I ran into is probably rushing to bring the rose petals to one of the sewing rooms for some reason.

I have to remember that, just because I'm on vacation, that doesn't mean these people are. I'll also have to find another way to entertain myself—and, whether she knows it or not, the woman with the basket gave me the perfect idea.

Town square. Now, I don't expect it to be like Fifth Avenue or anything, but maybe they have somewhere to shop. They obviously have somewhere to eat. I might be able to people-watch, too, something I like to do when I'm taking my lunch at the office outside.

Suddenly, things are looking a little brighter about my visit to this quaint and cozy small town.

On my third morning in Winter Creek, I finally decide to go check out the town square. The last two days, I picked up enough from conversations with my grandmother and the rest of the 'coven'—her name for the workers who live with her in the manor—to have a good idea of how to find it without asking for explicit directions.

I don't tell Marie I plan on taking the walk over. After one of the maids told her that I leave the house after breakfast every morning to feed the dog that comes to my window every night, she made a suggestion that I spend my visit inside of the house.

But it's only a *suggestion*. She follows it by telling me that she wants me to enjoy my time in Winter Creek, and how can I do that if I never see the rest of the town?

It's not so far. After the two-mile walk from the train station, the fifteen minutes it takes to go from the Coven House to the edge of the square seems like nothing.

The trip was totally worth it, too. Built like an outdoor, suburban mall, it's designed in a big square, with exits that lead to all four corners of Winter Creek. There are more stores than I can count at first glimpse, at least three different restaurants, and an array of filled benches.

Makes sense. When this is the one big gathering

spot in a tiny town, why wouldn't it be packed during mid-morning?

It's a little weird, though. I thought I got past how strange it was that this place barely has any modern tech. I haven't touched my phone in days. There are no cars, and everyone seems happy to walk wherever they have to go.

Then I start to see some of the other townspeople who live in Winter Creek and realize that my earlier Stepford vibe was spot-on. All the guys are walking around with short haircuts and business casual clothes. The women are all in dresses just a step down that the masterpieces Marie wears.

And everyone looks at me like I'm an outcast.

I guess I am. At the very least, an outsider. The townspeople are friendly enough, though, even if I get stared at in every store I visit. They wave and smile, probably because gossip has spread and they all know Marie's granddaughter is in town, but not one says more than a few words to me until I'm just about ready to head back—

"Look at you... when I didn't see you again, I was beginning to think you were nothing more than a daydream."

I know that voice. I've only heard it once before now, but it definitely lodged itself firmly in my memory. By the time I'm turning to greet him, I've prepared myself for Blondie's dazzling smile, pale blue eyes, and stunning features.

It's so good to see a friendly face—and one who actually looks happy to see me, too.

"Blondie! Hi!"

He's only stunned at my enthusiastic 'hello' for a second or two, though it might be the way I used my nickname for him out loud.

Whoops.

But he recovers quickly, I'll give him that, as he moves until we're within arms' reach.

Does he have any sense of personal space? I'm beginning to think not.

Surprisingly, I don't really mind. "How are ya?"

"I'm good, thanks. And it's Tristan, by the way." His lips twitch into a charming grin. "But you can call me 'Blondie' if you want."

He looks like a Tristan. If I could pick any name for this blond god, it might've been that one.

And, yeah... he's totally flirting with me.

Why not flirt back?

"Okay." I wait a beat. "*Blondie*."

"What about you? I don't think I caught your name the other day."

Probably because I didn't throw it. "Fallon. My name is Fallon."

"Fallon," he echoes. "I like it. It suits you."

"Thanks. Glad you approve."

His eyes light up. "Ooh... you got a little bite in you, don't you?" Tristan crosses his arms over his chest, leaning back on the heels of his shoes. "Are you trying to be my perfect mate or am I just lucky?"

Mate? What a weird way to say 'friend' like that, especially since I could've sworn Tristan is American. Isn't that a British or Australian thing?

It doesn't matter. He's just being a shameless flirt—and, not gonna lie, I'm totally digging it. After how strong Remy came on when we first met, his sudden disappearance stings a little. I'm not the best when it comes to rejection. Blondie—*Tristan*—seems like a sure thing if I want a whirlwind October romance.

That's why, instead of nipping this chat in the bud, I let it continue.

"You'll have to wait and see."

He raises his eyebrows. "That sounds like a dare to me."

I shrug.

His lips curve into a wicked grin. "A challenge. You don't know this about me yet, Fallon, but I love a challenge."

"Yeah?" It's another dare, but I'm having too much fun playing along to wonder if this is a dangerous game. "So do I, but I love to win."

"Another thing we have in common. Hopefully, that means you're sticking around for a while... I mean, if you're gonna play."

Again, I say, "We'll see."

"What do you think about Winter Creek?" he asks. "Not the type of place you'd want to make your forever home?"

Why does he say that like I'm a stray?

I don't know, but it rubs me the wrong way. Getting a little prickly, I tell him, "My phone doesn't work, I haven't seen any of my shows this week, and whoever named this place has a funny sense of humor."

At Tristan's confused look, I go on and explain: "The Winter Creek the town is named for? I've seen creeks. You just step over them without needing a bridge. That thing? That's a raging river."

Understanding flashes across his face. "Gotcha. But, you know... there actually is a creek. Hidden in the woods, there's a waterfall that feeds the creek before it widens into a river. It's close to my house. If you want, I could show you sometime."

Interesting. I snap at him about the things in Winter Creek that bother me, and he responds by inviting me to see the real Winter Creek. Flirtatious and good-natured? Plus gorgeous?

Sign me up.

"I'd like that. Before I leave, I'll have to—"

I don't know what it is that catches my attention so swiftly, or why I'm suddenly looking past his shoulder like a moth being drawn to a dazzling flame. I just... I can't look away.

On the far side of the square from where I'm standing with Tristan, I notice that someone is standing on the edge of the exit, backed by even more trees. I can't make out too many details. He's tall. A white guy with a notable tan, and black hair that matches his t-shirt and his jeans.

He's staring right at us.

At *me*.

I shiver. Like there's some kind of thread stretching between us, now that I see him there, I have to resist the tug I feel toward him.

Is it Remy? The dark clothes and tanned skin makes me think so, but I don't know. He didn't have a problem coming between me and Tristan the last time we chatted, but this guy hasn't moved a muscle.

"What are you looking at? Have I already lost your attention so soon?"

Tristan's teasing tone has me jerking said attention back to him.

"Sorry. I thought I saw something."

Following the direction I'd been looking in, Tristan glances over his shoulder before catching sight of the dark-haired guy watching us from a distance.

To my surprise, the figure standing in the shadows actually nods at Tristan.

Tristan moves closer to me before waving back.

Okay, then.

Definitely not Remy.

TRISTAN

Turning his back on the other man, Tristan clears his throat. "Where was I?"

Out of the corner of my eye, I watch as the dark-haired man disappears into the shadows of the trees. Only when he's gone do I meet the curious expression written on Tristan's pretty features.

"Sorry," I say again. "I was just thinking about how a much better name for this place would be, like, the Wooded Grove or something. There are so many trees here."

"It's part of the town pact. The trees were here before the rest of us. The creek, too. They should get to stay. Ask your grandmother. She'll agree with me about how important nature is."

He might be right. That maid carrying a bucket of rose petals was only the first one I've seen in the Coven

House. Sometimes they have other flowers, sometimes potent herbs, but they constantly bring them to the main sewing room that serves as Marie's office.

"Speaking of your grandmother," Tristan says, "I'm surprised she let you out of her clutches. And what about your bodyguard?" He takes a deep breath. "I could've sworn I scented him slinking around."

Bodyguard? *Scented*? "You mean Ponytail?"

He barks out a laugh. "You got a thing with nick-names, don't you?"

"Sometimes," I admit. "I wasn't sure if you knew his name."

"Remy? Oh, yeah. We go way back." Tristan shows me his teeth. You could call it a smile if you hadn't seen the way the two butted heads the other day. Since I did, I don't.

"I haven't seen him since he brought me to my grandmother's," I admit. "He's been busy."

"Sure he has." Tristan snorts. "That's his loss, even if I'm still surprised Marie doesn't have him trailing you."

"And why would she do that?" I ask.

Winter Creek doesn't just remind me of Stepford. It has a real small town, Mayberry-thing going on. Since settling in, I haven't felt like I needed to go reaching for my mace once.

And then Tristan says, "Because of the monster in the woods, of course."

He has to be joking. "The *what*?"

"The monster. Comes out when it's dark... you know. Because of the curse."

I'm sorry? "The what?"

"Don't tell me you haven't heard about the curse of Winter Creek yet."

Okay. He's just fucking with me now. I'm the new girl, and he's having fun making up stories to feed me. Like alligators in the sewers of New York or the Jersey Devil, it's probably some local legend he pawns off on every visitor, no matter how far and few between they are.

But because this is the most fun I've had in days, I go along with it.

"No. I can honestly say that she hasn't."

"She wouldn't, would she? Not if she wants you to come back again. But it's true. Whole town is cursed, thanks to the beast."

"A beast," I echo wryly. "What kind of beast?"

"Depends on who you ask. Some say a... werewolf, I guess. Some say it's closer to Bigfoot. Some say it's a *feral* who will haunt the woods until the curse that creates it is broken." He nudges me in the shoulder with his elbow. "Rumor has it that it'll take one special girl to break it. What do you think, Fallon? Do you have what it takes?"

I snort. "Hardly."

Tristan turns that dazzling grin on me. "I guess we're just going to have to see about that."

Uh, no.

No, we are not.

As much as I don't want to believe Tristan's stories, there's a part of me that remembers the strange dog watching me the last couple of nights—and the pretty big paw prints I find in the morning. All along, I've convinced myself it's an oversized stray. Who knows? Maybe it's a beast.

And, okay, maybe I'm just looking for an excuse to hang out with him just a little longer.

Either way, when Tristan offers to walk me back to the Coven House—another hint of that old-fashioned chivalry that just seems to suit the nostalgic vibe Winter Creek gives off—I take him up on it. And when he mentions that he's free Sunday afternoon and would like to have lunch with me... well, I take him up on that, too.

We separate when the high roof on my grandmother's home rises high above the trees in the distance. Even Tristan is confident I can find the rest of my way there. Since he has something to take care of at his own home, he explains he's going to use the shortcut through the forest to get there faster. With one last reminder to meet up with him on Sunday, he disappears.

Which is definitely a good thing because, when I start toward the Coven House, I find my grandmother waiting for me on the front steps.

Her hands are folded primly in front of her. It's the middle of the afternoon, during the time when she's usually in meetings, and she looks like she's been expecting me for a while.

Uh-oh.

I haven't felt like this since before I lost my mom and she caught me sneaking out to see my boyfriend of the hour back in high school. The expression on her face when she inevitably found me trying to climb into my bedroom is ingrained in my memory.

Adrienne Witt and Marie Bordeaux look nothing alike. They're not related in any way.

And yet... my grandmother has the disapproving look down pat.

"Did you enjoy yourself in town, jolie?"

Yup. Fifteen or twenty-five, it doesn't matter. The guilt twists my insides, warring with the need to remind Marie that I'm a grown woman.

Instead, I nod. "I did, actually. Thanks."

She purses her lips. "Make any new friends?"

There's something in the way she says that. She knows. No clue how, but she knows about me running into Tristan like that.

I immediately go back to the dark-haired stranger I caught watching us from a distance. It had been too far to see if he had a ponytail or not so while I doubted that it was Remy the second he nodded a greeting to Tristan, maybe I was wrong.

How nice. I haven't seen him since Monday, and the one time I do? He snitches on me to my grandmother.

"I wouldn't say friend," I edge carefully. I don't know what exactly Tristan is—or could be—but friend? Not quite. "He was just some guy who was telling stories to the new girl in town."

"Is that so?"

Yes, and it gives me the perfect distraction.

"Mm-hmm. He told me that the woods around your house has monsters in it. Is it true, Grandmere?" I purposely put a little tease in my tone. "Is Winter Creek really cursed?"

My ridiculous questions do exactly what I hope they would. Rather than look annoyed with me, Marie scoffs.

"Please. The only curse this town has is foolish boys taking advantage of my granddaughter. And in the square of all places."

Again. I'm twenty-five. It'll take a little more than sweet-talking and tall tales for a guy to take advantage of me. I haven't even had lunch with him yet.

That thought in mind, I decide not to mention my

date with Tristan to Marie for the moment. Someone definitely got back to her, telling my grandmother that I was spotted with Tristan, because how else did she know that my new 'friend' was a guy?

And why does she seem so put out that I visited the square in the first place?

"Was that wrong? Am I not supposed to go there?"

"No one owns the town square," Marie says cryptically. "But that doesn't mean you shouldn't be careful."

She does have a point there.

I nod. "Yes."

She clears her throat.

"Yes, Grandmere."

"C'est ma jolie."

I THINK I PISSED MY GRANDMOTHER OFF.

She's too classy—and, okay, arrogant—to say so. The most I get is a disapproving sniff whenever I mention taking another trip to the town square when we're sharing meals, but I lived with Jeannie Lipton for four years. She's mad, and I'm too wary of making her more annoyed by bringing it up or even informing her about my upcoming lunch date on Sunday.

The chasm between us is there, though, and it bothers me that I have no idea what I did wrong to create it.

At first, I think she's ticked off because she didn't want me wandering around on my own. Like it makes her look like a bad hostess or something.

But what did she expect me to do? Lock myself in my guest room and twiddle my thumbs until it's time to go home?

That's the thing. I never see my grandmother during the day. She's too busy with her work, and I don't need her to hold my hand to explore the rest of Winter Creek.

Maybe if I had had some way to tip her off to my visit before I suddenly showed up here, she might have taken a break of her own—and I don't know who I'm kidding. I've learned enough about Marie Bordeaux to know that her business is her life. I'm pretty sure the word 'vacation' isn't in her vocabulary. The French version, either.

She also isn't the sort of woman who window shops. If she wants something, she snaps her fingers and it's hers. Same thing with eating at one of the small cafes or restaurants. When she has a private chef in her own kitchen, what's the point?

Then I begin to wonder if she didn't like me having a chat with Tristan. I already knew he wasn't the biggest fan of the Coven House or Remy, and it seems as if my grandmother's distaste for Blondie rivals his.

But two days later, shortly after we finish dinner Friday night, when Marie comes striding into my room, followed by a pair of maids each holding a beautiful dress in front of her, I accept it might actually be something so simple as my grandmother having a reputation to protect.

With a nod, she instructs the two maids—Belinda and a grey-haired woman I haven't met yet—to lay the dresses out on the edge of my bed.

I was lying back against the mound of pillows at the headboard. As the maids curtsy and leave Marie and me alone, I climb out of the bed and move closer to her.

"Grandmere? What's this?"

"For you, jolie. I just finished making these. Something more fitting for my granddaughter when she visits the square."

I'm not an idiot. I know that I stick out like a sore thumb when every woman I've seen in Winter Creek is wearing one of my grandmother's elegant designs. I can't tell if it's because they all work for her or it's just the fashion of the small town that vintage-style dresses are 'in' right now, but my sweater, jacket, and jeans definitely marked me as an outsider.

Of course, when I popped my head into a boutique that sold Marie's designs, I almost had a coronary. Unless I wanted to drain my entire savings account, there was no way I could afford even the simplest-looking dress.

And now my grandmother had brought me *two* of them.

The one on the right is the same champagne-color satin that my grandmother seems to favor. The other is a soft lilac shade with a floofy tulle skirt that would hit my upper calves once I slipped it on.

Running my fingers over the tulle, I can't help but admire how gorgeous it is—and I tell Marie so.

"Thank you. These are for you. Daytime wear, and for your walks. I have another few designs in the works for you to add to your wardrobe. And, of course, I'll make you something more fitting for the evening soiree before it's held."

I look up from the dress I'm basically fondling. "Soiree? Like, a party?"

"That's right. To celebrate your return back to the family."

Oh.

Now, I made it clear that this was just a visit. It takes close to half a day of travel for the trains to bring me from New York to Winter Creek, and now I know that I'll have to be at the station before four when I'm ready to leave. It might not arrive every day, but it has to stop here sooner or later, and then I'm going back to the city.

I've said from the beginning that the longest I can stay is about a week and a half. But every time I mention that this is a *visit*—that I haven't *moved* to Winter Creek—she conveniently changes the subject.

It's not worth reminding her again.

So, instead, I ask, "When's this party?"

"Don't worry, petite fille. It's tomorrow, but I'll have your dress to you in well enough time."

What? *Tomorrow*?

There's no way I'm getting out of going to this party. I've only known her for five days now, but Marie is not the type of woman you refuse. If she says she's throwing a party for me, I'll be there.

I don't need another dress, though. This lilac dress should do the trick.

Patting the tulle skirt, I tell her, "You don't have to make me another dress. This one is perfect."

"Perhaps. But I think, yes... I think, with your face, a peach gown would be best."

If she says so. "I don't want you to go to any trouble—"

"It's no trouble at all," Marie insists. "Besides, what I can do with fabric, ma jolie... it's just like magic."

CHAPTER 7
CURSE

I assumed the party would be hosted at the Coven House.

Logical guess. I mean, Bordeaux Manor—the actual name for the huge house—has a closed-off ballroom specifically for when Marie wants to host parties. Since this one is supposed to be my 'welcome' into her family, it just made sense to me that it would be held here.

The next morning at breakfast, she mentions that we'll have to leave shortly after sunset to make it on time. That surprised me, until she goes on to explain that some of her dear friends—her *amis*—offered to act as the host so that Marie could be free to introduce me to everyone attending.

These friends don't live in the Coven House. Instead, they have a manor of their own not too far from my grandmother's. It's within walking distance, though the easiest way to get there is by taking a shortcut through the dark forest that guards the back of Marie's house.

From what I've learned these last few days, everything in Winter Creek is within walking distance. The town square is where most residents congregate, but while most of the locals who work under my grandmother live in the Coven House, not all of them do. There's another branch on the western border of town, near the far hills that cut Winter Creek off from the rest of... wherever we are.

I'd asked Marie on three separate occasions where precisely Winter Creek is located and, with a secretive smile, she'd given me a different empty answer each time. Between the raging river, the dense woods, the eerie Stepford set-up, and the hills in the distance, I've decided it's its own little hamlet. Almost like it's apart from the rest of the United States.

That would certainly explain the lack of street signs, why no one seems to use a car, or how there are no television cables, phone lines, and internet access. It's like time seemed to stop in the small town, or someone in charge simply forgot about this place—and no one else wanted to be responsible for it—so the residents continued to take matters into their own hands, leaving it as a monument to the past.

Like relying on telegrams, and having a train that

stops once a week if they're lucky. What's the point? No one ever visits, and no one ever leaves.

Except for me, that is. I accepted my grandmother's invitation to visit, and when my vacation is up in a week's time, I'll be taking that rare train right out of this place.

I arrived on a Monday. The train stopped then. Here's hoping that it'll roll into the station by next Monday at the latest so I can head back to my apartment—and that Jeremy won't be annoyed that I'll be a 'no call, no show' that day since I'll be due in to work that morning, hours before the train arrives and no way to give my boss a heads up.

But that's next week Fallon's problem. Current Fallon is hurrying to get ready in time for tonight's soiree. Marie brought me a dress that she—as she boasted—seemed to whip up by magic, insisting that I try it on to make sure it's my size.

It's gorgeous. A peach-colored chiffon dress that fits me like a glove, and makes me feel like I really do belong in the 1950s. Of course, that was what my grandmother was going for. This isn't just a cocktail party, she explains; it's a themed party, and the dress plus the white pumps she provided are perfect for it.

The rest is up to me. Using the small amount of make-up I packed in my luggage, I do my face. I try to emulate Marie's chignon, but that's a lost cause. The most I can do is twirl strands of hair around my fingers to give my wavy hair a little more oomph and hope for the best.

I think about removing my necklace. I can't remember the last time I took it off—probably back during my PE days—and I don't like the idea of leaving it behind even for one night. In the end, I decide to keep it on. My grandmother had complimented it before, and it's not like the old-fashioned opal doesn't match the vibe going on with my vintage dress.

During one of my infrequent chats with Remy—who seems to be avoiding me these last few days, not gonna lie—he mentioned that there isn't a single paved road in Winter Creek. I believe it. The path from the train station is stamped dirt, and the trail that led me to the town is a mix of pebbles, gravel, and heavily-traveled earth.

Did I expect there would be a nice road through the trees leading from one side of the woods to the other? Not really.

Would it have been nice so that I didn't spend half the trip trying not to break the heel on my shoe—or one of my ankles? Oh, yeah.

Do you know what the downside to leaving after sundown is? It's dark. Throw in the closely grown trees and it's nearly black beneath the caps of autumnal leaves. I'm already uneasy, and Tristan's teasing about a "curse" and a "beast" pops into my brain at the most inopportune moment.

Having crossed this way countless times, Marie knows what to expect. She has an oversize tote slung over her delicate shoulder, an honest-to-God lantern held in front of her. The flame flickers gently, giving just enough light to help guide our way.

We don't speak as I walk right behind her. She seems intent on leading us forward, while—and I'll admit it—I'm listening for some sign that we're being stalked by an unseen predator.

It's just the two of us. You'd think that another one of the 'coven' would have accompanied their matriarch and the outsider, but that isn't the case. Just another way my grandmother shows she's in control, I figure.

After we've been walking for about twenty minutes, she stops suddenly. Close on her heels, I do the same.

I can't see what she's doing ahead of me. Actually, I can't see anything at all.

The flame on the lantern has gone out.

A lump lodges in my throat. I swallow it roughly, then inch closer to my grandmother's back.

"The light's gone out," I say needlessly.

"Mm."

"Do you have... I don't know. A lighter? A match? I can help you relight it."

Please let me help you relight it.

The only response I get is the whisper of her skirt as she steps away from me.

My night vision is crap. Add that to how I'd gotten

so used to the lantern that, without it, I'm basically blind and the most I can see is the pale fabric of her dress as it gets swallowed up by the shadows surrounding us, and it's no surprise that my heart rate kicks up.

"Grandmere?"

Nothing.

"Grandmere? Where did you go?"

The lantern is still dead. How is she walking away without it? It's almost like she can see in the dark.

That probably should have been my first clue that something isn't right. Her continued silence is another.

And then her accented voice cuts through my rising panic, and I'm finally tipped off when she says, "Boys. Come out now."

Maybe I really am as gullible as Jeannie thinks because, for one bewildered moment, I get the idea that the themed costume party is actually a surprise party for me out in the woods. And then I hear a snapping sound, followed by a soft grunt, and sense movement.

I blink rapidly, desperate to get some kind of sight. It doesn't really work, but as though some higher power is looking out for me, the clouds covering the full yellow moon part, allowing enough light to filter through the leaves.

Two bulky shadows become a pair of men. The moonlight reveals their features, which is a good thing considering they're dressed in head-to-toe black. In the case of Remy, his hair matches the shadows. The other man has a head of hair more grey than black, and a familiar face that I don't really focus on because I'm gaping at the blank expression on Remy's.

There's no flirtatious grin. No smirk. No hunger, either. Like a robot waiting to be programmed, he steps out because my grandmother gave him the order and now he's expecting another.

My stomach drops to the forest floor. "Remy? What's going on?"

His gaze darts to the side. "Just do what you're told, Fallon. Okay? You're coven. You want to help us, don't you?"

Help them? Help them with *what*?

"Maybe. I guess. But—"

"I thought so. See? This doesn't have to be difficult—"

Remy is cut off when my grandmother says something in a litany of French. I don't understand a word of it, but the older man snickers while Remy hangs his head.

I hear a snap. The striking of a match, my nervous brain interprets, a split second before the lantern flickers back on.

I wince. Being plunged into darkness before had been rough, but the sudden flare of the lantern turned on high? It *hurts*.

Marie hands it off to the older guy.

Once I have my sight back, I notice that the light is illuminating the other man's face. It winks off the tanned skin, the deep lines, the wrinkles that make him seem even older than before. Next to Remy, I'd say he was at least the same age as Marie.

It also hits me why I thought he was so familiar before. I *have* seen him—and he looks like he's aged more than twenty years in the last two weeks.

"Wait. I know you. You're the one who helped me after I got cut on the street." Flashing back to that evening, I add, "You sopped up my blood with your hanky!"

He nods. "Dearie."

I just... what happened to him? He got so *old*.

He can tell from my expression what I'm thinking, too. Raising his free arm, he rubs his chin with his palm, then strokes his cheek with the back of his hand.

"Aye. I know. But if it breaks the curse and frees us all, it'll have been worth it."

Curse.

My back goes ramrod straight.

Curse.

Marie told me that Tristan was being ridiculous by mentioning a curse. That it was preposterous. Winter Creek was a quaint town. There was no curse.

So why is this dark not-such-a-stranger bringing one up now?

After my grandmother handed the lantern off to him, she began to root around inside of the tote she shimmied off of her shoulder. Before I can say another word about the curse, she lifts her head and says, "Armand. Enough. You volunteered to go searching for her. You knew the risks."

"I did, Madame."

"And you did well. You brought mon jolie home. And tonight this terrible curse finally ends."

I'm sorry—*what*?

"So there *is* a curse?"

"Mm," Marie says, drawing something out of her bag. "Further proof that you've been changed. A true witch would've known I was lying."

Am I sleeping? Did I doze off after my shower and I'm dreaming this insanity? Because that's the only logical explanation I have for what the hell is going on right now.

And then my grandmother sets her tote on the earth, her hands full of—

Rope? Why does she have rope?

Oh, no. Oh, no, no, no...

Okay, Fallon. You're in the woods, with people you don't know half as well as you thought you did, talking about curses and witches—and now you grandmother is looking at you with a gaze that is pure predator.

Almost like she's the big, bad wolf in an old fairy-tale instead of the kindly granny, and I'm about to be eaten up by whatever monster... beast... *thing* lurks out there because my naive ass followed her into the woods.

She knows it, too.

Holding up the length of rope, Marie smiles.

My hands shake even as I summon a nervous grin of my own. "Why, Grandmere, what big teeth you have."

I don't think she found any humor in my ill-timed quip. Pursing her lips, she nods at the two men.

And then she says, "Grab her," and I realize I'm in more trouble than I ever would have guessed.

It's the order that Remy was waiting for. He moves first, Armand only a split second behind him. Before I can react, they each have me by an arm. Jolting me, jerking my arms so hard it's like they're trying to rip them out of their sockets, they start to drag me away.

Flailing doesn't help. They're too strong. Digging my heels in the dirt just means I lose both of the pumps as they muscle me backward before slamming me up against the rough bark of the thick tree trunk that had been in front of me.

My grandmother watches it all with a calculating expression. It looks a lot more at home on her elegant features than any grandmotherly affection ever did.

"Keep her in place," she orders before marching forward with the rope.

There's enough of it to wrap around me and the

tree four times, keeping me trapped there even without the two men holding me down. However, I notice there's enough give to it that I can push against it, hopefully loosening the rope.

If I'd been thinking straight instead of panicking, I would have kept that to myself until I knew for sure what their plan was. Say they abandon me in the woods for some reason. Once they're gone, I could've tried to break free.

That's not what I do.

The second Remy and Armand release me, I throw my body forward, hoping the rope will just unravel and I can at least make a break for it. When that doesn't happen, I keep trying, begging them to let me go.

Marie sighs. With a flippant wave of her hand, she gestures at me.

I can't explain it. I don't know what happened. It *shouldn't* have happened, I know that much. But it did, and suddenly I'm completely frozen and quiet. My arms are tucked beneath the rope, hanging at my side. I can't move a finger. I can feel the dirt and the grass between my bare toes, but I can't even wiggle the baby one on the end.

I can blink. After a moment's panic when I fear that I'm forever paralyzed, I realize my jaw works, too.

I can talk again.

Screaming will probably only aggravate my grandmother. In a hoarse voice teetering on the edge of becoming another shout, I say, "What... what did you do to me?"

"You were acting like a child, jolie. I merely treated you like I would any witchling. If you won't act like you should, I'll make you."

Witchling?

A little more hysteria inches its way into my tone. "What is this? *Magic?*" This isn't magic. This is craziness. "Let me go. Whatever this is, I want nothing to do with it. Let me go."

"You might not want anything to do with this, but that choice was taken out of all of our hands a long time ago. You *are* the one we've been waiting for. And you're the one who will end this for once and for all."

"End what? Marie"—right now, I'd choke if I called her 'Grandmere' like she insists on—"I'm your granddaughter, right? Don't do this."

Whatever it is she's doing, *don't do it.*

"Madame," murmurs Remy. "Do we have to?"

"Yes." Her answer is short. Sharp. "And we must do it now. The moon is full, and we've already stayed on his territory too long. He'll be coming."

He? Who the fuck is *he?*

Marie folds her fist. She was empty-handed. I'd put my entire life savings down on that fact. After she finished with the rope, she had nothing in her hands—

but when she opens her fist back up, she has a silver dagger gripped lightly between her fingers.

The moonlight reflects off of the shiny blade.

I swallow my moan of terror.

Forget how she managed to conjure the sharp weapon out of thin air like that. I don't care where she got it from. The fact that she has one is bad enough.

Nothing good ever comes of someone wielding a knife like that.

And I can't do a damn thing to stop her since every last part of me is motionless against the tree. Even my mouth is locked up tight now, leaving me to scream inside of my skull as Marie nods at Armand.

The older man reaches beneath the rope, snagging my motionless arm. He stretches it out as far as it can get despite my bindings, presenting my forearm to Marie—and her knife.

She moves in front of me.

I try to will her to stop with my gaze.

She ignores it, choosing instead to place the tip of the knife against my skin, only a few inches away from the scar left behind in the crook of my elbow that last time I was cut.

And then she begins to speak again.

"For seventy years we've been trapped in time. Stuck. The world moved on without Winter Creek. We were a memory. Cursed. Jamais pardonné." She uses the point of the blade to gesture at the older man before putting it back against my inner arm. "To leave our borders is to pay the price. Time catches up to us all, jolie. I just want my second chance. I want my family."

Her family.

Her *coven*.

And that, I'm beginning to understand, was never me.

It takes all the grit and determination I have to fight against her hold on me enough to spit out four words: "My name is Fallon."

"So you say."

Another wave of her hand. My jaw clamps closed again with such force, my teeth click. And yet, when she drags the point of the knife along my inner forearm, I might not be able to scream out loud, but I still manage to make a loud, pained grunt. Just because I'm frozen doesn't mean that I don't feel it—or the rush of panic when I realize that I'm *bleeding*.

She's watching my arm intently, her lips pursed. As the hot blood bubbles to the surface, she nods and, after passing off the bloody blade to Remy, Marie takes my arm between both of her hands. Desperate not to watch what she's doing in case I see my blood, I feel it when she wrenches my arm, twisting it, squeezing it as she drips as much of my blood as she can on the grass in front of me.

"Tonight it won't be the moon's call he answers,"

she announces, "but also the singing of her blood. He won't be able to resist it."

I'm barely listening to her. After Marie lets go of me, she lifts her hand, tucking away a stray strand of blonde hair that had escaped from her chignon. Was the gesture on purpose? No clue, but it catches my attention—and so does the blood on her palm.

That's the last straw. That's what makes me realize that I'm absolutely, utterly fucked.

I was so, so careful not to watch the knife work, or to see her spill my blood on the ground. But when she raises her bloody hand up where I can't miss it?

No, no, no...

I see it. The moonlight reflects off of the smear of crimson on her skin, and I *see* it. Worse, I can smell the tangy, rusty stink of my own blood over the floral scent that normally clings to her.

There's not much I can do, inwardly hyperventilating while outwardly a damn statue, but I try to quell as much panic as I can. My heart is about to explode.

Marie clicks her tongue, oblivious to my struggle— or maybe she just doesn't give a shit.

"One day you'll understand, petite fille. I must do what's right for the whole coven, even if it means sacrificing one." She finally notices the blood on her hand. With an annoyed shake, she seems to flick it off. Magic or something else, who even knows anymore, but her hand is clean now. I'd be relieved if it wasn't for the way she adds, "Even if it means sacrificing *you*."

Then, before I can come to grips with her using the word 'sacrificing' and 'you' like that, Marie has two more for me, and something tells me that my life—as long as it lasts—will never be the same again:

"He's coming."

Without even a backward glance my way, Marie snaps her fingers. Armand lumbers forward, snagging her tote from the ground before offering his elbow out to her. As regal as ever, she takes it, letting him lead her away from me and my tree.

Remy did that, I think through my panicked haze. When he met me at the train station... he insisted I take his arm before he brought me to Bordeaux Manor.

To the *Coven* House.

I should've known. When my first instinct was to match the word 'coven' with Halloween and witches, I should've known better than to simply trust this woman because she claimed to be my grandmother.

What kind of grandmother is willing to sacrifice

her granddaughter like this? And, holy shit, what does that even *mean*?

I can't move. All I can do is watch as Armand and Marie disappear into the shadows, leaving the lantern behind. How thoughtful of them. When this monster in the woods comes following the scent of my blood, I'll be able to see my doom before it... what? Eats me?

Worse?

Oh my God. Oh my *God*.

Pleading is out of the question. So is begging. I'm not above trading anything for a chance to flee the woods before 'he' comes for me. Only I can't break through whatever Marie did to me to say another word, even though Remy's currently watching me with enough open desire and ill-disguised lust that I'm sure he'd be open to negotiations.

"Remy. Viens!"

I'm not wrong, especially since he glances over his shoulder at the sound of Marie's shout. Instead of trotting after her and Armand, he turns back, ponytail whipping around as he moves into me.

"The spell will wear off as soon as we're out of the beast's territory," whispers Remy. "If you survive, find me. Once the curse is broken, if the beast doesn't claim you, Madame has said that I can have you."

Maybe it's being tied to a fucking *tree*, frozen in place by my grandmother while listening to her and her 'boys' talk of magic and witchlings and spells, but as much as I'm freaking out, I can admit one thing: if he doesn't help me now, there are no negotiations. If he walks away, leaving me to the mercy of this *beast*, I'd rather die in these woods than ever let Remy think I'd allow him to touch me.

I want to tell him. Still frozen, I can't, but I hope if I think *'fuck you'* loud enough in my mind he'll get the hint.

And to think I had him high up on my list of prospective vacation flings...

Close enough that his rose and clove scent drowns out the rusty tang of my blood, Remy runs his dark eyes over me. A hint of remorse flashes across his striking face, but it's not enough for him to at least loosen the rope.

Before Marie can call his name a second time, Remy's gone.

And I'm left alone, keeping my gaze straight ahead so I don't see the blood while the word 'beast' runs on replay in my mind.

REMY IS RIGHT ABOUT ONE THING. BARELY TWO MINUTES after he abandons me with the lantern, I regain full control over my body. Still careful to avoid looking down at the burning slice on my arm, I immediately start to try to get out from the ropes.

It's not as easy as I thought it would be. The rope is tighter than it appeared, and with only one good arm and my eyes pointed high to avoid glimpsing my blood, I can't even find the knots to break free.

For a split second, I think about shimmying down and maybe using my toes to knock the lantern closer to me. It might be worth the risk of the flames escaping the enclosure to try to burn the ropes, but if I do end up lighting the whole damn forest on fire, I might go up in flames with the October trees.

Yeah. That's a nope.

Screaming is out, too. I doubt there's anyone around who could hear me, and on the off chance that 'he' isn't looking for me, I don't want to catch the attention of anyone who might things it's a good idea to be hanging out in the woods after dark.

Think, Fallon. *Think!*

There's nothing else I can do. My hemophobia has always held me back, but I'm not about to die because I can't handle a little blood. Gritting my teeth, hoping like hell my shrinks were onto something when it comes to immersion therapy, I look down.

Whoa. When I go light-headed, I'm not sure if it's my fear talking, or the fact that rivers of blood are streaking down my arm, dribbling past my palm, staining my fingers. Blood loss is a real concern. The knife cut deeper than I ever would've guessed.

But I deal. I have to. So, shoving my fear, my anger, and my urge to throw up dinner so far in the back of my racing mind that I'll need a crowbar to pry them back out, I use my bloody hand to twist the rope. It leaves a trail of red in the fibers of my bindings, but it's moving. I can just about reach the knots when the crackling of leaves seems to pierce through my determination.

I whimper, my heart pounding. Trying to tell myself to calm the fuck down does no good, but I have to find a way how. The faster my heart pumps, the more blood pulses from the open cut. It's flowing even more freely now, making my fingers slip on the tight knot.

"Come on, come on," I plead, ripping the tip of my index fingernail as I fight with the rope. The knot gives a little, but not enough.

And now I hear something *snuffling* nearby.

The sound is absolutely animalistic. It's a snuffle, then a low growl, and I don't know what I'm expecting this beast to be, but it's not what eases out from behind one of the trees in front of me.

The lamp light silhouettes a man-sized creature. A good foot taller than me even when its big body is hunched, all I can see is a pair of amber-colored eyes catching the flames, flickering as it watches me without blinking.

The growls grow in pitch as it steps into the light—

and, despite its monstrous appearance, I can't help but amend *it* to *he* for now.

The monster dick swinging between his muscular thighs makes it kind of obvious that the beast is male.

I've never been brave; reckless, sure, but never intentionally brave. I could pretend all I want, but given the choice between fight or flee, I'm running every fucking time. It's why I usually carry my mace and prefer sneakers. If I have to bolt, I will.

Right now? I *can't.*

My knees give out. Paralyzed by sudden fear, the only thing keeping me upright is the length of rope trapping me to the tree.

Beast... when Tristan teasingly mentioned the monster in the woods, or when Remy said 'beast', I couldn't quite understand what they meant. As the creature comes stalking closer, nothing I imagined is even close.

He's like nothing I've ever seen before. It's as though someone took a man and an animal—from the fangs jutting past his elongated muzzle, and the pointed, tufted ears on the side of his head, I'd say *wolf*—threw them in a blender and set it to pulverize. His back and shoulders are hunched, legs spread wide as he begins to circle my tree. Completely naked, walking on the balls of his fur-covered feet, half of his body is muscular, tanned, *human* flesh. The other? Patches of fur and old scars.

He looks broken, too. Mangled. His hands are more paw than anything, with thick, black claws curving around the tips of his fingers. Moonlight catches a few stray strands of saliva dripping from his muzzle.

I say my prayers then and there. Remy actually thinks I can survive this thing? If those claws and fangs don't get me, his dick might do the trick. Because I don't know exactly what this beast is thinking—and, apart from snuffles, growls, and snarls, he's not talking —but he wasn't erect when he first stepped into the clearing.

He is now.

Oh, no, no, no...

By the time he finishes circling the tree, sniffing so loudly it nearly drowns out my moan of fright, his dick is completely hard. It slaps his taut belly as he hunches further, drawing into himself though that doesn't do a fucking thing to hide his erection.

The creature snaps his pointed teeth once he's in front of me again, snuffling and whining as he edges closer only to howl and dance back out of my reach.

Almost as though he's scared of *me*.

That gives me a little bit of my nerve back. He's not going straight for me. When his cock bobs one way as he crouches low, he bats at it with the back of his hand like it's an annoyance instead of a guy ready to make use of the only female in sight.

Gulping, I pull myself up, putting my full weight

back on my bare feet. If he plans on having a little Fallon snack, I'm going to do whatever I can to at least cause him a bit of indigestion first.

He circles the tree again, sniffing wildly with his mouth hanging open, trying to catch a scent. He doesn't come any closer, but that doesn't stop me from trying to get away from that matted fur, those *talons* masquerading as claws. I press my back up against the tree, the rough bark biting into the exposed skin on my arm as I try like hell again to break free.

But I can't. I'm stuck, and the beast?

From the way he drops down all the way into a full crouch, snuffling at the grass now, it's obvious he just noticed my spilled blood.

Now I know what my grandmother meant when she said that my blood will sing to the beast. He seems almost entranced by it as he drops even lower, trailing one long, thick, black claw through the blood-stained grass in front of me.

Clamping my jaw closed, swallowing my terrified moan, this half-wolf, half-man *thing* lifts his bloody claw to his snout and sniffs.

He stiffens—and I don't just mean the most prominent part of him. His amber eyes flash as his chin tilts up, searching for me.

I nearly piss myself in fright when he rises up from his crouch, lifting his paw, reaching for me.

Easing closer and closer, I nearly stop breathing. There's no way in hell I can avoid his touch.

Instead of going for my skin, he crooks his claw beneath the gold chain of my necklace, mesmerized by the opal hanging off of it. At the same time, the head of his dick nudges my side.

Heat pours off of his naked body as he boxes me in. Trembling in place, my heart thudding against my ribcage, a fresh wave of blood warms my chilled flesh.

It catches his attention. Drawing away from me, he lets my necklace fall back against my chest. He reaches for my wounded arm instead, gripping it more gently than I would've thought the wolfish monster capable of as he bows his misshapen head over it.

The beast runs his snout along the bloody slice on my arm.

I stop breathing for real this time.

And that's when it finally hits him that I'm the source of the blood he scented.

Dropping my arm, he stumbles away from me and the tree. As if in terrible pain, the beast throws his head back and howls.

"Holy shit, holyshit, *holyshit*."

I'm crying. Tears of absolute terror fill my eyes as I tremble so violently, I rip open the skin on my upper arms.

This is it. I really am going to die in this nowhere place without anyone to know what happened to me.

The beast straightens to his full height, strange eyes flashing in the lantern light as he looms over me.

I'm gonna die. There's no way around it. I'm gonna die, and though I know it's as pointless as the tears, I finally let out a scream of my own.

It was my last weapon. I fully expect it to be the final thing I do—and it's everything a scream should be. Loud and long and so high-pitched, it could've shattered glass if I wasn't trapped outside in the middle of the woods.

His pointed ears flatten against his skull, eyes crossing as though the pitch caused the beast more damage than Marie's knife did me. The beast whines, throwing his mangled paw up in the air before the big creature spins on his arches, quickly loping off into the shadows.

My scream echoes around me. Throat raw and every part of me still shaking, I wait a few seconds to see if the beast will return.

Maybe... maybe this is what Remy meant. Maybe I somehow survived the beast, and now this stupid fucking curse is broken and I can get the hell out of Winter Creek.

Now, there's gullible and naive, and then there's being just plain delusional. I know better. Either that thing is coming back or my grandmother and her 'boys' are, and I still need to figure out a way to be long gone before they do. I have no idea why my scream scared off the beast like that, but once his ears stop ringing, he'll remember he's either hungry or horny, and I'm still tied to this damn tree.

I scream again. It's a sound of frustration more than anything, and it's followed by a broken sob as I rip the fronts of my biceps open with the friction between me and the rope. It helps, though. Every time I shift, the rope moves higher. I'm not looking forward to rope burn on my tits as it passes over my cleavage, but I'm making progress. There's some give to it, and I might just be able to shimmy out from beneath my bindings in one piece.

Please let me be able to escape...

Just when the rope gets caught on my boobs, I hear footsteps approaching. They're pounding against the dirt, heading right for me.

It's the moon that illuminates the new arrival as he bursts through the trees, and all it takes is one glimpse before sudden relief has me sagging against the rope.

It's not the beast.

It's a man.

CHAPTER 9
RESCUE

Shirtless and shoeless, he's wearing a pair of pants as dark as his hair and that's all. Brawny chest heaving as he comes to a quick stop, his face is shadowed in the darkness though I can sense the shock at finding me here wafting off of his big body.

It's not Remy or Armand, or any of the men I saw milling around the Coven House. Right now, that's all I care about.

"I heard screaming," he says, his voice a deep rumble that manages to soothe the panicked, jagged edges inside of me.

"Help me," I whisper. "Please help me."

He bounds toward me without another word, ducking his head as he reaches for the rope. He's at the side of the tree so I can't quite see what he's doing, but he must've had a pocketknife in his pants or something because the rope begins to slacken as he saws away at it.

"Beast." I spit out the word. Whether he knows enough about Winter Creek lore to understand what I mean, I can't tell, but I also can't just leave him to find out that we're not alone in the dark. "*Marie*."

He pauses, though I'm not sure which warning catches his attention. But then he returns to cutting at the rope as if he never stopped.

"Don't worry. I got you," he murmurs softly, the first loop snapping before he starts on the second. "You're safe with me."

Honestly? I'd be a fool to believe that. Not that it matters. Right now, all I want is to be free, and I damn near vibrate in place as he finishes cutting the last of the rope from the tree.

He turns toward me, but I'm already shoving off from the bark, my mind focused on running as far away as possible from this place.

That's what my mind wants to do. My battered and weak body has other ideas.

Without the rope keeping me on my feet, I crumple. My legs fail to hold my weight, and I hit the ground hard with my knees before falling forward. At the last moment, my instincts have me saving my cut arm. Of course, that means I don't have anything to break my unexpected fall except one weak wrist and my face as it hits the grass.

I could deal with that. Even if I busted my nose or sprained my wrist, it was better than being slaughtered by the beast.

But that's not what happened.

I land face-first into something that's cold and sticky and *wet*. It takes me one terrible second for the realization to hit me.

The rusty tang of the bloody grass helps.

Because that's what I landed in. The pool of blood that Marie squeezed out of my cut to summon the beast.

I push up, not caring about anything except getting away from it. That was my mistake. With blood on my cheek, on my chin, and now on my hands, my head is spinning. Moving at all is like trying to swim in quicksand. The stress and terror already made it hard for me to breathe. Light-headed and frantic, my poor sanity was hanging on by a thread.

After all I've been through since being led out into the woods, it's the stink of blood on my skin that finally breaks me.

The thread snaps, and I lose my fucking mind.

I HAD NO IDEA THAT I ACTUALLY LOST CONSCIOUSNESS until I come to with a violent start, a scream halfway to my lips before I instinctively strangle it.

My body jerks instead, sending fresh waves of pain all through me. My head is throbbing, my arm feeling tight and heavy. That's not all that seems to be weighing me down, either. As I jolt up into a sitting position, eyes springing open, I notice a thick orange and brown afghan pooling in my lap.

What the—

The second thing I notice is an overwhelming stink of wet dog mingled with pine slapping me awake, and the pine part is weird because I'm indoors. From the cushioning beneath my ass and my legs, I think I'm on a couch somewhere. Whoever dragged me in from the outside must have covered me up with a blanket. As I finger the edge of the wooly afghan, I figure out why my arm feels so tight.

The same mysterious someone also took the time to wrap gauze around my forearm, protecting the knife wound.

Lifting up my achy arm, I marvel at it.

How long was I out? Long enough to be moved, bandaged up, and who knows what else.

At that thought, my other hand flies to my chest next. The teeniest, tiniest bit of relief battles against my nerves when I pat my necklace and find the familiar shape of the opal. Daring to drop my gaze a little lower,

I see the hemline of the peach cocktail dress Marie sewed for me.

The instant I get my first glimpse of dried blood covering the bodice, I yank the afghan closer, covering myself up.

Okay. Not robbed, just moved, and I have no idea if I'm still in danger.

Because while I might be clueless when it comes to where I am, I vividly remember every single thing that happened before I had to have passed out. All of it, from being ambushed by Marie and the two men, to the beast prowling around me, the scream that saved my life, and the stranger who rescued me.

The stranger who is currently sitting in a wooden chair across the room, his head bowed, hands hanging between his wide legs. All I see is a mop of messy black hair, thighs as big as tree trunks encased in a pair of dark denim jeans, hiking boots, and a tight henley shirt that just hits the middle of his meaty forearms.

He must have changed after he brought me inside. Good. It'll be a lot easier to thank him for saving me now that he's wearing a shirt.

There's no dog to explain the stink, I notice. Who knows? Maybe he tucked the animal out of sight after he brought me here. Or maybe there is no dog at all and I was too busy freaking out to notice that my savior has questionable hygiene.

I almost laugh. Knowing that I'm out of immediate

trouble has me just about giddy with relief. Sure, I could be jumping out of the frying pan only to leap into the fire, but I've got to hope he didn't rescue me before only to hurt me now.

Of course, if I have any clue *why* he helped me in the first place, I'd have a better idea of what kind of trouble I've found myself in this time...

Welp. One way to find out.

I clear my throat, trying to alert him to the fact that I'm awake. A soft noise that breaks up the quiet has his head jerking up, eyes landing right on me.

The noise turns into a choking gasp when I get my first direct look at him.

You think that I would've gotten used to being bombarded by good-looking men since I've been in Winter Creek—and then there's this guy.

When I first met Tristan, I thought of him as beautiful. Remy was striking.

My savior is just my type.

I didn't think I had one until now. None of my boyfriends had anything in common except a tendency to use me for sex and fun before moving on. I've been attracted to all kinds—and some women, too, not gonna lie—but I've never understood the phrase "love at first sight" until right this very second.

It's just because he saved you, Fallon, I tell myself. That gut punch of attraction is gratitude. The sudden possessiveness I feel for a man I just met is simply ridiculous.

Right?

I mean, I can't even pinpoint what exactly it is about him that has my palms going sweaty. About five years or so older than me, he has a sharp jaw and high cheekbones that are contradicted by a lush mouth and dark eyelashes that almost look like he's had them done. They frame a pair of amber-colored eyes, too orange to be hazel. Unlike the other two guys I've met in town, he's not clean-shaven. He has a five o'clock shadow that develops into a closely-cropped beard that covers the knife's edge of that masculine jaw. It suits the slight scowl on his handsome features.

Because he's totally scowling now that I can see his face.

That doesn't bother me. More than that, I get the feeling that I *know* him and the scowl is pretty much his default expression. That we're not just strangers who met in the weirdest of circumstances... and it hits me why I feel like this: I've seen him before. Only just a flash, and Tristan distracted me from staring then, but—

"I know you."

He straightens in his chair. "You do?"

"I, uh, yeah. I think I saw you in the town square a couple of days ago."

On the edge of the square, when I shivered because I felt like someone was watching me only to see a guy standing there on his own, nodding at Tristan.

"Possibly." He returns to his slouch, glancing at a point over my head instead of meeting my eyes. "I was there."

Translation: I don't remember seeing you—and if I do, it doesn't matter regardless.

Fair enough. I'd gotten so used to Tristan's flirting and Remy's not-so-subtle interest—that I will never return now, thank you very much—that I think it went to my head. Just because those two were interested in the new girl, it doesn't mean every guy in Winter Creek will be.

Maybe it's better that the man who saved me doesn't seem to know what to do with me.

To be fair, I'm not so sure I do, either.

"Anyway, I guess I should thank you." Obviously. "For the woods. And, um, bringing me to—"

"My hunting cabin," he supplies.

I take the excuse to tear my gaze away from him, glancing around the room instead. Hunting cabin, he calls it. He isn't wrong. Opposite the chocolate-brown couch I'm perched on, there's a fireplace just behind his seat. A single wooden table is next to him, with a door to my right, and light brown walls covered with stuffed animal heads and weapons.

I notice a mounted stag's head—which, while

creepy, is at least understandable—and an honest-to-God wolf's mounted opposite of the stag that has me doing a double-take. An ax is resting on pegs over the fireplace, a crossbow is pinned next to the stag head like it's part of the trophy, and he has lines of arrows posted on the other side of the bow.

Okay, then.

I feel a little bit better now that I notice them. I've got no shot when it comes to using a bow and arrow, but if I can wrangle that ax down, I have some way to protect myself if I have to.

"Anyway, you don't have to thank me," he adds, dragging my attention away from the sharp, silver edge of the ax back to him. "Anyone else would have done the same."

His matter-of-the-fact attitude has me momentarily forgetting about the weapons.

Anyone else would've helped me? Considering it was my grandmother and a dude who made it obvious he wanted in my pants who trussed me up in the first place, I doubt that very much.

I shrug, leaving it at that.

My savior allows it. Nodding at me, he says, "Besides, I'm more interested in hearing how you ended up tied to a tree in the first place."

I should've been expecting this. Of course he'd ask.

"What?" I offer him a crooked grin. "That sort of thing doesn't happen in Winter Creek often?"

I'm trying to tease. It's my defense mechanism, making light of a bad situation otherwise I'll linger too long in the darkness. I've always been like this, but it's something I've clung to following my mom's death.

From the way his brow furrows, another scowl creasing his features, I don't think he gets it.

"I run through these woods almost every night, between my cabin and my home. I've never found a screaming woman tied to a tree before."

"First time for everything, I guess."

"Yes," he agrees, "and now I'd like to hear about how it happened."

I'm sure he would. "Who are you?"

A muscle in his jaw tics. "I'm the male who could have left you in the woods at the mercy of whoever hurt you first."

Ouch. I can't stop myself from wincing at his retort. I mean, he's not wrong, but still. Whatever happened to the gentle guy who cut me free while telling me that I'm safe with him?

He sighs. "Sorry. It's been a long night."

"Is it morning already?" I ask.

There are no windows in this room so I have no clue. I could have very easily slept through the night when I was passed out and be completely oblivious to that fact.

"Not quite. Closer to one a.m. last time I checked. It's probably two now."

No wonder his head was bowed before. He was probably dozing off himself after saving me. Depending on how long it took for me to walk halfway through the woods with Marie, plus the time spent tied to the tree, I could've been out for six or seven hours after he found me.

It's my turn to apologize.

"I'm sorry. For passing out on you, I mean. It's just… I have this thing about…" I gulp, and croak out, "blood."

Just the reminder has my stomach twisting. Oh, *God*. Do I still have it on my hands? Or my face? I didn't notice before, but I also wasn't really looking.

Bracing myself for the worst, I look now.

An exhale of pure relief escapes me. My hands are absolutely clean. No sign of blood anywhere that I can see.

"I figured," he admits. "Even if that wasn't what did it, I didn't think you'd want to wake up with it dried on you. When I cleaned up that cut on your arm, I got rid of that, too."

You know what? He can be snappish all he wants. He saved me, then washed the blood off of me. Who says heroes have to be all sunshine and smiles? Give me a grump any day.

And then he says, "But since you seem a little squeamish around blood, I doubt you gave yourself that cut. So, I'll ask again: who did this to you?"

It's in the rumble of his voice as he makes his demand. It's in the unblinking stare, and how his eyes go dark as he dares me to refuse.

I can't.

"My grandmother," I confess.

His lips thin. "Explain. Please."

CHAPTER 10
HUNTSMAN

He adds the 'please' almost as though it physically pains him.

Because he did—and because I'm pretty sure I'm not going anywhere until I do—I give him the Cliff's Notes version of how I ended up in this mess.

From the weird telegram three months ago to taking the train, finding out my estranged grandmother is a matriarch in this town I never heard of, then how she led me out into the woods on the pretense that we were going to her soiree before she turned on me, leaving me there for the beast that lurks in the woods. It explains why I was tied up, why I was bloody, and why I was so close to hysterical when he stumbled upon me.

There's only one thing I forget to mention: her

name. But whether I gave away one too many details or not, this man knows exactly who I'm talking about.

"Marie did this."

"Yes."

What else can I say? She *did*.

Something passes across his face, there and gone again. I don't know him anywhere near well enough to guess what it could mean, and he wrangles himself back under complete control between one breath and the next. As gorgeous as before, but it's like a door's been slammed closed between us, that's how effectively he shuts down his reaction to hearing what I told him.

But just because his expression goes emotionless, it doesn't keep his strange amber-colored eyes from darkening to a deep brown as he mutters, "The witches have gone too far this time."

Was I meant to hear that? Probably not.

Did I? Uh. Yeah. I did.

Normally, I would brush that off as a guy being a grade-A misogynist, calling Marie a 'witch'. Fresh from being frozen in place, my jaw screwed shut by some other power, and Remy talking about spells?

"Witches? You mean broomstick-riding, potion-brewing, Elphaba in Wicked *witches*?"

He doesn't say anything. He just gives me a look.

My stomach flutters. From nerves or attraction, I'm not sure, but I thread my fingers through the holes in the afghan, tugging it closer as if that'll protect me from his answer when I say, "There's no such thing as witches."

"Winter Creek is a supe town," he says flatly. "Not only do they exist, but half the territory is theirs."

Part of me wants to ask who—or what—owns the other half of Winter Creek. But the other part just has to know—

"Supe?" I echo. "What's a 'supe'?"

He huffs. I get the vibe that it's more his frustration at letting slip something he probably shouldn't have than me acting like a parrot, repeating everything he says. For a second, I doubt he's even going to answer me. He doesn't have any reason to—or to be honest with me at all, considering I have no idea what's going on or have any way to tell if he's lying straight to my face or not.

So when he says, "Supernatural races, like witches and vampires," I really, really want to believe he's fucking with me.

Only he's *not*.

I don't know why I trust this guy I just met—probably because I'm still so damn gullible, but also because I can't help but want to believe the man who saved me is a good one—but I do.

"And magic's real?" It's a whisper. That's about all I can manage right now.

Because it has to be. Even if I wanted to explain

away my grandmother's control over me, that does nothing to erase the memories of the half-wolf, half-man beast that prowled around me before my scream scared him off.

He nods. "Unfortunately."

Like everything else, he's so matter-of-fact about it, I can't even argue that he's wrong.

It all comes back to the beast. I notice that he conveniently doesn't mention it, and I take his silence as confirmation that the monster really did find me before my savior did. And if that thing is real? Then so are witches.

Marie Bordeaux is one... and, yes, I really should've known better when everyone called her home the Coven House instead of Bordeaux Manor.

Remy's probably a witch, too, since one of the first things he told me when we met was that he worked under my grandmother. An apprentice maybe? And Armand... he was in the city right before I decided to take the trip out to Winter Creek. How much do you want to bet she found a way to send him?

He was there just in time to sop up my *blood*—and now he looks like he aged a decade in a couple of weeks.

My breath catches in my throat. He didn't just bump into me by accident that day, did he? For all I know, he's the asshole who cut me in the first place, and... no. *No*. I'm gonna stop thinking along those lines right now otherwise I'm gonna lose it again.

But... Armand found me at home. How do I know they won't find me here?

"I have to go," I blurt out suddenly, kicking at the afghan with my bare feet. I don't know where I'll go, but so long as it's as far away as possible from the witches, that's fine with me. "Before they realize their plan to feed me to the beast failed."

"That's not what he wanted to do with you," my savior says in a firm voice. When I gasp, his implication obvious, he gentles it. "But he can't get you here, if that's what you're worried about."

The beast is only one thing worrying me right now. "But what about—"

"It's late," he cuts me off. Still gentle, though it's undeniably a tone that brooks no argument. "The witches won't come to this side of the woods. It's not their territory." *Territory* again. "You should get some more sleep. We can figure out what to do with you in the morning."

Sleep? Is he serious?

I wasn't even sleeping before, unless he counts stress-induced unconsciousness as 'sleeping'. Now that he's put the idea of witches back in my head—that my grandmother and the strange tricks she could perform might actually make her one—I can't see myself shutting down again anytime soon, no matter how exhausted I feel beneath my terror and confusion.

And what about him? Unless there's more to his cabin than this single room, there's only one place to lay down and I'm on it. He could leave me behind, of course, but would he? After all he's done to take care of the damsel in distress he found in the trees? Something tells me that, if I do try to fall back asleep, he'll be sitting in that wooden chair again the next time I open my eyes.

"I don't think—"

"That wasn't a request."

His deep rumble sends a shiver down my spine. "But—"

"Close your eyes. Get some rest. Don't argue, just do it."

Brisling at his tone, I put my weight on my uninjured arm and shift toward him. "Excuse me?"

He doesn't seem quailed by my glare. Instead, raising one of his eyebrows, he gestures for me to lay back down on the couch again.

When I fall back against the lumpy cushions, it's because my tired arm gave out, not because he told me to.

I guess I'm going to try to go back to sleep, huh? At least I won't feel the weight of the stranger's stare on me if I do.

The worst part is, it's not like I have any other

choice. Despite wanting to run before, going back out into the woods where that beast might still be lurking nearby is definitely not an option.

So is returning to the Coven House—at least, not right now, though I'm definitely leaning toward not *ever*. All my stuff might still be there, including my purse, my phone, and my train ticket back home, but I'd abandon it all just to put my time in Winter Creek behind me.

"Fine." I sound like a spoiled brat. I can't help it. "Whatever."

"So you think I'm an overbearing jerk right now. That's alright. Trust me, I'm used to it. But you'll thank me for it in the morning—"

"Fallon." My name just pops out. "I'm Fallon."

If I thought finally introducing myself to him would get him to share his name with me, I'm sorely mistaken.

Instead, he sighs. "Go to sleep."

"What about you?"

"What about me?"

"Aren't you going to sleep?" I ask him.

"It's the full moon," he replies, as if that's some sort of answer. Maybe I'm more tired than I want him to think because that doesn't make any sense to me. Especially when he says, "Someone has to keep watch."

Right. Because, whether he wants to admit that he knows about the beast or not, the thing's out there somewhere—and this guy already rescued me from him once.

And, okay. I *am* tired. My eyes are heavy, and I have this urge to pass out again if only to wake up tomorrow and discover that all of this was a bad dream…

I refuse to. Especially with him telling me that I should sleep, I just can't do it.

Instead, I glance around the room again, gaze darting from weapon to weapon, then finally back to the man hovering there. Something warns me that, despite all the sharp objects displayed on the walls, he's the most dangerous thing in here.

Shoving that thought to the back of my mind or I'll *never* sleep, I murmur, "You know, it's kind of fitting that this is your hunting cabin."

His voice sounds surprisingly amused as he says, "It is?"

"Yeah. I mean, if you think about it, it's like I'm in some sort of twisted version of Little Red Riding Hood. Right?"

For some reason, he doesn't have anything to respond to that.

I continue anyway. "You know. Instead of Little Red trying to save her grandmother from a wolf, I had mine trying to sacrifice me to one." I pause for a moment. "I guess that monster I saw… the beast… it was kind of wolfish. And then there's you."

"Me?"

"You saved me from the big, bad wolf. That makes you the huntsman." I gesture vaguely toward the mounted wolf's head. "See? That's why it's fitting."

"Are you tired yet?"

More than he knows. "Maybe. Are you tired of me asking questions?"

His jaw goes tight. "Yes."

Oh. If there's one thing I can say about Mr. Huntsman, it's that he's as blunt as he is honest.

"Sorry."

"Don't be. It's not your fault. Now sleep."

He was honest. I guess it's my turn because my bottom lip trembles slightly as I ask, "Is it safe?"

Am *I* safe?

And I don't just mean from the monster or from my wicked witch of a grandmother, either. As much as I *feel* like I know him, I don't, and maybe his intentions are good.

Maybe they're not.

For a heartbeat, he just looks down at me. Then, rising up from his chair, easing toward the couch so carefully, like he's eager not to spook me any further, he lowers himself into a crouch until we're on the same level.

"Look into my eyes."

I do. Despite his earlier glower, his eyes have softened. They're kind. Almost hypnotizing.

My breath catches. I was too far away from him

during that chance sighting in the town square to see his eyes, but this close? It's almost like my instincts from before are right. I really do know him—even though he still hasn't told me his name.

And then he does.

"I'm Lucas. And you can trust me to watch over you tonight. I give you my word that you'll be safe. Now sleep."

Only a fool would believe him. Only a bigger one would allow her eyelids to droop until they were closed, exhaustion settling over her as the last of my adrenaline leaves me sapped of energy.

And only a woman who sees something in a stranger that can't possibly be there would curl up with an afghan that stinks of wet dog in an old hunting cabin and actually expect to wake up again in the morning in a better state than I was when I left Marie's house all those hours ago.

But that's exactly what I do.

Sleep, he orders.

I sleep.

CHAPTER 11
LITTLE RED

When I wake up again the next morning, I'm alone.

And I'm *pissed*.

Way I see it, being angry is so much better than being afraid. I trusted Marie. To an extent, I trusted Remy, too; at least, I trusted him not to try to sacrifice me, which while pretty specific, seemed a given. But last night... they would've happily seen me slaughtered by that beast to break a stupid curse I don't even believe in, and now that I survived it, I'm furious. Hurt, too, but definitely pissed.

They tried to break me. Screw them. Witches or not, I'm going to do whatever it takes to make them regret ever trying to turn me into a happy meal for a creature out of my worst nightmares.

Even if I have to do it alone—because I am. Alone,

I mean. As I shove the afghan away from me, swinging my bare feet onto the chilly floor, I see that the chair sat across from me is empty. My dark-haired savior—Lucas, I remember, he said his name is *Lucas*—is nowhere in sight.

Good. This will make sneaking out of his cabin and finding my way back to the train platform a lot easier if he isn't here to demand more answers from me.

I stand up, daring a quick glance down at myself again. My necklace is still here, and the dark spots splashed along the bodice, dotting the material of my skirt are more a dirty brown color than the vivid red of freshly spilled blood. I swallow roughly, but that's the extent of my reaction. My hemophobia isn't so bad when the dried blood is old, almost like I can pretend it's spilled paint instead.

Besides, this old-fashioned dress I'm wearing is all I have. No phone. No shoes. No purse... I have nothing but the dress and my opal and a fervent hope that the conductor will take pity on me and let me on the train with an IOU.

Hey. Once I get back to New York, I'm good for it.

First, though, I have to reach the train platform. And while my sense of direction might not be the best, I just have to head in the opposite direction of the hills. Eventually, I'll find the river and, once I do, I'll keep on going until I hit the rope bridge.

I have until four o'clock to find it. Here's hoping

that I do—and that today is one of those arbitrary days where the train rolls in. It's Sunday, so I'm not so sure it will, but it's not like I can stay hiding out in this cabin. Lucas's disappearance is a pretty solid clue that he did his part, keeping me safe until morning. By now, it's gotta be daylight.

And I have to be on my way.

Before I head for the exit, I get up from the couch and walk over to the fireplace. The ax is posted over the center of the mantlepiece. On my tippy-toes, I can just about reach it. My fingers brush the bottom of the polished wooden handle. It's heavy. Solid. I'm not looking forward to knocking it off the wall and possibly having the sharp edge of the ax's head come crashing down on me if I don't catch it in time, but that's a risk I'm willing to take.

I need something to protect myself. If I'm going to march out into those woods again, Fallon's gonna be armed.

Too bad the ax isn't budging.

With a frustrated grunt, I jump a few inches off the ground, hoping to get a better grip on the handle.

Come on. I got this. I can—

"You'd have better luck with the bow. The ax doesn't come off the wall."

I let out a short shriek, clutching my chest as I land back on my heels before spinning around to find Lucas standing by the couch.

He's changed again. Wearing a black t-shirt and a pair of dark blue jeans, plus the same boots as last night, he doesn't look quite dressed for autumn weather. His hair is windswept, like he's already been for a morning jog, and there's a hint of pink riding high on his tanned cheeks.

In his arms, he's holding a bundle of fabric, a deep red color that reminds me of blood. I'm not sure if that's on purpose or not, but he has it looped easily over his folded arms, leaving his sculpted biceps on display as he watches me with an amused expression that's finally replaced his usual glower.

My heart racing for more reasons than just being caught, I snap, "Don't do that!"

He must walk like a damn cat. I never heard the door open or his boots crossing the threshold. He was just there, and I'm not sure how long he watched me struggle with the stupid ax before he said something.

His brow furrows. There's that glower again. "You're the one trying to steal my weapons, and I'm the one who gets yelled at? That doesn't seem quite fair."

"I wasn't going to steal it. Just... borrow it."

"You weren't going to chop me to pieces with it, were you? Like in your story."

My story? Oh. That's right. Little Red Riding Hood.

He's teasing me, I think. Not in a malicious way, but to help keep my mind off of the situation I'm in. It's morning, so I have to face it head-on, but maybe it can wait a few minutes more. I've got time. The train doesn't roll in until at least four.

Stepping away from the dark fireplace, I point out, "It's the wolf that gets chopped to pieces at the end. The huntsman does the chopping. Little Red gets a new fur cloak out of it, plus her granny back." With a rough shake of my head, I admit, "I don't want to see my grandmother again."

He nods, conceding that point. "So if you weren't planning to turn that ax on me, why did you need it?"

I shrug. "Dunno. I guess I thought it might come in handy on my way back to the train."

Lucas drops his bundle of fabric on the nearest seat cushion before hooking his thumbs in the loops on his jeans. "Why would you be going to the train?"

His casual question doesn't fool me. His disapproval of my escape plan is obvious, but what else can I do?

"My grandmother tried to kill me. I don't know about you, but where I'm from? That's kinda not okay. Then you expect me to believe she's a witch. That's even worse. I'm not about to stick around and let her or her goons try again. I'm going home, and if I have to wait on the train platform and flag the damn thing down myself, that's what I'm going to do. It's not like I have anywhere else to go."

I thought about it last night before I fell asleep. In Winter Creek, I thought my grandmother was untouchable because she employed half the damn town for her fashion business. Now that I know she's a witch? I have to assume everyone who works under her is a witch, too.

Like Remy, who seemed so proud to call himself 'coven' when we first met. Sure, he told me I was 'coven', too, since I was Marie's granddaughter, but I guess family loyalty only goes so far.

One day you'll understand, petite fille. I must do what's right for the whole coven, even if it means sacrificing one. Even if it means sacrificing you...

I can't go to the cops for help—and that's assuming they even have cops here. I could ask Lucas if I can hide out in his hunting cabin for a few days, but that's too much. He already saved me last night—doing way more than one stranger should for another—and I'm not sure I'll be comfortable staying here when I know what dangers lurk out there in these woods.

No. It's much better for me to just get the hell out of this place. Since the only way to leave is by train, I thought it was obvious that I'd be taking the first one out as soon as possible.

Until Lucas says, "Don't you know?," and my stomach goes tight.

There's already so much I don't know. I'll be the first to admit it. But what is it I don't know *now*?

"Know what?"

"That the train only rolls into town once a week... if

you're lucky. More like twice a month, if I'm being honest. You'd be waiting a while for it to stop."

What? "You're kidding."

Please tell me you're kidding.

Lucas shakes his head. "I'm sorry, but everyone in Winter Creek knows the train is unreliable. It comes a few days before the full moon, and usually when the Luna goes dark. That's it."

Luna. What a strange way to refer to the moon.

Whatever. He can call the moon 'Fred' if he wants, that doesn't change the fact that Lucas is telling me that I'm stuck here indefinitely.

I don't know why I'm surprised. Even Sheila couldn't confirm the exact date for my return trip when I booked the trains, telling me instead that my ticket will work whenever I want to go home. Add that to how everyone I spoke to in Winter Creek was careful not to give me a train schedule to follow and yeah...

No wonder my grandmother seemed convinced I'd be sticking around. I don't think she ever expected me to leave, and that was *before* she tried to serve me up on a silver platter to the beast in the woods.

Well, joke's on her. I survived. I made it. And hoping that the beast only comes out when the moon is full, I just have to wait about two more weeks for the next train.

Might not have a job to go back to, but at least I'll be alive.

Hopefully.

Hmm. He said the ax is stuck to the wall. Maybe I should grab the bow instead, like he suggested.

"Lucas—"

"Besides, you're wrong. You have somewhere to go until the train arrives."

I blink. "I do? Where?"

"With me."

"What?"

"It's an option. I told you. This is my hunting cabin. I don't live here. My friends and I... we have a house on the other side of the woods. There's plenty of room. I went back after sunrise to tell them about you. Majority rules. You're more than welcome to stay with us."

That sounds way too good to be true.

Call me a skeptic, but guys usually have a motive for inviting me back to their place. Lucas hasn't given me any hint that he's interested in me like that, but don't think I didn't hear the way he slipped *my friends and I* into his offer—or *majority rules*. Someone doesn't want him picking up a stray and bringing her home with him, but the rest don't seem to mind.

Why is that? I wonder, my mind already jumping to the worst-case scenario. And while not much can be worse than being tied to a tree, bleeding out like a stuck pig, I'm not sure signing up to be entertainment to a house full of dudes is a good idea.

Trying not to sound too suspicious, I ask, "How many friends live with you?"

He doesn't seem surprised at my question. "There's five of us total. Three guys, two girls. We've known each other for ages and I'd vouch for all of them. You'll be safe with us, Fallon."

I don't know what does it: the solemn and sincere tone of voice he's adopted, or how I'm pretty sure that's the first time he's actually said my name. Either way, I know that I can't see any reason to refuse.

Still, I have one more question for him: "Why are you doing this? Helping me so much, I mean. You don't have to. You don't even *know* me."

I'm watching him so closely that I see it when his jaw tightens. A muscle jerks right along the edge.

"This is our territory," he says after a moment. "My friends and mine. We protect what's ours. I told you. The witches went too far last night. They left you in *my* woods. So now you're under my protection."

Oh. I get it. It's a pride thing. For whatever reason, Lucas and his buddies have beef with the witches. Maybe it's because they're some of the only humans in this 'supe' town—unless he's hiding a pair of pointed fangs and a thirst for blood from me—and this is his way of fighting back against their magic and the curse that probably affects the rest of them.

Only one problem, and it's something that's been bothering me since I discovered witches are real.

"What about me?" He obviously views this rivalry against witches as an 'us vs. them' situation—and I don't know what side I fall on that little divide. "Am *I* a witch?"

Lucas doesn't even hesitate. "No."

"How do you know? She's my grandmother—"

"And maybe she is, but you don't smell like them."

What? "I don't smell like a witch?"

He shakes his head. "They smell like flowers and —" He stops short. Snorts through his nose. "You don't smell like them. I don't know what you are, but you're not a witch. They can't claim you as one of theirs anyway, not if you accept being under my protection."

I want to. I'm not so sure what Lucas and his friends can do against a coven of witches, but I'll take any help I can get right now.

"I don't have any money," I tell him. "Clothes, either. It's all back at my grandmother's, but if I can get my stuff back, I can pay you—"

"I don't want your money."

Pity. If he took payment, I could stop obsessing over whatever it is he really wants. "Then what—"

"Put this on." He picks up the red fabric he brought with him to the hunting cabin. "I just want you to cover up with this."

Bristling at his command, I'm so close to coming up with a retort—but I stop short when he shakes out the fabric and I see what it is.

It's a cape. No. It's a *cloak*. Complete with a hood.

Just like in the fairy tale.

"Oh, you've got to be kidding me," I mumble under my breath. Then, shaking my head, I tell him, "I'm not wearing that."

"Your dress is unique. So are your eyes. If any of Marie's witches see you, they'll run to tell the head of their coven. Unless you want to go naked, this was the best I could come up with on short notice."

"A red cloak with a hood," I say wryly. "That's *all* you could come up with?"

His lips twitch. Holy shit, I think that might've been the first smile I've seen since waking up last night to find him watching over me.

"I might've mentioned your analogy to Eleanor. I wanted a coat, but she had this in her closet. She insisted I bring it for you. She thought it would be a fun way to welcome you to the... to our family."

Eleanor. Family.

Oh.

Wow. I totally misread this whole situation, didn't I? No wonder the gorgeous hunter didn't seem to make any kind of move on me. He's already taken, and obviously a loyal guy.

And Eleanor is a lucky chick with a good sense of humor who can actually get the glowering grump to smile.

Besides, he's right. For all his talk of me being

under his protection now, I can't expect him to stand between me and my grandmother and her witches if they try to find me. If I'm covered up in Eleanor's red cape, walking with Lucas, maybe they'll think I'm her and leave us alone.

It's worth a shot.

I take the red cloak from him. "In that case, just call me 'Little Red.'"

CHAPTER 12
ARGUMENTS

I'm beginning to think the people in Winter Creek all have a tendency to undersell their homes.

First, there was the Coven House. That sucker definitely was more of a manor. And Lucas's house...

It's a fortress.

Three stories tall, it's surrounded by an iron fence that reaches my boobs. The house itself looks like it's made up of big slabs of a dark grey stone, though that might just be the design. It's narrow, reaching higher than the trees, with a single widow's walk wrapping around the uppermost floor.

I almost expect it to have a moat dug in front of it. It doesn't. Like Marie's manor, it has a grassy knoll for a front yard, with trees bordering it. Because unlike the Coven House, it's not set on a street. It's literally tucked into a clearing just big enough to fit it and have enough of a patch of grass around it to be considered its yard.

Welp. I feel a lot better about staying here now. Maybe the witches will be able to follow the windy path we took to find this place—and considering how many fallen trees Lucas had to help me over, and closely grown copse of trees I had to wiggle my way through, I doubt it—but even if they did, this sucker seems like it was built to withstand whatever magic a bonafide witch could throw at it.

As I gape up at it, Lucas falling into a companionable silence a few steps behind me, I can't help but breathe out, "This is *your* house? You *own* this?"

I don't know much about Lucas. Despite the good half an hour it took for us to reach this place, I was lucky if I got about twenty words total out of him. Five of them were: "You ask too many questions". The rest were simple 'yes' and 'no' answers to the questions I couldn't keep back.

He can't be that much older than me. I don't even know if he has a job. I highly doubt he works for Bordeaux Designs, and unless rescuing damsels in distress is a paying gig—and he already refused *my* offer to pay him—then I can't imagine how the hell he could've paid for this... this *castle*.

I should've known better. With my history, I really should've known better than to bring it up.

But I didn't, and I wince when Lucas says, "My parents did. They're gone now so the house is mine."

Oof. "My mom's gone, too."

He doesn't say anything to that. I'm kinda glad that he doesn't.

Instead, he raps his palms against the top of the fence. "Stay here. Okay? I'm gonna let everyone know you're here. They already knew you might be coming, but you probably want to have a few minutes to yourself before you meet everybody."

He's not wrong.

"Sure. But, hang on..." Reaching up, I remove the red hood from my head. The cloak itself has a button that clasps in front of my throat. I unsnap it, shrugging it off. Once I have it in hand, I hold it out to Lucas. "You can tell your friend 'thanks' from me."

"You can tell her yourself later," Lucas points out, but he takes the cloak. Tucking it under his arm, he uses his free hand to push open the iron fence. It eases out with a groan, though he doesn't act as if it's heavy at all. "Don't move. I'll be right back."

With a shove, he sends the fence flying back toward me. It *clicks* shut, the slam echoing around the clearing.

If his friends didn't know I was already here, they do now.

Stay here, he said. Don't move.

Fine.

I watch him stride across the yard, heading toward

the front entrance. Already I regret giving him the cloak back. It was surprisingly warmer than it appeared and, just my luck, it's one of those freeze-your-nips-off days in Winter Creek.

Because I need the distraction, once Lucas is inside, I let my curiosity get the better of me. I try to push the gate open.

It doesn't budge.

He didn't lock it, but maybe it has a catch where it shuts up tight once the fence is closed. Forgetting for a moment that I don't have any shoes on, I give the bottommost bar a good kick.

Shit. That's solid iron. Even with the kick, it didn't move a centimeter, and I'm lucky I didn't crack a couple of toes. If I'd put a little more oomph into the kick, I would have.

Just how strong *is* Lucas?

I bend over to get a better look. Maybe if I find the locking mechanism I can figure it out—

"Fallon?"

My head shoots up.

I do a double-take when the front door swings open and the man who comes bounding out of the house isn't dark and brooding Lucas but, instead, a blonde Adonis who seems stunned to see me.

Tristan. This is where Tristan lives.

He's one of Lucas's friends—or family.

I never would've guessed that. It was pretty

obvious that Tristan had a thing against my grand-mother and her people, and it's kinda funny that he's the one who warned me about the monster and the curse in the first place... but, I don't know. It just never occurred to me that Tristan would be one of Lucas's housemates.

From the expression on his face, he didn't expect to see me, either.

"What are you doing here? I know our lunch date is for this afternoon, but you didn't have to come all this way to pick me up."

Oh, crap. It's Sunday, isn't it? I told Tristan I would meet him in the town square for lunch. Not surprisingly, it totally slipped my mind.

Before I can admit that it did, Lucas appears in the doorway. "Tristan," he calls out. "I told everyone to scatter until I got her settled in."

Huh. Good to know I'm not the only one that Lucas bosses around.

At the sound of his name, Tristan pauses between the iron fence and the entrance, giving me his back as he turns toward Lucas.

"I know. But I thought I scented— wait." He looks from Lucas to me and back. "This is her? The girl in the woods?"

Lucas gives a short nod.

In an instant, Tristan changes. His easy posture stiffens. Instead of that prowl he uses when he's around me, his body shifts, bringing him to his full height as he faces Lucas.

"I wasn't sure. I mean, I *wondered*... wow. And Marie turned on her?" Glancing over his shoulder, Tristan looks back at me again. "Hey. Are you okay?"

I give him a half-smile. "Put it this way: you were right. There's a beast *and* a curse."

"Oh, Fallon—"

I'm not done. "But I was right, too. I told you I couldn't break the damn thing."

That's for sure. I still don't have any fucking idea what this curse *is,* but it doesn't matter. If the beast is real, so is the curse. I didn't survive that monster. I escaped with Lucas's help. The witches will want more blood when they find out.

Good thing I have a castle to hide out in, and a huntsman to protect me.

Plus Tristan's here.

It could definitely be worse—and I don't realize how much until it's too late.

At a signal from Lucas, Tristan heads back into the house. I notice it, but stay quiet as Lucas passes him on his way to the fence. He eases it open with one hand.

He didn't unlatch it or anything. He just yanked and pulled.

So I have my answer, then. He is *very* strong.

Once the two of us have walked inside together, Lucas doesn't seem the least bit surprised that the front room is empty. So is the kitchen we pass through, and the game room he leads me by. I only know that's what it is because I peek inside and see the huge billiards table in there. There's a game currently in play, cue sticks tossed haphazardly on the green felt. A couple of opened soda cans litter the edge, but there's nobody in there.

Just at the end of the hall, there's a staircase. Lucas gestures for me to go first. I shake my head. It might be a little too late to learn any lessons since I'm already in his house. I don't care. I'm going to be more cautious than I have been. He can go up the stairs first, just in case.

He doesn't argue. With a shrug, he starts up the stairs, taking them with a fluid, lazy grace that I have to admire.

His ass in those jeans don't look half bad, either.

"Your room is up one more flight," Lucas says, pausing on the landing. There's another flight of stairs and a hallway leading off of it. He gestures that way. "This is where most of the house has their bedrooms. The—" A dark shadow passes across his face a second before his signature glower takes over. "Luna damn it. I *warned* them."

He spins on his heel, marching down the hall. From right behind him, I can see the lines in his back through his t-shirt, the way his muscles have gone taut. Lucas is pissed, and he's muttering to himself as he storms away.

"I told them to scatter. To their rooms, to the woods, it didn't matter. I didn't say the library."

Oh. When he mentioned earlier that I probably wanted a few minutes to myself, he didn't mean while I waited outside. He was arranging it so that the people who live in this house vanish and I can sneak inside without being the center of everyone's attention.

It was thoughtful. Pointless now, but incredibly thoughtful.

I follow him if only because I heard the word 'library' in his low mutter. Besides, better the devil you know, right? He saved me and brought me here. Until I have a better option, I'm sticking by him.

Together we pass three rooms, all with matching closed doors. I take it all in, curious about this house and Lucas's friends. That's pointless, too. Except for a pair of muddy sneakers kicked in front of one of the doors, I don't see anything.

Until we reach the fourth room on the left, that is.

It's the only one with an open door. That explains how he knows that something was up. From his spot on the landing, he must've seen the open doorway and figured there was a reason it wasn't closed.

There is.

Lucas doesn't say anything at first. Sidling closer to him, I can feel the tension in his big body. I was right when I thought he was pissed, and super glad it's not directed at me.

Standing on my tippy-toes, I look around his bulk.

Holy *shit*.

He said 'library'. I had an idea what a library in Lucas's house would look like. Similar to his hunting cabin, maybe, with a few books here or there.

I've never been so happy to be wrong.

Except for one small square window to let in some natural sunlight, every inch of the four walls is covered in shelves that house hundreds and hundreds of books. At least six oversized beanbag chairs and matching low-rise tables lay scattered over the thick shag carpet. In the far corner, there's a mocha brown couch stretched out, inviting me to lie down on it. The library itself is dark and cozy and smells musty like old books with a hint of cedar thrown in.

I'm immediately in love with it.

Lucas can just stick me in here. With enough books that I'll never run out of reading material, and a window too small for anyone to climb through, so long as the door locks, I'm good. Leave some food for me, point out the nearest bathroom, and you won't have to worry about me.

Too bad there's already some kind of stand-off going on in the middle of the room. If it wasn't for the three people arguing quietly amongst themselves, I might've dropped into the nearest chair. I was in severe need of comfort and this library promises to deliver it.

Or maybe I just want to lose myself in something other than my own troubles for a while...

On one side, there's a couple standing together. The man is around my age, with deep black skin, dark brown eyes, and his hair cut close to his scalp. He has a similar build to Lucas, with wide shoulders and a brawny chest, and a soft voice.

The woman in front of him is a lot more animated. Compared to his height, she seems dainty, though I'm pretty sure her size is closer to mine. Skin as pale as the man's is dark, her hair is a light brown color styled in big, bouncy curls that sway as she argues. Her eyes are the same shade as her hair, though her annoyance might be making them look darker.

And then there's the chick they're facing off against. She *is* petite. At least four inches shorter than me, she has delicate features that give her an innocence that's completely at odds with the nasty twist to her expression. Like me, she's a blonde, though her hair is more golden than mine is. Her eyes are totally different.

They're such a vivid green shade, I almost swear she colored them in with a marker.

The first woman is animated, but the second delivers her side of the argument with precise barbs. They're still too quiet for me to make any sense of. It doesn't matter. She spits out her retorts, fire in her emerald-colored eyes.

It's the man who finally catches on to the fact that they're not alone. Glancing over the first woman's head, he jerks his chin toward Lucas, his eyes darting to each of the women in turn.

It's almost as if he's saying: *I didn't want to get dragged into this in the first place, but here I am. Here you are. Deal with it.*

Lucas steps into the library. Unsure what exactly I should do, I edge closer to the room. Not quite inside of it, but not so far away that I don't get to watch what's going on.

The woman with the curls notices him next. Her face slips into an expression that I'm familiar with; it's the same one Jeannie wore whenever Lorelei caught her borrowing clothes from her side of their closet. It's the *Oops, I thought I'd get away with it, too* look.

Only she hasn't, and her newly sheepish grin tells me she knows it.

Emerald Eyes makes one final remark—as heated as it is, it's still a whisper and I can't hear it—before she follows the direction of her opponents' stares and notices that she has company.

If anything, she looks more furious to see us.

Yes, yes. Lucas is here. You've been caught.

Took you long enough.

He clears his throat. "I thought I settled this argument already. And I also thought I told you all to scatter until Fallon is settled in. Would someone like to explain to me what exactly is going on here?"

His voice is steady and calm as he addresses the other three, though there's a stormy look blazing in his eyes so fiercely, I can't help but shiver. He has a river of rage under his carefully crafted mask—and everyone in this room knows it.

Three heads turn toward Emerald Eyes. Not wanting to be left out, I stare at her, too.

She perches her hands on her hips, a defiant tilt to her head as she looks at a point just past Lucas's shoulder, almost like she can't bring herself to look him in the eye. "Nothing was settled," she snaps. "You just came in and barked orders at us like usual. The argument didn't even begin until you left again."

"Jade." It's a low warning that even I recognize. "Don't."

"What?" she shoots back. Jade... *ha*. Not so far off with my Emerald Eyes nickname, was I? "I'm not the only one who thinks so." Looking past me now, she scoffs. "Where is Tristan anyway? He was on my side."

I'm sure he was—until he knew I was the woman that Lucas was playing 'white knight' over.

"Tristan knows better than to challenge me. Which is more than I can say for the rest of you. What about you two?" he says, addressing the others. "Care to explain?"

The woman starts to open her mouth. The man lays his hands on her shoulders. She closes her mouth, shaking her bouncy curls.

"Didn't think so." Lucas dismisses them, all of his attention back on the tiny blonde. "And you, Jade? Are you challenging my authority?"

"No, A—"

"Then explain yourself."

For a moment there, I really thought she was going to ignore him. Just excuse herself and leave the room. But then she dares a quick peek over his shoulder again, her glittering gaze landing right on me this time.

Her upper lip curls in instant dislike.

I can't say the feeling isn't mutual.

Jade grows bold. With a royal shake of her head, she continues to stare at me. "She shouldn't be here. You promised you wouldn't upset the house by bringing in another stray. And, look, here we are. Again." She huffs. "And to think I actually believed you after what we got stuck with last time."

The other woman lets out an offended squeak.

The man at her back keeps his hands on her shoulders. "What's that supposed to mean?"

"You're the one who brought her in, Kirk. You tell me."

Another warning from Lucas as he rumbles out, "*Jade.*"

"Eleanor is my mate—"

"Your wife," corrects Lucas, head snapping back to Kirk. "She's your wife."

"Right." The woman with the curls—Eleanor— leans back against her husband's chest. "We're married."

At the word 'married', I immediately drop my gaze down to her left hand. No ring, but I do notice the way the fingers on her right hand are lightly stroking a mark on her neck. When Kirk lifts one hand off of her shoulder, taking hers in his, I get a better look at it.

It's not just a mark, I notice with a start. It's a *bite*. Like she got bit by a wild animal and it scarred.

Okay, then.

I blink away my surprise, gaze darting away so that I'm not staring. It lands on Kirk and Eleanor's intertwined hands.

Wait. *They're* married. And unless there are two Eleanors floating around—and Lucas already told me that two women live in this house so I can't see how— then she isn't his girlfriend or wife. She's Kirk's.

I glance over at the other woman.

Eleanor is married—

"I'm not," Jade says flatly before giving a pointed look over at Lucas.

Oh.

Yup. I got that one way wrong. It isn't Eleanor that Lucas is involved with. It's the other one, and suddenly her nasty attitude makes a whole lot more sense.

"Jade." He bites out her name one last time. "Enough. Drop it."

Though dropping it is probably the last thing she wants to do, she screws her jaw shut and pouts for a moment before sighing. "Fine. But since there's no talking sense into anyone, I'm going on patrol. Someone has to make sure the witches don't cross into our territory." She dares another glance up at Lucas. "And I'm doing that for you. Not *her*."

He scowls, even after she's flounced out of the room and down the hallway and can't possibly see it. "What makes it worse is that she's *right*." He blows a breath out through his nose. "We managed to avoid running into the coven on the way to the house. If I know Marie, she won't let this go that easily. Someone else should be patrolling with Jade."

"Tristan?" suggests Eleanor.

Lucas shakes his head.

She turns into her husband, laying a hand on his chest through his shirt. "Kirk, why don't you go? Last night was the full moon. We should give Lucas a break."

"I appreciate it, Ellie," Lucas says, cutting off Kirk with a gesture of his big hand, "but I promised Fallon my protection. I'll do a better job of it making sure the witches stay away from our house tonight. Why don't you two do me a favor and show her to her room? Then, later on, we can trade off."

Translation: take over babysitting duty for me, all right?

I don't blame him. Guy's just trying to do a good deed, and what does he get? His friends giving him grief.

As if finally remembering—or even just *realizing*—that I'm right here, he turns to look at me. "How's that sound? You okay with that plan?"

Like I can really say no. "Sure."

"Good. Then I'll see you later."

He's gone before I can even process what just happened. When I finally do, I look into the library.

"Do I want to know what all that talk of patrolling means?" I ask, more to myself than the two strangers Lucas left me with.

"Nope," chirps Eleanor.

Hey. At least she's another honest one.

"Fair enough."

Later that afternoon, as I look down at my new change of clothes, I have two thoughts: one) it's better than wearing the blood-stained chiffon dress, and two) I'm going to fucking freeze.

It's the middle of October. For a town called Winter Creek, we haven't even hit the real *cold* yet, either. I'm hoping to be long gone by then, but since I'm stuck here for a while, I had no choice but to borrow some clothes from Eleanor and Jade.

Well, probably Eleanor, and not just because Jade clearly doesn't want me here. I just managed to stuff myself into the bra, tank top, and cut-off shorts that she brought to my room a half an hour ago; no panties, because while I'll share everything else, I'd rather go commando than wear a stranger's underwear. Everything fits kinda the same—the tank is a little short, the bra a little more padded than I like, and I had to wiggle to get the shorts buttoned—but if I tried to squeeze my butt into something in Jade's size, it would never work.

I almost gave up on the bra, too. Only after seeing how my nipples poked through the tank top without me wearing the damn thing had me sighing and reaching for it. In spite of the stony exterior, the house is warmer than I expected so I'll be fine inside. Doesn't change the fact that my outfit is a summer fit instead of autumn.

But that's all Eleanor owns. Seriously. I guess it's hard to get clothes when you're boycotting the witch-run stores—because, surprise, my grandmother is a witch *and* a seamstress—though it still doesn't explain why every piece of clothing that both of these women have are loose cotton dresses, shorts, tank tops, and the odd pair of sweatpants.

She gave me a set of my own to sleep in, promising to scrounge up some more clothes that might be closer to my style. I'm grateful, even if I feel half-dressed for the moment.

But I'm clean. At Eleanor's sweet yet blunt insistence, I took a forty-minute long shower. I had to. I didn't realize how nasty my feet got, tromping around the woods without any shoes on, until I noticed my mud-covered toes leaving marks behind on the hardwood floor of my borrowed bedroom.

It's a nice space. It has a bed. Not as luxurious as

the one in the manor, of course, but the sheets are fresh. The bathroom had a brand new bottle of both shampoo and conditioner waiting for me, plus an unopened toothbrush. I don't really know why they're so prepared for unexpected guests, but I'm grateful enough that I don't question it.

Same thing with the clothes. If there's one thing my mother taught me, it's not to be a choosing beggar. I'll take what I can get and leave it at that.

It's for the same reason that I leave it alone when it seems like I've been shoved into an empty room on the third floor and then forgotten. And maybe I'm being a little facetious. Someone brought me up a plate of lunch, placing the ham sandwich with a pickle on the side on my bed while I was locked in the bathroom, scrubbing up. It was probably Eleanor, though seeing the sandwich made me think of the lunch I could've been having with Tristan in the town square if my grandmother hadn't, you know, tried to feed me to the beast in the woods.

Same thing happens at dinner, only this time I'm sitting cross-legged on the bed when the door flings open.

Just like I thought, it's Eleanor who is carrying a plate of spaghetti with meatballs on it. Kirk is right behind her, utensils in one hand, a glass of water in the other.

At this point, I'm starting to get just a little weirded

out. As though the shower washed away some of the shock clinging to me, I'm finally looking at the situation with a clearer head. There's no denying that my grandmother hurt me. I removed the bandage Lucas put on my arm before I got under the shower spray and while the cut clotted over, it's still there. I didn't imagine it.

There's also no getting around the fact that I agreed to basically move into this stone fortress in the middle of the woods with a bunch of people I know nearly nothing about. Sure, it was my best option at the time, but while I basically know their names and that's about all... it almost seems like they know *me*.

I could forgive the ham sandwich. It's a classic for a reason. The pickle, too. Who doesn't love a good pickle?

Same thing with spaghetti and meatballs. That's a safe dinner, right? Anyone would eat them, unless they had food restrictions or a meat-free diet.

But when I notice that the glass of water has an orange slice on it... not lemon, not lime, but an *orange*... I can't get past the coincidences. How did they manage to serve my favorite lunch sandwich, my favorite dinner, and my preferred beverage?

I have no idea, and that bothers me more than knowing that my grandmother might still be out there, searching for me.

Add that to how they just walked into my room

without even knocking and there's only one thing I can think to do once I finally get rid of them.

I lock the door to my room, hoping like hell that I'll be back home and safe in my apartment before I know it.

IT DOESN'T TAKE LONG FOR ME TO ADMIT THAT LUCAS clearly wants me out of sight, out of mind until it's time for the train to roll in.

Fine. I can do that.

To be fair, he didn't actually *say* that. He didn't have to. Actions speak louder than words, and at his first opportunity to pass me off to someone else, he did. With the excuse that he was "patrolling"—and I still don't know what that means, but following Eleanor's lead, I don't ask—I don't see him again the rest of that first night. The next day, either.

In fact, the only ones who take the trek up to the third floor are Eleanor and Kirk. Eleanor, because she's taken to the role of playing mother hen to me, and Kirk, because it doesn't take a genius to figure out that he's so besotted with his wife, he follows her everywhere.

Of course, right when I'm starting to get used to this new routine, everything changes...

It's my second morning in the house, on the third

day after I first arrived to stay with them, when I hear the doorknob rattle. I'm already up, wearing the same shorts as the first day along with a forest green tank top that brings out my eyes—according to Eleanor, at least—so it doesn't surprise me. Once she realized I felt more comfortable with the door locked, Eleanor would rattle the knob, then wait for me to answer.

The person on the other side of the door doesn't.

They knock, then call out, "Are you awake?"

Lucas. That's Lucas out there.

I'm already halfway toward the door, almost sprinting toward it when it hits me how quick I was to move when I knew Lucas was on the other side of it.

That should've been a big ol' honking warning sign.

Should've been, except I purposely ignore it.

Instead, after fluffing my hair and checking to see where my opal hits my cleavage, I take a deep breath and open the door.

He must've just showered before he came upstairs to see me. Most of his mass of dark hair is dried, though there are a few stray tendrils that are damp curls, clinging to his forehead and the nape of his neck. He's wearing another impossibly black t-shirt that matches his hair, bringing out his unusual eyes.

He's frowning. It should be illegal for a man to look as gorgeous frowning as Lucas does.

"You locked the door."

No use denying it. "I did. Why? Was that wrong?"

He shakes his head. "No. Just unexpected. But it's fine. Anyway, I've come to see if you want to come down to breakfast."

Wow. A personal appearance and an invitation to leave my prison cell? He must be in a good mood today—and, no. I'm not being fair. Just because Lucas agreed to keep me safe from my wicked grandmother, that doesn't mean he has to hold my hand and keep me occupied. Being protected should be enough.

I wish it was.

Too bad my heart skipped a beat when I heard his voice, my stomach doing a little flip-flop when I opened the door and saw his face.

I can't pretend I'm not attracted to him. This is getting dangerously close to 'crush' territory, too, and that's the last thing I need. Infatuated Fallon gets herself into trouble, and I think I've already had my fill of that since I've come to Winter Creek.

"I'd love to." And then, because I can't help myself, I ask, "What's for breakfast?"

"It was Tristan's turn to cook. He went with pancakes, fruit, and bacon for the carnivores among us."

I don't know a single meat-eater who doesn't love bacon. As for the pancakes...

"Buttermilk pancakes?" I verify. "Sliced straw-berries?"

"Actually, no. We're having chocolate chip with bananas."

What a surprise. Not that Tristan cooked—though that definitely catches my attention—but that he miraculously picked chocolate chip pancakes with sliced bananas on top of all types and toppings.

"Really?" My voice comes out weaker than I intended it to. "That's my favorite."

It's a full kitchen when I follow Lucas downstairs.

From my quick tour of the first floor the other day, I remember that this place has a kitchen huge enough to fit a dining table built for eight inside of it. The cabinets, stove, and massive refrigerator take up half the room; the wooden table and all its chairs are in the other. Of the eight chairs, four are filled.

Everyone is scarfing down their breakfast, though they all instinctively stop when Lucas walks into the room.

He nods. Without a word, they dig back into their food.

That was... weird, right? Almost like they needed his permission to eat, even though they must have already started when he ran upstairs to get me.

And why was it *Lucas* who asked me to join them

for breakfast anyway? Since he brought me to stay in his house, it's been obvious that he planned on making Eleanor and Kirk responsible for me. Too busy with whatever it is he does, he was happy to delegate any responsibilities he believes he has to the little lost lamb he found in the woods.

Because that's what I feel like. That's what I've thought of myself as from the moment Marie's goons muscled me up against that tree. I was the prey for a monstrous beast. A lure.

A sacrifice.

And surrounded by Lucas and his friends? Who seem friendly enough, but what the hell do I really know? I can't shake the feeling that I'm still being hunted—or that I'll be looking over my shoulder long after I'm back safely in the anonymity of Manhattan.

For now, I hover on the other side of the threshold, hesitating to join the others for reasons I don't really want to look too closely at.

Sensing my hesitancy, Lucas turns to me. "Come on in. You don't want your breakfast to get cold."

Jade snorts. "Maybe if you'd let Ellie bring it up to her earlier, it wouldn't have been."

Lucas ignores her, keeping his eyes on me. "Go on. Sit down."

He points out a seat for me. I'm not surprised that it's as far away from Jade as it can get—or that he seems oblivious that his order might just rub me the wrong way.

It's also sat exactly opposite of Tristan. Who, I notice, is so busy with his breakfast that he doesn't even bother to lift his head and say 'hi'.

Message received, Blondie. It was fun to flirt with me when it was just the two of us, but throw in his friends and, suddenly, I'm invisible.

Good to know.

Eleanor spares a tight-lipped smile. Her cheeks are stuffed with food, chipmunk-style, so I know that's the only reason I don't see her teeth. Kirk, following his wife's lead, uses the coffee mug he's holding to gesture a greeting at me.

Ah, well. Three out of the five of them don't seem to mind my presence at the table. I guess that's the 'majority rules' Lucas was talking about.

Once my hand hits the back of my chair, Lucas moves to the counter. He picks up an empty plate, shooting a look my way. "What would you like? I'll make you a plate."

Clank.

Jade's fork falls from her grip, hitting the table with a clattering sound. She picks it up quickly, though there's no missing the heated glare she sends Lucas before muttering something I can't quite pick up under her breath.

Lucas ignores that, too. "Fallon?"

I get the sensation that, for some reason, it's a much more loaded request than my savior just offering to slap some pancakes and bacon on my plate for me. Which is ridiculous, but if this is the only way to show that I'm not a damsel in distress, then I'm damn well going to get my own breakfast.

I join him by the counter, holding my hand out so that I can take the empty plate. "Don't worry. I got it."

He doesn't hand it over. "Are you sure? 'Cause I don't mind."

I waggle my fingers. "It's fine."

With a shrug, Lucas passes me the plate. Then, grabbing his own, he backs up so that I can get my breakfast first.

Pick your battles, Fallon. If this is his way of being chivalric, I can give him this concession.

With as many people to feed, breakfast is served buffet-style. There's a towering stack of pancakes on one counter, a mound of sliced bananas next to it, and still plenty of bacon left on a third plate.

Once I take enough, I go back to my seat. It's next to Eleanor, who nods approvingly when she sees that I didn't skimp on the bacon or the syrup. Tristan is still staring down at his plate as if the last few banana slices are fascinating. Kirk is humming to himself on the other side of Eleanor, while Jade—sitting opposite of Kirk—is glaring at me from across the diagonal.

I expect Lucas to slip into the seat between Jade

and Tristan. I don't know why, especially since it seems like the most obvious thing in the world when the big, brooding man takes the seat at the head of the table.

Which, unsurprisingly, is the one on the other side of me.

It's his protective nature again, I tell myself. This way, he can keep an eye on me while also making sure that Jade leaves me alone.

And it works, too—for maybe three minutes.

Though Jade's done with her plate, she doesn't rise up from her seat. Instead, she stays at the table, alternating her pissed-off stare between me and Lucas. And then, though I'm almost sure I imagined it, she growls.

Tiny little thing and she *growls* at me.

Lucas places his fork down. "Jade."

There's a warning note in his voice that makes me admit that: no, I didn't imagine that, did I?

Her expression is one of pure innocence. "What? I'm not challenging you, Luc. You never said I can't challenge *her*." Innocence turns to open annoyance as she furrows her brow and wrinkles her nose... and, even so, she's still so freaking pretty. It's not fair. "Besides, it's not like I even can. She's a—"

"She's our guest," he says firmly. "I offered our protection. She accepted it. End of story."

Eleanor leans into me, bumping shoulders. "Don't listen to Jade. She's all bark and no bite."

As if to prove Eleanor wrong, Jade snaps her teeth at the other woman.

Okay, then.

You know what? Jade doesn't like me. I got that vibe from her the moment we met. She only cemented it when she point-blank told Lucas that she doesn't want me here. I might've been able to avoid her when I stayed upstairs. Sitting at the breakfast table, it's a lot harder.

But if she thinks I'm going to just sit here and take her mean girl bullshit, she has another think coming.

I might have the other day. After everything my grandmother put me through, I'm done with putting up with other people's crap.

"Is there something you want to say to me?" I ask her. "Because, so far, you've taken your attitude out on almost everyone else when we all know I'm the one you have a problem with. Go on. I'm a big girl. I can take it."

I spent four years in a dorm with Jeannie Lipton. I can take anything Jade wants to throw at me.

"Fuck you."

Jade's answer is short and to the point. Because of course it is.

Tristan's head shoots up from his plate.

Lucas starts to rise from his chair.

Oh, no. I did this. I got the reaction I was looking for, and I'm feeling a lot more like myself than I have in days. No way I'm going to let these two guys fight my battles for me.

"Sorry," I toss back easily, "but you're not my type." Then, to rub it in, I sneak a peek toward my right. "When I do chicks, I prefer brunettes with pretty smiles, not blondes with a stinkface."

Right on cue, Jade's lovely face twists again, right into an expression of outright dislike. But she doesn't say anything.

Eleanor breaks the silence. "Um. Thanks. But I'm mated—"

"Married," murmurs her husband.

"Right. So I'm gonna have to pass."

I don't know her all that well, but there's a hint of a tease there that tells me she's going along with it.

I like her. We've only just met the other day, but I really like her.

Shame I can't say the same for Jade.

CHAPTER 14
KISS

After breakfast, I offer to clean up but Lucas points out that it's Jade's turn to do the dishes. Since not even getting my hands wet and dirty will get her on my side, I let it go with the caveat that, for our next meal, I'd like to do something to help.

He won't let me pay him. The least I can do is scrub some dishes, right?

With a slightly amused expression on his face, Lucas promises that he'll put me into the chore rotation for as long as I stay at the house. Figuring that's as fair as it's going to get, I agree.

Then he suggests that I spend the rest of my morning in the library instead of returning to my third-floor bedroom and I don't care why he's acting so strangely all of a sudden. I've been dying to return to the library. I'm not about to let my chance slip through my fingers.

It's more amazing than I remember. Strolling around the library, reading the titles on the shelves, I notice that most of them are from decades before I was born. Almost like the bulk of this library was built around the early part of the century to about the 1950s or so. I see a few modern titles, including a couple of big name romance authors that I'm immediately interested in, but I like how far back it goes even if it takes me a minute to understand why.

Considering this house was his parents' before him, odds are that it belonged to his parent's parents before that. This is a library that's been lovingly built over a hundred years or more—similar to the stony fortress it's a part of—and it's a monument to time.

It's *fascinating*.

When I see a book of Grimm Brothers' fairy tales, I decide to grab that one first. After checking the index, I snort to myself when I see it has the story of Little Red Riding Hood in it. You'd think I'd want to avoid it after what happened to me.

Nope. Plopping down on the sofa, I prop up the book on my knees and begin to reacquaint myself with the old legend.

And if I'm comparing it to these last few days? Why not? I might've started it, but Lucas fed into it by making me wear the red cloak on our journey from the hunter's cabin to his freaking castle.

For the next day and a half, I spend nearly all my time in the library. It's as cozy and comforting as I thought it would be, and I'm often joined by Eleanor on her own or, more often than not, with her husband. At first, I thought it was because they're back on babysitting duty, but Eleanor insists that this is just something the two of them like to do. Each in their own chair, leaning up against each other as they read a different book, they're happy just being together.

And, man, do I envy them.

They're also the only two who seem to enjoy the library as much as I do. At the very least, no one else except for Eleanor and Kirk have made a point to stop by and say 'hi' since I've left the third floor.

Not Jade. Not Tristan.

Not Lucas, either—until after an uneventful lunch on Thursday, five days after I came to stay with him and his friends.

I'd already finished reading two different books of fairy tales, a book on witchcraft, and an over-the-top forced proximity romance book from the 90s before turning my attention to an old Agatha Christie book when the door eases open that afternoon, a pair of big shoulders appearing in the doorway a moment before I realize that it's *Lucas*.

"You doing alright?"

Keeping my finger between the pages as a marker, I nod. My heart rate's kicked up a bit, getting a head-on look at his darkly handsome face when I wasn't prepared for it, but I will myself to calm.

"Yeah," I tell him after a few seconds. "It's so nice and quiet in here. Peaceful, too. I really like it."

"Would you mind some company? I was thinking about getting a little reading in, but if you'd rather be alone..."

Are you kidding? Give up a chance to spend some time with the enigmatic Lucas?

Yeah, right.

"Come on in."

"You're sure? You don't mind if I join you?"

An overprotective if slightly overbearing man who revs my engine *and* likes to read? And who, Eleanor confirmed, has nothing going on with Jade and—in spite of her best efforts otherwise—never has?

"Not at all."

Lucas walks over to one of the shelves, grabs a book seemingly at random, then heads toward the sofa. Before I know it, he's sat on the furthest cushion from me. It's a three-seater, so there's only one place between us... and, yet, I feel like we're almost touching.

I didn't expect him to actually sit on the same sofa as me. For some reason, I thought he'd pick out his book and plop down on one of the beanbag chairs like Eleanor and Kirk usually do. Silly in retrospect, but now that Lucas is so close, I'm intimately more aware of him than I am the book in my own hands.

For a few minutes, all you can hear in the library are the sounds of our breathing and the whisper of pages being turned. I can't say for sure when that changed, when the breathing picked up a little or the pages slowed down, but it doesn't take long before I have to admit that Lucas is one hell of a distraction.

I think I've read the part about the kimono being found on the Orient Express three times before I glance up to find that Lucas has stopped reading, too.

In fact, when I look at him, I see that he's looking at *me*.

If only I could read his expression as easily as one of these books. I have no idea what he's thinking—or why he's staring at me.

His close attention makes me a little anxious. "What?"

"Nothing."

It's not nothing.

He closes his book. "It's just... you're not anything like what I thought you'd be."

Considering his first impression of me was when he stumbled upon me tied to a tree, blood everywhere, and that I fainted as soon as he freed me... I can only imagine what kind of woman he thought I'd be.

Case in point: how he immediately seemed ready to shield me from Jade's cattiness at breakfast the other morning before I took care of myself, or how he's been careful to keep us separated since.

Still, I can't say I'm not grateful for his support, and since he's the one that started up a conversation when we're supposed to be reading, I tell him so.

Lucas brushes aside my gratitude with a casual sweep of one of his big hands. "What Ellie said the other day... about how Jade is all bark and no bite? She wasn't wrong. Once Jade gets to know you the way I do, she'll get used to having you around. She always does."

I think about the comment Jade made regarding Eleanor and Kirk's relationship—*you're the one who brought her in, Kirk... you tell me...*—and how she seems to get along with the other woman now, albeit begrudgingly. That must be what he means.

I shrug, not so sure I believe it. Eleanor had to marry into the friend group for Jade to finally accept her. If that's the case, I haven't got a prayer.

When Lucas stays quiet, I pick up my book again. I reread the same paragraph for a *fourth* time when he breaks up the silence by clearing his throat.

"So..." His deep voice has my breath catching. "Was it true?"

I don't look up from the page. I *can't*. Whenever I meet his gaze, I'm afraid Lucas will see just how attracted to him and... yeah. That could be a mess. Between Tristan and Jade making everything undeniably awkward when all of us are together, and Lucas noticeably keeping his distance from me to the point that I'd just leave if I had anywhere else to go… my fanciful idea of a vacation fling went out the window when Remy turned out to be a jerk and I missed that lunch date with Tristan.

So forgive me for not quite understanding what Lucas was getting at right away.

"Hmm?" Oh, wow. So that's whose luggage they found it in…"Was what true?"

"What you said about your type."

Huh? My type? "I have no idea what you're talking about."

"When we were all at the table for breakfast," he says in an attempt to jog my memory.

Considering how that first one went, I know which breakfast he's referring to since one or two of his friends have been on "patrol" during mealtimes every time I'm asked to join the table.

He must mean when I snapped back at Jade, and—

Oh.

Oh.

Sorry, Poirot, I think to myself, letting the book close before placing it on the arm of the sofa. I'll get back to you later.

Then, shifting in my seat so that I can face Lucas, I prop my chin up with my folded fingers. "Are you asking me if I was just riling Jade up by mentioning that I've banged girls in the past or if I really meant it when I said I was into Eleanor?"

Lucas blinks.

Look at that. I think my candor stunned him.

He recovers quickly, but I don't miss the way the heights of his cheeks go just a little pink there. "Yeah. I guess it's something like that. Because, you must know, Eleanor is ma—"

"Married. I know."

Lucas nods. "She's been very happy with Kirk for a long time. And our kind… we don't believe in divorce. When we get together, it's for life—and we're not wired to cheat."

Kind? Ah, jeez. I'd wondered what was up with the five of them living together in this big house. Sure, Kirk and Eleanor are a married couple, and even if Lucas and Jade never had a thing going on, it's obvious that it's not for a lack of trying on her part. As for Tristan… I don't think there's a single soul in all of Winter Creek who'd turn him down if he flashed his gleaming smile their way. Still, it seems as if the three of them are single—and their friend group is very insular.

Then there's the strange way they refer to things, almost like it's in code. I've overheard them calling themselves a 'pack', and they all have this strange obsession with patrolling their territory. If I had to guess, I'd think they were trying to rise up against the witches, keeping my grandmother from taking over the entire town, but, honestly, I have no idea.

But the way he says 'kind' like that? Is this like a religious cult or something? Not gonna lie... the whole "no cheating" thing sounds pretty dope, but I really hope that's not a dig on me coming out to him.

That's the thing with being openly bi. Most of my relationships have been with dudes, but I've had more than a few girls that I thought might be the "one". But just because I'm attracted to both genders, that doesn't mean I'd actually expect Eleanor to cheat on Kirk with me—and if he really thought I meant my teasing, he might not have gotten as good a read on me as he thought he did.

"I'd never try to come between a committed couple," I tell him. "That's not my style."

Lucas puts his closed book to the side. I'm not even sure he read more than a few pages. Probably not, since I'm getting the feeling that grabbing the book was just his cover story to have this chat for some strange reason.

And that's when he asks me, "Then what is? Your style, I mean," and I'm sure I'm right.

How to answer, though? Part of me wants to toss a flippant retort back at him. But the other part?

It's like when I first came to in the hunting cabin all over again. I look over at Lucas, and I can't shake the feeling that I know *him*—and I want him to know me.

I give him another shrug, and an honest answer. "I've been with a couple of different people in my time. Mostly guys, but some girls. No big deal. It's all about attraction to me. If I'm attracted and they have a good personality... and they're into me, too, of course... why not, right?"

Lucas goes still—again, he stays quiet—and I have to wonder if maybe I said too much. Apart from quips and jokes to deflect, when push comes to shove, I've never been the type of woman who shies away from her past. Of course, I'd rather talk about my old relationships and sketchy one-night stands than dredge up the old memories of my mom's illness I prefer to keep repressed.

Still, considering I just can't seem to resist this tug I feel toward Lucas, I'm suddenly wondering if there's such thing as being *too* honest and open.

Whatever happened to him in that moment when he froze in place, he shakes it off as quickly as it affected him. Leaning into the arm on his side of the sofa, he relaxes—and he continues the conversation. "That's all it takes? Attraction and a good personality?"

I snort. "I hope you're not implying that I'm easy, big guy."

"Not at all. Just making sure I understand what you said."

Right. "Then, yeah. That's all it takes. But it's not just sex for fun, you know? I have a reason for dating as much as I do, hopping from relationship to relationship when it's obvious that it's not gonna work out."

He raises his eyebrows. "Really?"

There's something in the way he's watching me now that has me ready to backpedal.

"Maybe we should change the subject," I say. "You probably don't even want to hear this—"

In a throaty voice that tells me that I have his complete attention, Lucas says, "I absolutely do."

Oh. Well, in that case...

"I've been looking for the one for a while. And, like, I know I'm only twenty-five, but I've always had this... I don't know... feeling that there was someone out there meant just for me. Man, woman, someone who is neither... it doesn't matter *who* they are so long as they're my person, if that makes any sense." I wait a beat. Lucas nods, so I continue. "I just haven't found them yet, so I keep looking."

Jeannie used to make fun of me for that. In high school, it was more of a light-hearted tease, but by the time we were in college, she thought I needed to give up my fairytale fantasies of my Prince Charming and a happy ending.

Considering she had a front-row seat when my relationship with Danny imploded, she probably has a point.

But Lucas doesn't look at me like I'm being childish. He's peering over at me now as if I said something he identifies with.

"Do you mean that?"

"I do. And I guess you could say all my flings have been me getting one step closer to finding the *one*. Not that I regret any of them"—I don't because each one had a hand in making me the woman I am now—"but they're all done and over with and I'm still searching."

Does that sound pathetic? It kinda does, but if Lucas thinks so, he doesn't give it away on his face.

Rather, he looks almost... thoughtful.

"What about now? Are you looking for forever, or..."

His voice trails to a close, leaving his question open-ended.

I'm not sure how to answer. Honestly, I'm looking for my happily-ever-after. Not like I can tell Lucas that. I'm leaving in a couple of days so it's not like *forever* is even on the table, but if he seems interested in getting to know each other a little better...

"I'm not seeing anyone right now, if that's what you're asking."

Is that what he's asking?

"Brunette females are your type." His voice drops. "What type of males are you looking for?"

I zoom right past the way he said 'females' and 'males' like that. In the short time I've known Lucas, he has a weird way of talking about a couple of things.

Like referring to the moon as the 'Luna'… why wouldn't he have a different way of discussing men and women? That's just Lucas. He might be different, but there's no doubt he's giving me a clear signal here.

And me? I've been dying to do something like this since the moment I woke up and discovered he not only saved me from Marie, but he washed the blood from my skin.

So, matching his throaty tone from before, I murmur, "Why don't I show you?"

He gulps. "Yeah? And how would you do that?"

Following his lead, I scoot next to him. Then, lifting my hand, I curve my palm around the edge of his jaw. His stubble is softer than I expected; it's not scratchy at all. There's also no resistance as I guide his mouth toward mine.

"Like this," I whisper a split second before I dart out my tongue, swiping it along his bottom lip.

It's like an electric shock rushing through me. That's the sort of jolt I experience simply from touching my tongue to his lip. Eager to feel that again, I shift my body. My hand stays on his cheek, keeping him right where I want him, as I climb up on my knees, leaning into his side.

In this position, I can really kiss him. Starting with nibbling at the corner of his mouth, I wait to see if Lucas is going to be an active participant or if I made a colossal error, mistaking his curiosity for interest. Just when I'm about to pull away from him, he lifts his own hand, bracing the back of my head.

After that, it's not a matter of who is kissing who. We're both kissing each other, the gentle kiss becoming deeper as Lucas holds me to him.

That's okay. I'm not letting go of him, either. If I could climb right onto his lap, I would—and when he moves his lower body, spreading his legs to brace his feet against the carpet, I realize that I *can*.

I start to follow the instinctive sway of his body, going light-headed from his addictive kiss, and I might've ended up showing Lucas just how damn easy I am if it wasn't for what happens next.

Something creaks. I don't know what it is, but it's loud enough to cut through our kiss as we both under-stand at the same time that we're not alone anymore.

We break apart. I flop down on the cushion right beside Lucas while he straightens up in his seat.

And that's when I see who walked in on me and Lucas in such a compromising position: Jade... and Tristan.

Of course.

Jade is standing in the doorway, hand curved around the jamb. She's digging her long nails into the wood, her expression simmering with ill-disguised rage.

Tristan's pretty face is blank. He gives nothing away as he leans against the nearest bookshelf.

"Sorry for disturbing you, Luc. Jade—"

"I know what Jade was doing," Lucas says. "And I thought she knew better. You, too, Tristan."

He swallows. I watch his Adam's apple bob with action. "Yes."

Lucas squeezes my thigh, a quick touch, then he's already on his feet again, leaving me on the couch.

"Jade. Go on a run. Cool off. Take over for Kirk if you want, but don't come back to the house until you're ready to have a conversation."

She tilts her chin up, though she's not looking at Lucas. She's glaring at me.

"Is that an order?"

"What do you think?"

With a frustrated huff, she releases her death grip on the door jamb, spinning around so quickly that her hair fans out behind her. As she storms off, I can't help but think that all she's missing is a little foot stamping. Otherwise, that was a grade-A tantrum.

Lucas lifts his hand, running the back of it over his mouth. I try not to be too offended that he's basically wiping my kiss off of his lips, but it's tough. Two seconds ago, I was ready to shift onto his lap and see what would happen next.

And now he's acting as though nothing happened between us at all.

As soon as Jade disappears, Lucas and Tristan lock eyes. A charged moment passes between them, so electric that the hair on my arms stand on end. There aren't any words, though. The eye contact doesn't last more than a split second, either. Tristan breaks the stare, dropping his gaze to the carpet.

Still silent as the grave, Lucas stalks out of the library.

I take that as my cue to go. Being rejected by Lucas is bad enough, though I probably should've been expecting it. Having it happen in front of an audience? Yeah. That sucks.

Tucking my hair behind my ears, purposely looking anywhere but at Tristan, I try to make my escape.

I get as far as the open doorway before he murmurs my name.

"Fallon?"

Crap. I should've been expecting that.

I turn to glance up at Tristan, swallowing a gasp when I discover he's *right there*. He's so close that I can smell the outdoors on him as he bows his head over me, forcing me to look up at him.

I suck in a breath as my head tilts back, eyes locking on his steely gaze.

His lips part.

I get the insane idea that he's going to kiss me. With Lucas's taste still on my tongue, Tristan seems to vibrate in place, our mouths mere inches away from each other.

All I have to do is give him some sign that I want this. A soft sigh, a whispered 'yes', even a delicate brush of my lips against his. I could twine my fingers with Tristan's, press our bodies together, give in to the attraction that's crackled between us since the moment he first stepped out of the woods... and use this nice guy to forget what just happened between me and his best friend.

I step back.

Tristan follows.

Reaching out, his hand hovers over my bicep. He doesn't quite touch me, though the heat from his palm scorches my skin.

I see the resignation on his face. For a split second, he thought I was going to kiss him.

Not gonna lie, so did I.

"I should be heading back to my room," I squeak out. "Goodnight."

"Fallon, wait."

I haven't moved yet. "Yeah?"

"I want you to know something. Okay?" At my nod, he leans in and says, "There's always a choice."

Gone is the flirtatious, easygoing tone I'm so used to from him. He sounds earnest. Sincere.

Desperate.

I meet his eyes again. As blue as ever, they're a darker shade than normal. "Tristan?"

"Remember that, Fallon. Okay? When you

remember everything else, don't forget this moment right now. You don't always have to do what you think you're supposed to. You have a choice."

I always have a choice. And if he thinks that I always do what I'm supposed to, then he hasn't gotten to know me at all.

Only one of us acts the part of a trained soldier when it comes to being given orders—and it sure the hell isn't me.

But he looks like he needs me to agree with him, so I nod.

He exhales softly, drawing away from me. "That's all I ask."

Good. Because, right now, that's all I can give him.

Even if I can't help but feel like it should be more.

Like a scolded puppy with her tail between her legs, I slink upstairs to my given bedroom.

Lucas is gone. I don't want to think that he chased after Jade, but I don't see him as I head toward the staircase. Giving me my space, Tristan lingers in the library while I make my quick escape.

The rest of the doors, as usual, are closed. I figure one of them has to be Lucas's, but I have no idea which one it can be. Since I'd be even more pathetic than I already am to knock on each one until I force him to come out and face me, I shake off the last of the daze that settled over me during our kiss and scurry up the stairs.

My opal bounces as my bare feet pad up the hard-wood steps. I quiet it with my palm, stroking the familiar curve of the stone as I shudder out a breath.

I still taste Lucas. Something a little bit spicy, something a little bit fresh—his toothpaste, most likely—and something undeniably *him*.

I almost head straight for the bathroom to rinse out my own mouth. The fact that I don't, that every instinct inside of me wants to hold onto that kiss a little longer no matter how abruptly it came to an end, I know I'm big trouble... but I still turn toward the bed instead of the bathroom.

Sleep it off, Fallon. Just pretend it didn't happen. Wake up, and maybe this time it'll all be a dream.

It isn't. And as much as I try eagerly to nap myself into a new reality, when I wake up a few hours later, groggy and grumpy and hungry, I scowl to see that I'm still in the impersonal guest room that's been mine for days now.

A peek outside reveals I slept even longer than I thought. It's dark out, the waning moon a dim spotlight on the backyard behind the house. Like in Marie's manor, my room overlooks the back end of Lucas's home.

Unlike Marie's manor, I haven't seen a single big dog begging for scraps since I left.

Poor stray. I hope someone else is taking care of him since I'm not. And I know feeling bad for the dog I only tended to for a handful of days is kind of ridiculous—at his size, he was clearly eating well before I came onto the scene—but that's who I am.

Good to know my stay in Winter Creek hasn't completely changed me so far...

This late, I definitely slept through dinner. With my doors constantly locked, if Eleanor drops a plate off for me, she leaves it just outside of my room. No matter how many times I tell her it's not necessary, that I won't starve if I skip a meal or that I can go down to the kitchen and fend for myself, she insists.

Then she let slip that she does it on Lucas's orders and I gave up fighting her on the whole food issue.

Tonight's different. When I ease open the door, there's nothing waiting for me on the other side. And that's only surprising because—whether I join them downstairs or not—I haven't missed a single meal since I arrived here.

That's the problem with eating regularly. Back at home, if I'm too busy with work or, honestly, I just don't feel like it, I might eat a protein shake or a granola bar—or a bowl of ice cream—if anything at all. Being here has spoiled me. First, Marie's private chef, then Lucas's friends all taking turns to cook for each other. My stomach has expanded.

I'm starving, and that means I finally have the chance to go down to the kitchen to feed myself.

Technically, I'm allowed to. I might have chosen to camp out on the third floor by myself for most of my stay, but Lucas assured me that I have free rein of the house when it comes to the common areas, like the game room, the library, the kitchen, and a few others. I can go to the kitchen if I want.

Too bad the door is closed when I reach it.

That gives me a reason to pause. Most kitchens I've ever seen are a part of an open floor plan; if not open, they usually have a swinging door. Not this one. It has a solid door just like all the others in this place and I hesitate a moment before reaching for the knob.

And then I hear a voice coming from the kitchen and my hand falls to my thigh.

As muffled through the wood as it is, I can hear Lucas clearly as he tells someone to take a seat. Probably because he's not bothering to keep his voice low.

Why should he? He doesn't know I'm standing right on the other side of the door. Good thing, too, because I can tip-toe away without anyone thinking I was eavesdropping on him and whoever else is in there with him.

One step. I take one step before he speaks again and, damn it, I go still when it's obvious that he's talking about *me*.

"I told you to stay away from her. I thought I made myself clear. It wasn't an order because I trust you to do what you're told. So why are you challenging me?"

I know what this is. I guess it's finally time for Jade to get the lecture from Lucas she's earned by going all mean girl on me.

I should walk away. Sure, it's about me, but it's not my business.

I should walk away—

A sigh, and then a male voice says, "You know why, Luc."

My breath catches.

Tristan.

That's *Tristan*.

I honestly thought that it was Jade who was about to get reamed out by Lucas in there, but I was way wrong.

"And I respect that. Luna knows I respect the goddess, but I had the first claim. You know that, don't you?"

"I found her," argues Tristan. "At the train. I'm the one who told you she was here. But then... I told you what it felt like. How can it be wrong?"

"I'm not saying it is. I'm saying that, you found her first this time, but my claim still stands."

Claim? What?

What is he talking about?

I inch a little closer, cupping my ear before pressing it to the door. I'll regret it later, but I can't walk away from this. I just... I *can't*.

"Fine." Tristan exhales. "You're right."

"I usually am. Besides, you don't have to worry about this. It's not your business."

"If it affects you, it affects the pack. That makes it all of our business."

"Maybe."

"Luc... I'll stay away. You could be right about everything. The pull, the draw... maybe it's because we've all been together so long, it's an echo of your bond I'm feeling because I'm still alone. That doesn't explain what you think you're doing—"

"I *know* what I'm doing," rumbles Lucas.

It's a warning, but one Tristan ignores.

"For your sake, I hope so. But if you're not going to tell her—"

"I will." A rush of air. Is it a sigh of resignation or one of frustration? Without seeing Lucas, I can't tell... and I'm not so sure I want to know. "I have to. Just... it's only been one Luna. There's time."

"For you, maybe."

A low chuckle from Lucas this time, without an ounce of humor in it. "For all of us, Tris. You know that. And you know why."

"Lucas." A chair shifts. Tristan must have gotten to his feet. "It wasn't your fault—"

"There you go. Smoothing the edges of your wild leader." Another meaningless laugh. "What the fuck would I ever do without you guys?"

"I don't know. But what are you going to do about her?"

Her again. There's absolutely no doubt in my mind that they're still talking about me.

And when I hear a deep sigh coming from Lucas, then, "Luna only knows," a part of me wishes that they weren't.

Forget dinner. With the way my stomach is flip-flopping from all I overheard, I'm not all that hungry anymore.

***

"No. Absolutely not."

Lucas stands with his shoulder leaning against my doorframe, arms crossed over his chest, legs crossed at the ankles of his boots.

He knows what he's doing. Wielding his undeniable sex appeal against me like this... he knows exactly what he's doing. We haven't been this close since our kiss, and as though he got the idea that he can just show up all gorgeous and untouchable and think I'll jump to obey him, he's blocking my way out of my room—

—and it's *working*.

Damn it. After the way he rejected me after that kiss, I basically holed up on the third floor. I haven't left it in days. The only exception was when I would sneak down to the library whenever I was sure that Lucas was out of the house.

No way in hell did I want to chance running into him again.

It's so weird. Since arriving to stay with him and his friends, I'm becoming slowly adapted to his schedule; either that, or I can... I don't know... *sense* it when he's gone. Like the air is a lot less charged as soon as he heads out to the woods for another patrol.

He's always patrolling. If he's not, then Kirk is. Tristan. Jade. The only one who seems to be as much a prisoner of this fortress as I am is Eleanor, and she seems to enjoy it. I run into her more than anyone else, and though it's usually in the library, she dragged me to the game room yesterday evening after I finished the dinner she brought me.

Because... yeah. I'm back to eating my meals alone in my room. It's funny, though. Every time she brings me the plate, she makes sure to tease me. Something about me not taking it the wrong way, that it's just food, and she's happily mated.

It's always 'mated'. I've given up wondering why she refers to her marriage like that, assuming it has something to do with her family. She's not Australian, but her parents were from London before they moved here when she was a kid.

I asked her once why she doesn't have an accent and she just shrugged. It was during last night's pool game, actually, and since the smiley Eleanor proved to be one hell of a pool shark, I was too distracted by getting my ass kicked to really focus on why she sounds like every American on television. Even I have a more noticeable accent than her.

Same with everyone else in the house, too...

Right now, I'm listening to Lucas's accent-free drawl as he looks down at me, a closed expression on his face. He said 'no', and he expects me to abide by it.

Funny, Lucas.

I keep my voice light and friendly despite the aggravation threatening to rise up. "I think you got it wrong. I wasn't asking for permission. I was telling you that today's Monday, and I'm going down to the train station to see if I can finally hitch a ride out of Winter Creek."

I've been here for two weeks. Regardless of how Lucas tried to explain that the train doesn't roll in on a predictable schedule, I won't be able to forgive myself if I don't at least *try*. It dropped me off on a Monday at four. Why couldn't it reappear at the same time?

So he said it has something to do with the cycles of the moon. I call bullshit on that. I arrived a good couple of days before the full moon, and if I'm meant to wait until the new moon—when it's hidden in the sky—I have, like, five more days.

I don't think I can stay here that much longer. With Jade's catty comments whenever I see her, the sting of Lucas's rejection hurting anew whenever I think about how quick he was to leave me behind in the library...

not to mention Tristan's hot-and-cold attitude... I've never felt more like an outsider.

Tristan makes it even harder. One second, he's acting as if I'm a ghost. Others, he looks at me as if he's dying to kiss me. That, if it wasn't for Lucas warning him off, he would've.

I know that's what's going on. I may be gullible, but I'm not naive. Tristan's loyalty is obviously to Lucas. If Lucas wants him to stay away from me, he will.

But then Lucas did the same thing, so I really don't get what the hell he thinks he's doing.

I don't care. I'm lying, of course, but I pretend if only because the complication with Lucas and Tristan is one I really don't freaking need.

Which is exactly why I have to get out of here. Then I can put this whole trip behind me, forget about everything that happened, and move on.

I'm good at that.

Now, call me a coward if you want, but my plan was to scrounge up some paper and a pen so I could leave a 'thank you' note behind. Still feeling raw from being so vulnerable in front of him the other night, I decided that just disappearing would be the best for all of us.

I asked Eleanor for the paper. The pen, too. She didn't blink. But I think I might've gone too far when I wondered if she might have a pair of shoes I can borrow. I haven't had any since I lost those pumps in the woods, and though I traveled through them once before in bare feet, I'd rather not have to do that again.

Plus, I don't know how picky the train is. It's bad enough that I'm going to have to sweet talk my way onboard. If they stick to the 'no shirts, no shoes, no service' BS, I'll really be screwed.

It's the shoes that tipped her off. She might've brought me a pair she could spare, but she obviously told the leader of the house.

Lucas's dark gaze—more burnt orange than amber right now because, yup, he's nowhere as casual as he's pretending to be—dips to the black strap sandals I have on.

"Permission or not, you're not leaving."

Like hell I'm not. "I'm not your prisoner—"

"No, but when you accepted my invitation to stay, you put your safety in the hands of my pa... my people. It's not safe for you to cross out of our territory yet. The train belongs to all of Winter Creek, but you'll be on witch land to reach it. You can't go."

He thinks so, but I have a backup plan.

"Come with me, then. You got a hard-on for protecting me so bad? Walk with me to the train station. Once I'm onboard, they can't get to me."

Lucas's laugh is so low, it sends a shiver up and down my spine. It reminds me of the laugh he gave during his conversation with Tristan in the kitchen—

only with a much blacker edge. "Please, Fallon. Don't tell me that you're *that* naive."

If that doesn't ruffle my feathers... "What?"

"Didn't you tell me that the witches already found you where you were? That they took your *blood*?"

My stomach drops. Thanks, Lucas. Like I needed the reminder. "Yeah. So?"

He raises his eyebrows. "Think it over."

"What? You think they'll follow me back to New York?"

"Marie thinks you're the one to break the curse on the town." He's never explained it to me, but even Lucas acknowledges that it exists. "I've known her a long time, Fallon. If she believes that, nothing will stop her from getting to you."

I mimic his expression. "Not even you, Mr. Protector?"

"Stay on my territory. I'm the only one who can keep you safe from your grandmother."

He believes it, too.

With a frustrated huff, I snap, "You can't honestly want to keep babysitting me, Lucas."

"If that's what you think this is, then yes."

"I don't know what any of this is!"

My shout doesn't do anything to move him—and I don't just mean his body. He's still blocking my door, sure, but there's something else. Something more.

I'm beginning to think I hit the bullseye when I told him I wasn't his prisoner.

Holy shit. I just might be.

A muscle ticks in his cheek as he remains unmoved. "It doesn't matter anyway. I already told you. The train won't be here until at least the Luna is gone. The new moon. That's its usual schedule... unless Marie changes it."

That catches my attention. "What did you say?"

He meets my gaze purposely. "The witches go too far sometimes. I told you that, too. If Marie controls most of Winter Creek, why wouldn't she control the train?"

I rear back on my heels as if someone had shoved me. That's how strong my reaction to Lucas's simply stated question is. It's the secret suspicion that I kept buried deep down in the time since I learned my grandmother was the wicked witch in my story, and he just put it out there like that.

What makes it so much worse is that I'm pretty sure he's right. That everything he's said is right.

But I don't want to hear it—especially not from him.

So, regaining my footing, I march into him.

"Move."

"Where are you going, Fallon?"

"*Out.*"

He doesn't budge.

I ball my hands into fists at my side. "Lucas—"

"Where are you going?" he repeats.

Okay. We can do this all day, or I can give into his overbearing dominance and just tell him so that he'll finally get out of my fucking way.

"For a walk. Is that okay? You said I'm safe on your land. If I stick to the house, can I just take a damn walk? Get some fresh air? Is that okay with you, boss?"

For a split second, I think I might've gone a little too far. What really do I know about Lucas except for the fact that he seems to have a bit of a savior complex, he lords it over a houseful of his friends that he orders around like his personal soldiers with all of his chores and theirs patrols, and I inexplicably feel complete when he's around?

That last one should be enough for me to recognize just how dangerous he is, but that doesn't stop me from going on my tippy-toes so that we're on an equal footing.

Of course, that also puts our faces right in front of each other, with me breathing heavy, and Lucas... I'm not so sure he's breathing at all.

Until his tongue darts out. He runs it over his bottom lip and I know—I just *know*—that he's reliving our kiss the same way that I am.

If he tries to initiate another one, I don't know what I'll do... and, yeah, that's another fucking lie because

I'm already imagining the heat from his hands on my skin.

Too bad Lucas seems to remember himself at the last minute. Closing his eyes, shuttering them for a moment, when he opens them again, it's like that charged moment never passed between us.

He swallows roughly, rising up from his not-so-casual lean. "Don't go too far."

I'm so glad he's relented, I ignore the continued sting of rejection I can't keep from feeling. "I won't."

"I mean it, Fallon. I'll know."

I nod. "Got it."

Because if there's one thing for sure that I *do* know about Lucas, it's that I one hundred percent believe that he will.

CHAPTER 16
WHOOPS

Starting out, I don't really have a destination in mind. Away from Lucas and his mixed signals is about as far as I'm ready to go... until I go a little deeper into the woods than I probably should have and chance upon a babbling creek with crystal clear water and plenty of rocks dotting the floor of it that spans about six feet across.

Too wide for me to jump over, it's an obvious boundary to Lucas's "territory" that we must've detoured around the other day.

It's chilly out. I tugged on my sleep sweats before I made my escape so that I didn't freeze my ass off, though the water makes the temperature seem even cooler as I go ahead and walk alongside the creek, following it.

There's no coin in my pants so I can't flip it to figure

out which way to go. The way I see it, I'll either walk for a while and end up at the rope bridge, or I'll find the waterfall in the woods that Tristan once told me about.

Either way, I need some time to myself without feeling like I'm the sixth wheel, hiding out so close to the attic, it's as though I've gone from Little Red Riding Hood straight to Jane Eyre.

When the creek stays about the same narrow size instead of widening anywhere near close to how big the river near the rope bridge is, it makes sense to think I'm heading toward the waterfall. Good. The last thing I need is for Lucas to accuse me of purposely disobeying him after our little spat.

Though, to be honest, I begin to get a little nervous when I start spotting a couple of paw prints similar to the ones I once found outside of the Coven House. It starts out as a few here or there, but whenever I see a patch of mud or dried-up dirt, inevitably there's an impression that catches my eye—and makes my stomach jolt.

My only saving grace is that, every single time I get a closer look, I remind myself that they're obviously animal prints. Dog, wolf, maybe even bear. There's no way they belong to the massive half-human beast with his arched foot tipped with talons, and that's all I care about.

At least, until I peek my head through another

copse of closely-grown trees that I'm pushing my way past and, following the sounds of splashing water, discover that it's not just the beautiful cascading waterfall that Tristan told me about I've finally stumbled upon.

It's a beautiful cascading waterfall, surrounded by large boulders, leading into the stream I just followed —and there's a massive dog with golden fur frolicking in the pool made by the waterfall.

Seriously. That's what it's doing.

Frolicking.

Splashing its massive paws against the water, throwing its bulk around so that it's making a splash, before getting up to all fours and shaking off... and then doing it again.

I watch in amazement. The dog hasn't noticed me yet, which is a pretty good thing since I'm beginning to think that it's not a big dog.

That sucker is a *wolf*.

I fucking *knew* there were wolves in this place!

Oh, boy. Okay, Fallon. This is what we're gonna do. Take one step back, then another, and hopefully we can slip into the shadows of the trees and that creature will be none the wiser.

The wolf's pointed ears twitch. Its head swivels, looking right in my direction.

Does it see me?

I really, really hope not.

I swallow my tiny squeal of fright. My mace might not do much against a wolf that size, but it might've bought me some time to escape the wild animal—if it wasn't back at my borrowed room in my grandmother's manor, that is.

"Nice wolfie," I murmur. "You don't want to eat Fallon. She's too stringy, and with this amount of fat on my ass... yuck."

Did it hear me?

Did I just sign up to be a wolf's dinner?

Oh my God...

As though it didn't hear me at all, the wolf busies itself with snorting some of the creek water out of its snout. Shaking its head, it looks away, and I let out a soft sigh of relief.

It didn't see me.

I'm okay.

I can *escape*—

Before I can take that step back, something happens. The wolf begins to rise up on its hind legs, but it doesn't stop. Rearing back, it's almost like it snaps and, out of nowhere, a woman with soaking wet blonde hair and a shapely ass is standing in the exact place where there had been a giant wolf a split second ago.

I like to think my reaction to seeing that is pretty normal, even if it probably wasn't the smartest one.

Bursting through the trees instead of turning and

sprinting in the opposite direction, I snap out, "What the *fuck*?"

The woman spins around slowly, lazily, obviously not the least bit concerned with me standing at her back when she can turn into that huge golden wolf in a blink of an eye.

My heart thudding, fingers trembling at my side, I have to swallow another curse when I recognize who she is.

Jade's green eyes glitter in a dare as she—without even bothering to cover herself at all—mockingly says, "Whoops. Sorry. Didn't see you there, human."

IN MY TIME, I'VE SEEN MY FAIR SHARE OF TITS. NEITHER Lorelei nor Jeannie was all that self-conscious, and while I was never attracted to the twins, I can appreciate a nice rack. Same thing with any of my past flings that happened to have a pair.

Jade's are nice. Not gonna lie. But when I stand there, staring at her, it's not the fact that she's completely naked that has my mind on the fritz.

Oh, no. I'm still stuck on the fact that she was a fucking *wolf* about two seconds ago.

My hand flies up to my mouth. It fell open when she spun to face me, but as freaked out as I am that

Jade can turn into a *wolf,* she's still Jade. I don't want to give her the satisfaction of seeing she rattled me.

But she did. She definitely did.

With her smirk widening as I stand there slack-jawed, I manage to close my mouth with a gentle push from my thumb as my mind spins all on its own.

And, I have to admit, a lot of things that I just thought were super weird about Winter Creek *finally* make a little sense.

How did I not see it before? Running the last week or so through my brain at high speed, I can't say that all the clues weren't there.

Eleanor and Kirk referring to each other as 'mates' before someone reminds them that they're married. Not 'mates' like friends or partners, but *mates,* like how wolves mate for life.

How about the bite on her neck that Eleanor seems to touch in an almost absent gesture? I thought it was strange neither of them had wedding rings, but maybe that's what her scar is? A wolfy way of saying she's taken.

And then there's Lucas's fixation with the moon... and all the patrols, the talk of territory, and a fierce rivalry with my grandmother and her coven that I'd understand a lot more if they're both supes.

Most importantly, all of the times I could've sworn I heard one of my hosts mentioning something to do with the 'pack'. I just brushed it off, assuming that had a meaning I didn't get—like I did with a lot of things, I'm realizing.

Because there's no damn way that Jade's a fucking werewolf and the rest of them aren't.

That's gotta be what she is, right? Like... like a different type of 'supe', not a witch or a vampire, but a chick who can turn into a wolf when she wants to— and then shapeshift back to her smirking human self when it'll make the most impact.

Like, oh, when I accidentally stumble on her bathing in the creek?

Didn't see you there, human, I re-run through my head.

Right. I'm a human, and Jade... she's obviously *not.*

On that note... yeah. My sense of self-preservation catching up to my spinning head, I decide this is my cue to go. Maybe if it wasn't Jade daring me to say something while standing there, bold as brass, dripping water as she drops her hands to her hips, I might've stuck around.

But it *is* Jade, and no way in hell am I staying here to ask her any of the hundreds of questions running through my skull right now. So I don't, spinning on my heel and flying through the woods as fast as a spooked human can go.

Panic and shock give me tunnel vision. I'm only staring right ahead, hoping like hell I can find my way back to the house without any trouble—or Jade deciding to go wolf again and chase after me before I can get to the others. No matter what, stumbling onto the witches' territory is out of the question for me, though part of me has to wonder if I'm making a gigantic mistake trusting *wolves*.

I hope not. If so, I'm completely screwed when, somewhere off to my side, I hear someone call my name and I realize that Tristan is here.

How? No idea.

Why? Same answer.

Does he know that I just found out Jade's secret? I can't tell, but I wouldn't be surprised.

But in case he doesn't...

I jerk my head over my shoulder, trying to pinpoint where I heard his voice coming from as I put on the brakes. I almost fall—thanks to Eleanor's slippery sandals—heroically managing to stay standing... though I do stumble a little again when I see Tristan running toward me from the opposite side of the creek I'd inadvertently been trailing earlier.

I gape, and while part of my stunned silence—over my frantic breathing that is—has to do with how absolutely beautiful his physique is without anything covering up his chest, it has more to do with a sense of deja vu slamming me over the head.

Tristan is shirtless. Shoeless, too.

In fact, all he has on is a similar pair of sweatpants

to the ones Lucas was wearing the first time I ever saw him.

Of course. If these supes come out of their wolf shape with their dick swinging, why wouldn't they grab a spare change of sweats they have stashed somewhere in the woods so that us non-supes don't label them a perv and a flasher?

Jade might not have minded showing me all her goods. Tristan, at least, had the decency to cover up before he came running after me.

Because, yeah. I don't know for sure, but it seems pretty obvious now.

Tristan is one of them. So is Lucas.

Everyone in his house is probably just like Jade.

And I'm *not*.

"Holy shit." I take a few hurried steps backward. We still have the creek between us, but suddenly it's not enough when I think about how much I *did* trust these strangers, and how much at their mercy I've been since I came to stay at their house. "Holy *shit*."

Tristan holds up his hands.

"Fallon." His voice is gentle. Soothing. "Fallon... it's okay. It's me."

Is that supposed to help calm me down?

Spoiler alert: it *doesn't*.

Jade was one thing. I haven't gotten along with her since the moment we met. But Tristan? There was a time—before I met Lucas and felt an undeniable connection with him—that I thought *maybe*. We had a lunch date.

He called me *pretty*.

I'll get over it. Like everything else that's happened to me since I decided to take Marie up on her invitation, I'll continue to accept that the world is nothing like I thought it was; at least, not in Winter Creek, it isn't. But I need a minute, and I need Tristan to stay on his side of the running water.

Just as I have that thought, Tristan's gaze flickers toward the water, then at me. With a graceful leap, he clears the creek. It's nowhere near as wide as the raging river near the train station, but it's still a jump that only an Olympic athlete should be able to clear.

And Tristan does it easily.

A hysterical laugh bubbles up inside of me as my mind flashes back to that day I met him in the town square. How he told me he'd bring me to see the waterfall that led into the actual Winter Creek. I somehow found it on my own—and obviously learned his wolfish secret, too—but here he is.

He found me.

Probably because he was *following* me.

Another laugh escapes me at just how freaking naive I can be.

Did I actually think that Lucas would let silly, little Fallon meander around on her own? Not really. I guess I just thought he'd pass the task on to Eleanor or Kirk or maybe even himself before he'd give babysitting duty to Tristan.

And yet, here we are, and I laugh because, if I don't, I'm gonna start screaming. Not because I'm scared, either, but because I can't think of any other reasonable reaction to discovering that—on top of everything else—werewolves are *real*.

Poor Tristan. I'm pretty sure my unhinged laugh worries him.

He's lucky that I went with laughing. If he's anything like the beast, my shrill scream will kill his ears.

Though he's on my side of the creek now, he stops when a few feet separate us.

He taps his bare chest. Once, I would've envied that hand. Now? I wonder what it looks like as a paw...

"Fallon? It's me. Tristan. I know this has to be a lot right now... that you saw something you weren't supposed to see. But it's okay. I'm still Tristan. I'm still me."

His voice still has that soothing edge. He sounds so earnest that it does what I would've sworn was impossible a few seconds ago: it settles me enough that I can wrangle my laugh, turning it into a few gulps of air as I force myself calm before he can reach out and touch me.

He wants to. That much is clear.

Like the day in the library when his hands hovered

over my arms without quite making contact, he extends his, leaving it up to me if I want to close the gap between us and let him embrace me.

I don't, which is probably why I use the first thing I can think of against him to keep the few feet between us.

"What are you doing here? I thought Lucas told you to stay away from me."

I'd put money down he expected me to bring up the thing I wasn't supposed to see. Instead, completely disregarding it, I throw in his face a conversation I wasn't supposed to hear.

Good one, Fallon.

His eyebrows arch in recognition, and he smartly doesn't deny my accusation. He also doesn't move any closer. Tristan stays exactly where he is, my words freezing him in place almost as effectively as Marie's spell kept me trapped against that tree.

And then his lips curve, a sad smile tugging down the corners of his mouth. "He did. And now you know why."

Yeah... I don't think I do.

"He's the Alpha," Tristan explains when I proceed to stand there with a blank expression on my face. "The leader of our pack. If he gives a command, not even the Beta can refuse."

So it looks like, while I glossed right past the whole

'Jade being a werewolf' thing, he's going to dive head-first right into it.

Okay, then. If he's going to accept that there's no shoving this bit of knowledge back into Pandora's box, I'm going to do the same thing.

"The Beta… is that you?"

"Lucas's right-hand wolf, yeah," he confirms before he sighs. His chest moves with the motion, causing my gaze to dip toward the bare skin between his pink nipples.

When I realize that this is not the time to be staring at him, I snap my head back up.

He's watching me closely. "Fallon… I wanted to tell you. But, like I said, when the Alpha says 'no', it's a 'no'."

Because Lucas is the Alpha.

Because Lucas *is* a wolf.

They *all* are.

And despite thinking that from the moment Jade smirked at me, it's one thing to suspect it.

It's another completely to have Tristan confirm it.

"Holy sh—*oh*."

Ah, crap. There go my wobbly legs. I didn't even see any spilled blood this time, but I'm dropping down to the grassy floor of the woods like a sack of potatoes anyway.

As I crumple, Tristan doesn't wait for my permission. Moving so he's a blur on the dark edge of my hazy vision, he's suddenly *there*, hooking his hands under my armpits, hoisting me back to my feet as though I weigh nothing to him.

Heat floods through me. Whether from embarrassment or something else, I don't know, but I tell him in a firm voice, "Thanks. I'm alright."

From the shadowed look on his gorgeous face, I'm not so sure he buys that. He does, however, let me go.

Something tells me he doesn't want to, but he steps away from me.

Then, in a soft voice, he murmurs, "I'm not going to hurt you, Fallon."

"I never thought you would."

I mean that. There's something about him. Something about all of them, except for Jade. Even she's all bark, no bite, according to the others—and I believe that, too. If she's been a secret wolf all along, she could've kicked my ass easily, no matter that I'm bigger than her when we're both human.

And isn't that a fucking awful thought? I've been baiting a damn *werewolf* all along.

"It's just... it's a lot to take in." I exhale roughly. "Shit. I thought witches were bad. Now I'm learning werewolves are real?"

"Shifters," he corrects gently.

"What?"

"That's what we are. Wolf shifters. It's a type of supe."

Figured that. "Supernaturals," I say, to prove that I'm not completely clueless.

"That's right. In our world, there are a couple of different shifters... shapeshifters... though our pack is all wolves. Witches, you know about, obviously. We don't have bloodsuckers in Winter Creek, but Fang Cities are full of them."

"Bloodsuckers... you mean vampires?"

"Yeah." For a second, I see a glimmer of the Tristan I met before I came to stay at the house. "We're lousy with witches here, but at least we don't have any of the corpses near our territory. Small mercies."

It's that glimmer that makes me realize just how... how *insane* this back and forth is right now—in a good way, though. I went from feeling like an outsider in all ways, like everyone in Winter Creek was in on some inside joke except for me, and finally... *finally* I'm allowed to know the secret.

And it's one hell of a *doozy*.

But, hey, if he's willing to talk... I knew about supes. Lucas told me about them, and Marie dropped the facade that she was just a seamstress when she used her magic against me. There is one thing that I've tiptoed around for a while now, and maybe I'm pushing my luck bringing it up, but I just gotta.

"And the curse? The one on this town. What about that?"

Tristan hesitates for a second. I'm pretty sure he's about to shut me down—or maybe use his charm against me to change the subject—but then he exhales roughly.

"It's real," he confesses. "Just like I told you it was." A small, hollow laugh escapes him. "For Luna's sake, even when I was supposed to keep the curse to myself, I couldn't help but mention it in front of you."

Yeah. I remember.

That's why I asked.

"But what *is* it? What is the curse? It's not just that you're all supes"—at least, I don't think it is—"so what is it?"

He blinks. "You don't know?"

If I did, I wouldn't have asked. "No. Everyone's been so damn vague about it. Even you were, slipping the curse in when we were talking without saying any more than that. I always thought it had something to do with the witches, but now that I know your secret... maybe it's time to hear about that one."

At this point, I do expect him to shut me down. Lucas has before. Marie did, too, before throwing it in my face that, if I were a witch, I would've known she was lying when she haughtily told me there was no such thing as curses.

But whether he's trying to make this all up to me— or trying to get me on his side—Tristan glances behind him, then turns back to tell me, "Seventy years ago, something happened. Something bad. Someone got hurt, and the supes in Winter Creek paid the price for it. The wolves blamed the witches. The witches blamed the wolves. No one knows exactly which side is responsible for the actual curse, but since it happened, we've been... stuck."

I lick my lips, my mouth suddenly dry. *Seventy years ago...* "We... you mean, like, your parents? Grandparents?"

He shakes his head slowly.

I was afraid of that. "You mean... *you*. Lucas and you and—"

"The others, yeah. Our pack. The coven. Marie was the head witch back then, and she's only built her coven up since, hoping it'll help break the stasis spell that's kept us all stuck here. For seventy years, we've lived just like this, but nothing has changed. Not yet."

Because I'm here now.

Because my grandmother searched for fifteen years because she thought I might be the one to break the curse.

"But why me?" I ask. I hate to turn the idea of a whole town—or the supe side of it—being cursed into a 'me, me, me' situation, but it's hard not to after all I've been through. "Why did she think I'd be able to break it?"

Before Tristan can answer me, I come up with the solution on my own.

"Because I'm her blood, right? Maybe not her actual granddaughter. Seventy years ago... I could be her great-great-granddaughter or something, but she needed my blood." For the beast, I remember. "The beast... he's part of the curse, too."

"He is." And that's all Tristan has to say about that. "And I know it sounds crazy. I lived it, so I know how unbelievable this must be to a non-supe. So maybe you *are* human, Fallon, but you're also a part of this."

Whether I like it or not, I think I am.

He huffs, gaze darting to the side instead of meeting my eyes. "And maybe Lucas might disagree, but I'm glad you finally know what's going on. Why he's so determined to protect you from the witches, and why he..." He darts a tentative look back at me. "Why he's the way he is."

You know what?

For the first time since Lucas glowered at me after being so gentle, washing the blood from my face and wrapping the slice on my inner arm, I think I do.

Across from me, Tristan is waiting for my response.

Pushing everything aside so that I can unpack it later, I decide to give him a perfectly in-the-moment-Fallon one.

"You look good for seventy-plus," I tease, a sense of relief washing over me when Tristan chuckles, letting out the breath he'd been holding at the same time.

That's my dark sense of humor at work again. I *have* to tease because the alternative is freaking out that all my snide thoughts and comments about Winter Creek being like Stepford—like being a monument to the *past*—were far more spot-on than I ever would've thought possible.

He sobers up a little, though his voice has a hint of his own tease in his response. "If I ever leave Winter Creek before the curse is broken, you might not think so." The tease vanishes as quickly as it arrived. "But time… it didn't just stop. It dragged. I don't think I'm ninety-eight. I'm twenty-seven." He pauses, holding my gaze. "I've just been twenty-seven for a long, long time."

Is it weird that I kind of get that? I'm twenty-five, but I feel like I've been around a lot longer than that. Probably because watching your mother die days before your twenty-first birthday ages a girl, but still.

"I guess you really hoped that I would be the girl to break the curse, huh? What happens then? Does time start all over again?"

I think it finally hits Tristan that we've gotten so far off the track, we couldn't find it if we tried. And while that's probably good for me, since I desperately need the distraction to put off processing everything I just saw and learned, there's clearly a reason why Lucas sent him to watch over me while I took my walk.

Assuming he did, of course. Which, yeah… he had to, and I'm even more convinced when Tristan straightens.

Eyes on his face, Fallon. Eyes up.

"I'm going to have to tell Lucas. About all of this."

My head jerks up again. "What? Why?"

I know why, but I'm hoping that Tristan doesn't.

"Jade disobeyed him." He tightens his jaw. "In Winter Creek, humans aren't supposed to know about supes. Just because the witches revealed themselves to you, it didn't mean he wanted us to. But she did."

"Jade didn't do anything," I argue. "It's not her fault I stumbled upon her. I was just looking for the waterfall. She didn't know I was out there."

It pains me to defend her after how shitty she treated me since I came to stay in Lucas's house with his friends—with his *pack*—but I don't want her to get in trouble because I snuck up on her the way I did.

The slightly exasperated yet definitely amused look Tristan gives me tells me that, like so many others, he thinks I'm as naive as I have to admit I probably am.

"Fallon... one thing you should know about shifters? Our senses are unparalleled. We can see in the dark. Even in our skin, we're fast. And our noses? You'd be amazed by what I can scent, even from a distance. She-wolves are just as powerful as the males, too. I can't speak for Jade's motives, but trust me on this: she knew you were there."

Oh, great.

Lovely.

If Jade wanted me to know what she was, she had a reason; especially if she went against Lucas to do it. I don't like that Tristan admits he doesn't know what her motives are because, if one of her fellow wolves doesn't, what hope do I have?

That's not all that has me worried all of a sudden, either. Sue me, but I'm a little stuck on that tiny tidbit he just said about wolf shifters being able to scent things from a distance.

"Hold on. Your nose... what about when I'm sitting right here? Can you smell me then?"

He nods. I'm sure he thinks I'm nuts for steering the conversation in this direction, but he lets me.

In this moment, I get the feeling that Tristan would let me do *anything*.

He takes a deep breath, that gorgeous chest rising and falling with the motion. "One sniff and I can tell what soap you used in the shower. Shampoo, too. I know what you ate for your last meal. And that's not all. Emotions give off a scent, too, Fallon. So I know when you're happy. Scared. Nervous and confused, like before. Or now, when you're—"

I stop him right there by blurting out the only thing on my mind since he started his list: "What about if I'm turned on?"

"Fallon?"

He has to know what I mean. "Yeah. Like, if I'm with a guy and I'm attracted to him... can you tell?"

He gulps. "Yeah. I can tell."

Oh my God. And he's sitting here with no shirt on and, despite learning the truth about what he is, I can't stop myself from glancing down at his chest every few minutes.

Not even that, but I was into him back when I called him Blondie and had no idea what his first name was.

And what about how I'm basically walking around

with damp panties anytime Lucas turns his attention my way...

"Good to know," I say weakly, backing away. How far can his nose reach? I'm about to find out. "On that note, I think I'm going to go back to my room and, I don't know, crawl under my bed and hide there for the next seventy years. See ya."

Before he can stop me, I begin to get my ass as far away from him as possible. I can't help that, either. Flaming embarrassment is like jet fuel to me, pushing me to put as much distance between Tristan and me as I can.

Until he calls out, "Wait," in a ragged voice and something inside of me twists. "Fallon, please—"

Damn it. Against my better judgment, I turn around.

Tristan's expression is hard to read. As our eyes meet again, that whitish sheen I've seen so many times before rolls over his icy gaze. I always managed to convince myself that I was seeing something that wasn't there.

Now I know better. Whatever that nifty little trick of his is, it has something to do with his being a wolf... man... shapeshifter supe.

Because that's what he is... and, the more I think about it, the more that doesn't seem to faze me.

Maybe it's because I've been in Winter Creek for a while now and seen enough shit that nothing surprises me anymore. I mean, I did turn and bolt when the wolf turned into Jade, but was it because she basically slapped me upside the head with her supe status, or because it was *Jade*?

This is Tristan. Running his fingers through his thick blond hair, leaving track marks behind with his... yup, those are inch-long claws at the tips of his fingers... with his *claws*, all I see is the charming guy who flirted with me when I first rolled into Winter Creek.

Only he's not flirting now. Body purposely held in a pose to make him as non-threatening as possible, he's watching me as if waiting for me to start that unhinged laugh again, or maybe to start screaming after all.

I'm not going to hurt you, Fallon.

Once upon a time, I thought he was the more dangerous of the two between him and Remy. I was wrong—obviously, since Tristan hasn't tried to sacrifice me yet—but it's almost like I sensed the wolfish side of him all along.

"Yeah?"

"You don't have to go," he tells me. "Not yet. If I made you uncomfortable... I didn't mean to."

Is that what he's worried about? "I know. Besides, I'm the one who asked."

He inclines his head, admitting that. Then he begins to say, "Lucas, he..." before his voice trails off notably.

I should let it go.

I *should*, but that's not my style. "Lucas *what*?"

"Never mind. If I know the Alpha, he's going to be wondering where you are. Maybe it's better that you go back." He nods, almost as though he's trying to convince himself more than me. "Yeah. You go. I'll catch up."

"You mean you'll *follow*, right? Like you were earlier?" His fingers flex at his side. Seeing the slight gesture, I know I was right. "Tell me, Tristan... was it Lucas who told you to follow after me like that?"

He doesn't say anything.

That's okay. I got my answer in his silence.

And, because I'm *me*, I push it.

Tapping my opal with one of my normal, regular human fingernails, I say, "Kind of weird, huh? Since he is the one who told you to stay away from me."

Tristan swallows roughly. "That's only because he knows no one else will protect you better than I will if he can't."

Whoa. That's not what I expected him to say.

My hand falls back to my side. "I—"

"It's getting late, Fallon. Let's go back."

Know what? I'm suddenly not in such a rush to head back to the house. But since this topic is a dead-end...

"I have a question," I blurt out. "About your wolf. If... I mean, is that okay?"

Does he know what I'm doing? Probably.

Does he play along anyway? Of course.

"Anything for you."

There's that twist again. Hm. Maybe this isn't such a brilliant idea...

Gonna do it anyway, though.

"Jade's wolf has golden fur. Almost blonde, like her hair color. What about you?" I don't know why I want to know that—but I do. "What does your wolf look like?"

He reaches for the band of his sweatpants and heat rushes to my face. "I could shift right now and show you."

Okay. I might've made a big mistake here without realizing it.

To be honest, part of my interest is piqued when it hits me that, in order to do just that, Tristan plans on stripping off his sweats. That definitely has a certain appeal, but leading him on is probably the worst thing I can do right now.

That's exactly what I would be doing, too. Whether he meant to or not, he gave himself away when he told me about a wolf shifter's senses. If Jade knew I was out here, there's no way that Tristan—and Lucas—didn't know they had an audience for their little discussion.

So I threw it back in his face, letting him know I was out there. Too bad he would've already known.

Was it staged? Or did neither one care if I over-heard them as they talked about me?

Did Lucas want me to know that he warned Tristan away from me?

Did *Tristan*?

Well, that little charade is over. He's here, and if I give him permission, he'll drop his pants right in front of me. And maybe nudity doesn't seem like a big deal to a group of supes who clearly end up naked when they go between forms, but I'm human.

It won't just be Tristan stripping down so he can show me his wolf. It'll be a guy showing off his body to a woman—who despite liking what she sees—isn't inexplicably drawn to him the same way he is to her.

Oh, no. For some silly reason, I can't stay away from Lucas...

I hold up my hand. "Maybe later. I don't know if I can handle being face to face with a wolf again so soon."

Tristan pauses, his fingers—no more claws in sight, though I'm positive I saw them before—resting on the top of his waistband. We both know I'm full of shit with that sorry excuse, but he lets me have it.

Dropping his hands to his thighs, he rubs them through his sweatpants. "Let me know if you change your mind."

"I will," I promise him, and I mean that in more ways than one. I have to, considering we both also know that he's not just talking about showing off his wolf when he says that. "But," I add, knowing I shouldn't but unable to stop myself, "what about Lucas?"

That strange whitish sheen rolls over his icy eyes again—and it finally hits me that what I'm seeing is the animalistic nature of his wolf peeking out through his eyes while he's standing on two legs in front of me.

Oh, yeah. Another clue I totally misread. Good going, Fallon. It's almost like I *wanted* to be completely unaware of what was right there all along.

He clears his throat. "What about the Alpha?"

It's so strange to think of Lucas as that, but if he and his friends really do make up their own version of a wolf pack, he would definitely be the one in charge. The alpha wolf.

Wolf...

"I mean, his wolf. What does his look like?"

"You can ask him. I'm sure he'd show you."

I highly doubt that. "Or maybe you could just tell me."

"It's pretty common that our wolves match our human coloring. Take me, for example. My wolf's fur is a couple shades darker than Jade's. My eyes are blue in either form. So Lucas, he's a black wolf with eyes that match his. And since he's the Alpha, he's more dominant than the rest of the pack. Bigger, too. Trust me, you'll know him when you see him."

Why am I not surprised to hear that—or to agree that, in retrospect, Tristan is absolutely spot-on?

Oh, that's right. Because now I know for sure that Lucas spying on me and Tristan that day in the town square isn't the first time I caught him watching me before he took the chance to rescue me from the beast in the woods.

He was there my first night in Winter Creek, wasn't he? Probably right after Tristan told him I arrived on the train, and that Remy came to intercept me, bringing me to the Coven House, he was there.

He was there, and when I saw the big, black wolf watching me from my window, I innocently thought he was an oversized stray and fed him some of my steak.

Tristan is so convinced that Lucas will be looking for me that I'm almost a little offended when I finally make my way back to the house and he's not waiting on the back porch with a glower on his handsome face, muscular arms crossed over his brawny chest.

With or without a shirt would've been fine by me, too, but he's conspicuously absent. He's not the only one, either. There's been no sign of Jade since I saw her at the waterfall, and while I know for a fact that Tristan kept a close eye on me my entire walk back, he disappeared just as seamlessly.

I glance over my shoulder before I reach for the door handle. He's not there. I guess, now that I've made it back in one piece, he's gone back out on patrol, rejoining his post on the edge of witch territory.

Letting myself inside, I expect to run into *someone*. Unless Jade came back and ratted on herself, no one knows that the Fallon that left about an hour or two ago is totally different than the one slipping in through the kitchen.

I don't, though. No Kirk, absently sipping his coffee while he strokes one of Eleanor's curls. No Eleanor as she leans into her husband—her *mate*—as though she can't bear the thought of being away from him for too long.

No Lucas, watching me eat as though making sure I don't starve myself or something equally as ridiculous...

No one is around, though. Not in the kitchen, and not on my trek up both flights of stairs to reach my room. Once inside, I kick off Eleanor's sandals, shrug off the sweats so I'm back to wearing her shorts, and— letting my anxiety take the lead—talk myself into believing that the whole pack abandoned me.

That thought in mind, I'm suddenly eager to track Lucas down. It probably should say something that the one I'm most worried about leaving me is the one who treats me like a babysitting charge instead of a woman, but I shake that sensation off as I go in search of him.

Hey. If he's not looking for me, I'll look for him.

Stepping down from the final stair that leads me from the third floor to the second, I'm just about to go down to the main one when music drifting down the hallway catches my attention.

And that's not all.

I didn't go down this hallway before though I did peek down the length of it on my way upstairs. I can't remember if the door at the end, past the library, was open then—but it is now.

That's where the music is coming from. It's a classical piece, played on the piano, and unless I'm wrong, it's not a recording.

The curse, I remember. While I now understand why they don't bother with television or telephones, I have to wonder what else it affects. Did they even have recordings of piano music seventy years ago?

Records, I think, shifting on my bare feet, padding toward the open door. It might be a record, though my gut says it's not.

I've never seen the door to this particular room open before, but if there's one thing I've learned living here, it's this: an open door is an invitation.

I accept it.

Without a moment's hesitation, I walk into the room. Instantly, I know that my gut was right. While the music stopped when I was halfway down the hall, there's no doubt in my mind that someone was playing it.

He's still sitting behind the piano, amber eyes locked on me as I step into the space.

It's nowhere near as crowded or cozy as the library, though it has its own charm. The walls are a pale cream color, offset by the black piano that takes up most of the space. On the walls, I see two distinct paintings of sunsets—and one that is a large portrait of Lucas, wearing a greaser-style haircut that reminds me of that old movie musical my mom used to love, made in the 70s but set back in the 50s.

You're the one that I want—

No, Fallon. Down girl. Lucas from the past is just as sexy as Lucas from now, and after everything Tristan told me... I need to cool off.

I take a deep breath. Fake a smile. Exhale.

Turn toward the piano.

Lucas waits for me to stop avoiding his stare, finally looking at the modern version of the man immortalized in that portrait.

Only when I do does he jerk his stubble-covered chin over my shoulder.

"Close the door behind you."

Yup. This was an invitation meant specifically for me—and, suddenly, I think I understand why the house was so empty.

They scattered, didn't they? Their Alpha gave a command, and they're gone.

If I was smart, I would go, too. I don't. With a gentle nudge, I push the door closed, then stalk over to the piano.

It's a Grand, one of those iconic black pianos with the top held up. If it's as old as I think it is, it's gotta be worth a fortune. Just in case, I hook my fingers through my belt loops, keeping my hands to myself.

I nod at him. "I didn't know you could play."

"I taught myself a long time ago." He lifts his hands from the keys, looking at his short nails. "It's a good reminder that I'm more than claws. I needed that tonight." Dropping his hands, he closes the lid over the keys. "I think I needed you to know that, too."

I suck in a breath.

And that's it, then. The cat—or, in this case, the *wolf*—is out of the bag. I'm not sure how. Either Tristan beat me in or Jade did, making their confessions to their Alpha, and now he's just put it out there.

I shrug. "I guess you know that I know, huh?"

He nods. One sharp jerk of his head before he grates out, "I know."

"Cool."

His jaw tightens. It's not his glower, though the way his brow furrows tells me that it's on its way. "Cool? Is that all you have to say?"

"Well, yeah."

"Most non-supes scream and run when they find out shifters are real."

Looking over the piano at him, I can't get a real read on Lucas. Is he relieved that the truth is out there? Pissed that it got out?

Oooh... is Jade in trouble? That would be one nice thing to come out of tonight.

He's watching me closely. Before I ask, I think better of it. The air is charged between us. That *something* that seems to tug me toward the mysterious dark-haired huntsman... my savior... this *wolf* is hard at work at the moment.

It's just him and me. Just the two of us in this room. Why should I waste this opportunity asking about *Jade*?

So, instead, I smile before pointing out, "Most non-supes don't see a wolf in the woods, think it's a big dog, and toss it her scraps."

It's Lucas's turn to go still before he finally says, "You knew that was me?"

"Yes."

A pause, and then, in a soft voice I've never heard from him before, he asks, "You knew all along?"

"You mean, when I gave you the steak and started saving you my bacon from breakfast?" He nods, and I snort. "Hell, no. I legit thought you were a dog. But"—and there's no avoiding it, so I might as well make it undeniable—"now I do. I know that you're a wolf shifter."

He doesn't deny it.

"The Alpha," I add.

He doesn't deny that, either.

"I'll have to show you my wolf in person sometime," Lucas says, rising up from the piano. "When you're ready for it. Then you'll see the difference."

"I'd like that."

And I definitely don't tell him that Tristan offered to shift for me already.

He moves around the piano. Giving me the excuse to break away from the behemoth, I step closer to him. "To tell the truth, there's so much I want to know."

Lucas gives me a half-grin, and the hint of humor softens the almost teasing complaint that follows. "Luna. I should've known the questions were coming. Tristan warned me you already had plenty, but knowing you... those were only the tip of the iceberg."

Later, I'll look back and admit it was the grin curving his lush lips that did it. That, and the powerful rumble in his chest—so dominant, so *Lucas*—as he told me to close the door behind me.

If I want to find out if he feels this *thing* sparking between us the same way that I do, I just... I have to do *this*.

After all, you never know unless you try, right?

"So it was Tristan who came in and told on me?"

"My packmates are loyal to their Alpha," is all he says.

"Did he tell you everything we talked about?" I ask him.

"He told me enough."

Probably not. And don't think I didn't notice the confirmation there, Lucas.

He's grinning. It's only fair that I grin, too.

Another step closer to him, and while it's probably risky, playing with this predator, I can't stop.

"What about how he told me that wolf shifters can tell when humans are turned on? How they can smell it with their wolfy noses?"

Lucas's half-grin fades away. I already miss it. "Tristan talks too much."

That wasn't a yes. And from the growl in his voice, I know the answer.

Of course, he didn't—but I just did.

Making sure he notices, my eyes dip to his groin. Unless I'm wrong and he's that impressive when he's limp, I see a noticeable bulge pushing against his jeans.

Please don't let me be wrong. Because if I make this gamble... if I *lose*... this situation is gonna turn real awkward, real fast.

"Oh?" I give him my best innocent, damsel-in-distress look. I draw the line at fluttering my lashes, but I don't have to. His gaze is already darkening. "Maybe I misunderstood."

My innocent look becomes a pointed dare as I turn slightly, glancing at Lucas over my shoulder. "Maybe I should go find him. Go double-check with him how I'm feeling right about now."

Should I be teasing a wolf shifter? An *Alpha*? Probably not, especially when I forget one of the things that Tristan did tell me. So focused on his nose, I totally disregard his shifter speed.

That was my mistake—or maybe it wasn't.

When Lucas moves quick as lightning, snagging my hand, tugging me toward him with enough force that I land cradled against his hard chest, my back to him, I know that I rolled the dice... and I *won*.

His chest is an immovable object at the top of my back, but there's something even harder nudging me a little bit lower.

Curving his big body around me, he bows his head so that his stubble brushes against the height of my cheek.

As I resist the urge to squirm, Lucas's breath is hot on the shell of my ear as he says in a low voice, "Ah, sucre. Don't you know better than to tease the big, bad wolf?"

Sucre? Sugar?

What?

I must've misheard him. But so long as it's not another woman's name he's calling out right now, I could care less what he calls me. Not with his heat a brand through my tank top, and my body aching for more of his touch.

So I roll my hips, pushing my ass against the bulge

that's *definitely* there. "That's the wolf. What about the man?"

His laugh is a bark that has my pussy clenching. Oh, yeah. She's aching, too. "Trust me. You don't want to know what the man wants to do to you."

He's wrong about that.

Before I can tell him so, Lucas swoops my hair over my right shoulder. Shoving his nose against the point where my neck connects to the rest of me, he breathes in deep. "Luna, I forgot how fucking amazing your scent is."

I shiver, more from his words than the tickle of his nose against my skin. "You shifters and your sense of smell," I tease, breath coming quick no matter how hard I try to hide how he's affecting me. Probably pointless since I've never been so turned on, but if this is how he wants to play, I'm game. "It's probably just my shampoo."

"It's not."

"My deodorant?"

"Not unless you don't wear any."

Oh.

"It's you. It's always been you." He breathes in again, exhaling with such a force that the warmth of his breath reaches me all the way down to my bare feet. "You smell divine, sucre. But I wonder... do you taste as good as I remember?"

I have no idea what he's talking about, but if he means what I *think* he means...

My tongue darts out, dampening my lips.

Well, Fallon. It's now or never.

If you want him, take him—or let him take *you*.

"I don't know, Lucas," I purr, shifting slightly so that he knows I want him to let go of me. He does, a silent signal that—while he may be an Alpha—it's the human who has all the control right now.

Shaking my head royally, purposely meeting his eyes though his are undeniably locked on my glistening lips, I ask, "Why don't you take a lick and find out?"

He was looking at my lips, but the second those words are out, his eyes snap up. He's staring right at me, allowing me to see it when his irises become a brilliant orange color, hot like lava, and just as dangerous to my health.

It's a dare. We both know it, and it triggers his wolf.

Because it wasn't just a dare. It was a *challenge*.

And if there's one thing I learned in my short time living with wolf shifters, it's that you *never* challenge the Alpha.

You never challenge Lucas.

You know how I get a prompt reminder of that fact? Easy. I provoked the wolf—and despite still standing in front of me as a man, I think the wolf answers.

Faster than should be humanly possible, he slams the upright lid on his piano, closing it so that he has a flat surface to work with. My ears are still ringing with the slam before I realize that he has my shorts off, tossing them away from him.

Lucas pauses for a second to growl again when he notices that I'm not wearing any panties for him to rip off before he grips me gently around my naked waist.

Then, while my head is still whirring with how this is actually happening—that this is actually happening with *Lucas*—he sets my bare ass down on the closed lid of his antique piano.

Humanly possible, I think to myself as the chill from the lid does nothing to cool down the heat raging through me. Of course it isn't humanly possible.

Lucas isn't exactly a human, is he?

And the way he muscles my legs apart, widening the gap until he can squeeze his big shoulders between them before devouring my pussy just further proves my point.

I let him. Obviously. When he mentioned 'taste' and I dared him to 'lick', I didn't expect him to run his tongue along the length of the column of my throat.

Not saying that wouldn't have been sexy as hell, but having him lap at my pussy like he's never tasted something so sweet... it's everything I wanted—until, suddenly, it's just not enough.

I finally gave in and started to squirm. I try not to

think about what kind of mess I'm leaving behind on his piano, and when I first tried to edge as much of my pussy off of it as I could, Lucas gripped my hips again, shifting me right back to where he put me in the first place.

He rests his chin on the edge of the piano, trapping me in place with his hands. I instinctively know that, if I tell him I've had enough, he'd stop. The only reason he moved me was because it gives him a better angle to nuzzle my clit before dipping the point of his tongue inside of me, then spreading his tongue out flat and gathering as much moisture as he can before diving back in.

Lucas only breaks to peek up at me and make sure I'm still on board with this. Considering I start to keen under my breath anytime he gets near my clit, it's obvious that I am. His eyes are burning with lust and pride when I flutter my eyelids open and catch him watching me.

"Grab my hair if you have to." His voice is rich and throaty as he ducks his head again, returning his attention back to my pussy.

I do. Threading my fingers through his hair, forming curls with the strands as I wind through the strands, scratching at his scalp with my nails when another jolt of pleasure rushes through me, I hold on until my soft pants turn to anguished pleading.

"Please, Lucas," I whimper. His tongue breaching

my entrance is a tease that has me tightening up. I squeeze my calves against his shoulders, ignoring the burn in my thighs. "I need *something*."

He doesn't even question it. Giving his head a quick shake, letting me know to let go, I release him and he moves his body so that he's crouching a little higher instead of eating me out on his knees.

Lifting up his arm, I watch his shoulder muscles bunch right before he dips the knuckle of one finger inside of me. Gasping at its intrusion, I scoot a little closer to make it easier for him to work the rest of it inside of me as he returns his attention to lapping lazily at my clit.

The single finger helps a little, but—not gonna lie—while Lucas got the gist of what I was saying, I have to admit I was hoping for something a little more... substantial than his finger.

That doesn't stop me from jerking my hips slightly, enjoying the feel of his finger even as I moan in frustration when it's not enough. As though his mind-reading is some shifter skill I don't know about—but the determined Alpha still wants to make me beg for it—he takes a second finger and... *yes*... he starts to stretch me out.

Smart. God knows I'm tight as hell. I haven't had sex in months and, so far, the two fingers are my limit. Considering I can only imagine what he's packing in his jeans, I need to be a little more ready for what happens next.

If it happens.

Please let it happen…

"**P**lease, Luc," I murmur, echoing the 'please's playing on repeat in my pleasure-filled brain. I'm squeezing him again as he begins to slowly fuck me with his fingers. It feels amazing, but I still need more. "I need *you*."

My confession gets the exact opposite reaction than the one I was hoping for: Lucas *stops*.

Fair enough. He wanted a taste; that doesn't mean he signed up for whipping his dick out. I should be grateful to get the chance to be intimate with him at all.

Who knows? Maybe this will finally help me get over my strange fixation with him. The kiss didn't do anything to get him out of my system, but maybe a little oral and some finger-fucking will?

He withdraws his fingers, resting his hands on the edge of the piano instead. Figuring Lucas has hit his limit and he's putting an end to our little fun, I immediately try to unhook my limp legs from around his head.

With the hand that's sticky from being inside of me, he grasps me by the ankle before I can.

I look down at him. "Lucas?"

"Do you mean it?"

Huh? The endorphins must be getting to me because I have no idea what he's talking about. "What?"

His fingers stroke the underside of my ankle. "You said you need me. I have to make this clear. Are you asking me to mate you?"

Shifter lingo. When he says 'mate', he obviously doesn't mean like what Kirk and Eleanor have. He's not asking me to wolf-marry him or anything, but while 'mate' has a bunch of different meanings, I forgot the most obvious one.

Fuck. He basically wants to know if I want him to *fuck* me.

And I do.

"Well, yeah. If you want to. If you don't, that's okay, I'll—"

"Want to?" Releasing my ankle, Lucas slowly rises to his full height. Oh, he's a big one. "I've wanted to mate you since the moment you were laid out on that couch in my cabin, asking all of your incessant questions while pretending like you weren't scared of me."

I sputter, and I lie. "I wasn't scared of you."

"You were." Lucas gazes down at me with an expression that I can't quite read. "But you're not now."

That's true, at least.

I'm not.

And I'm still not scared when he tears off his t-shirt before unzipping his jeans, shoving them and his underwear down past his ass, leaving him mostly naked. With that second swift move, he frees his cock. As thick as I expected with a length that's impressive though not intimidating, he grips it in his hand.

Already erect, with a bead of precome beading up on the head of his cock, there's no denying that he's more than ready to mate.

I guess he was just waiting for me to ask.

"Put your arms around my neck," he orders.

Of course he would be commanding in bed. That's so like Lucas—so like an Alpha, I bet—that I don't even think of teasing him any further.

Reaching out, I throw my arms around his neck. Once I'm holding on, he slips his hands beneath my bare ass.

"Wrap your legs around me."

I do.

Now, I always knew Lucas was strong. Even before discovering he was a wolf shifter, I'd marveled over his strength. He carried me easily to his cabin after I passed out. He could swing the same iron fence open and closed again that didn't move a single centimeter when I used all my force to push at it.

So why am I surprised that he can hold my entire weight in one palm as he uses his other hand to line up our bodies before shoving himself inside of me?

Maybe I'm not surprised by that. Maybe it's his single-minded devotion to claim me, his big hand sliding up my back until he collars my neck, holding me effortlessly as he pins me on his length. Like he can't imagine being anywhere else, and once I gave him the go-sign, he wasn't going to waste a second before I'm his.

And, whoa, do I like the idea of being Lucas's more than I probably should...

Tilting my head back, my mouth falls open as I whimper out a moan. I've never been so full, whether it's this angle or just *him*, but I'm completely dominated by this powerful Alpha.

Lucas doesn't waste this opportunity, either. Swallowing my gasp, he kisses me with such delicious force, I know that he's claiming my mouth as much as he is the rest of my body. It's a possessive kiss, frantic and messy, with teeth clashing and another moan getting caught in my throat as Lucas tightens his grip on my neck.

I swear I feel something prick my tongue, and when the rusty, tang of blood fills my mouth, I swallow it. So long as I don't see it, I won't be afraid of it, and I'm determined to do anything to keep this going.

Lucas pulls back. For a second, I think it's because he tasted the blood, too... until I get a good look at his satisfied face, wolfish eyes gazing down at me, and a pair of elongated canines biting down into his lip.

Oh. Whether he meant to or not, he must've got me with his shifter fangs.

And I... I'm surprisingly okay with that.

So much so that I can't help but remove my hand from his neck, caressing the edge of his jaw with my thumb before running it along his bottom lip.

"Oh, Lucas," I say, my voice gone throaty with need, "what big teeth you have."

It's the same thing I said to Marie in a completely different situation. And, unlike Marie, Lucas knows just how to respond.

He runs his tongue over one of the fangs, eyes glittering with something I can't quite place—but I know I *like* it. "All the better to eat you with, sucre."

The pleasure that shivers down my spine at his answer has me clutching his thick neck again, squeezing his body with all the strength in my taut body.

I swear to God, I nearly come from that look on his face alone.

It's not just that, either. A sense of humor while he's inside of me, possessing me in a way I'd never thought possible? For fuck's sake, if I didn't already think Lucas was one of the most tempting guys I've ever been with, that seals it for me.

"You already ate me," I remind him, my breath turning choppy as my body screams for one of us to just fucking *move* already. "I thought you had something else in mind now?"

"Oh, sucre... you really just can't help tempting the beast, can you?"

I shake my head wildly, sending my hair falling over my shoulders. "Not even a little."

"Good," he growls, and without another word, he pulls out just enough to slam his way home inside of me.

The sensation is fucking *delicious*.

As he builds up a rhythm, never fully out of me as though he can't bear the separation, all I can think is that it's a good thing Lucas played with me with his fingers and tongue first. I'm so hot, so slick, so *wet* that there's only the slightest hint of resistance in the beginning before he's stretching me out, making me his, making me pant his name in adulation.

Am I loud? I might be. I'd completely forgotten that I currently live in a house with four others that aren't the male I'm fucking, and with their shifter ears, they might hear more than they bargained for. Sure, they all seemed to have disappeared, but did they stay gone?

I have no idea, but when Lucas moves his palm so that he's cupping the back of my head, guiding my mouth against the nook where his neck meets his shoulders, I let him.

To be fair, I'm letting him do whatever the hell he wants to me.

This new position muffles my moans and shrieks as he begins to rock inside of me. His strokes are short and frantic, almost like he's expecting me to put a stop to this at any moment so he's trying to get as much pleasure out of our fucking as he can.

That doesn't mean he's a selfish lover. Not even a little. I was so damn close to coming myself from his teasing when he gave me head before, but the big Alpha takes it one step further. Releasing his hold on the back of my head long enough for me to sit up against him, bouncing on his cock as he pistons his hips wildly, Lucas slips his hand beneath my tank top.

One quick shove. That's all it takes. One quick shove and he has both my shirt and my bra over my boobs, baring them to him.

Lucas buries his face against my tits.

"I've missed you." His voice is muffled, the heat of his breath causing another shiver to explode down my back as he pants against me. "Luna, I've missed you so fucking much, sucre."

What is that supposed to mean? Since he's rescued me, I've been right here. Except for when I went for my fateful walk, but if he wanted to keep an eye on me, why did he send *Tristan*?

I shouldn't ask. I should accept his murmurings as nonsense he's spouting in the heat of the moment, and I try to do just that by simply asking him in a near-breathless voice, "What was that?"

He tugs on my nipple with his teeth—blunt human teeth and not fangs because he's back to letting his human side have control—then looks directly at me. "You feel so fucking amazing around me. Like you're made for me. Like you *belong* to me."

"I do." It's dirty talk, I tell myself. At this moment, I'd probably say anything to reach the orgasm I'm so close to chasing. "I'm yours."

"Say it again." He pulls out, bucking up into me. "Luna damn it, *say it again*."

With his ferocity so fucking hot, that's no problem. I've grown used to the cold, stoic Lucas, and this hot, demanding hunk of man is almost enough to push me over the cliff.

I dig my nails into the back of his neck, clinging to him.

"I'm yours, Lucas." My voice is trembling. My legs are shaky, too. I'm so close to coming around him, and from the way his pace has only picked up, he's gotta be about to finish, too.

"You always have been," he promises, bucking into me again.

Before I can say anything to that, his big body begins to shake as he fills me up.

Knowing that he's nutting inside of me sets me off. It dawns on me way too late that we definitely didn't stop to grab a condom or anything, and while I'm on the shot so there's no chance of him knocking me up, this is the first time in my life I let a guy come inside of me without at least seeing his test results first.

Which just goes to show how far gone I was because, instead of inwardly freaking out that he's still coming, I join him as my own orgasm slams into me.

Since I'm a screamer, the moment I feel myself begin to come apart in his arms, I start to shriek. Lucas immediately has me by the back of my head again, gently pushing me against him so that he can muffle my screams this time.

And then, as fast as it started, it's *done,* and I'm not sure what exactly I'm supposed to do.

Lucas does.

Before he pulls out of me, he lets go of my head so that I can move if I want to. For a moment, I don't—until he reaches behind him, taking my wrist and slowly pulling it away from the back of his neck. With a gentle tug, he moves my limp arm until it's in front of him.

I finally lift my head, just in time to see Lucas run his nose along the half-healed slice on my inner arm. It's more scab than anything; thankfully, the cut wasn't as deep as it could've been, and Lucas's first aid that night in his cabin kept it from getting infected. As though checking that for himself, he takes a deep breath before angling my arm so that he can reach it with his mouth.

He presses one hot kiss to the middle of the old cut, a sweet gesture so at odds with how completely he just owned my body, then lets go of my arm.

A little stunned by what he did—and feeling as weak as a kitten—I'm simply clinging to him as he trails his blunt fingertips down the length of my spine before easing my legs from around his waist. With one hand settled possessively on the small of my back, he grips my chin lightly between the fingers on the other, kissing me so deeply that I barely remember being cut by his fang before.

Panting slightly, branded by his kiss, Lucas lets go of my chin, dropping his hand, reaching for my tender pussy.

With one last possessive stroke up my slit, as though the dominant male in him is checking to make sure that his come is still deep inside of me, marking his conquest, he grunts out a sound of satisfaction, then drops to one knee.

"Lucas?" My voice is hoarse. I might've muffled my screams against his thick neck, but that doesn't mean I didn't shout my throat raw as he played my body even better than he did that piano. "What are you—?"

He doesn't answer me. Naked and utterly intoxicating, he also doesn't snatch his own discarded clothes up. Instead, after pressing an open-mouthed kiss to my upper thigh, he grabs my shorts. His expression is one of intense concentration as he guides me to lift up one leg by my ankle, then the next. Once he has me step inside of my shorts, he slowly tugs them back up my body.

It's such a contrast to the way he pulled them off of me in his haste to bury his face in my pussy. Like he's making up for being so rough by being incredibly gentle in the aftermath of our sex.

Lucas moves his big hands behind me, pulling the denim shorts up and over my ass. When I reach down to do the buttons and zipper myself, his hands are suddenly covering mine. He taps my fingers with his, then does the job himself. A quick squeeze to my midriff before he tugs Eleanor's old bra and tank top down over my boobs.

Once I'm dressed, he yanks up his own pair of jeans, tucking himself inside of them. He doesn't bother with his button. His shirt, either. That should've been a clue since I now know that a male shifter coming out of a shift only needs pants on to be considered decent, and he probably wouldn't bother getting fully dressed if he was preparing to go wolf.

But I'm still surprised when he tells me, "I have to go."

I blink. "What? *Now*?"

I don't know what exactly I was expecting. Considering I noticed that he was already starting to recover when he shoved his semi-hard dick back inside of his jeans, I guess I was hoping that we could move this thing we're doing somewhere a little more private. My room or his, I didn't care, but preferably somewhere with a bed instead of a piano.

Now that we already had sex once, I couldn't see any reason why we can't do it again. I'm also itching to get my hands on his cock, and to find out just what Lucas tastes like.

So, yeah. I'm basically ready to continue this while I'm still hot and horny and in the mood—and before the endorphins wear off and my body starts to ache— but that's obviously not the plan.

Careful to keep his eyes off of me, he shakes his head, almost regretfully. "I can't. I have something to take care of." And, then, the death knell: "I was out of control anyway. I... we shouldn't have done that."

We.

Boom.

Shouldn't.

Boom.

Have.

Boom.

Done.

Boom.

That.

The words echo in my brain to the beat of my suddenly pounding heart which, hey, is kind of surprising since I didn't know a shattered heart could still fucking *beat*.

I move so that he's forced to look at me before I say, "Lucas?"

No way I can deny that he's purposely avoiding my gaze when he instantly turns his head from me, giving me his profile instead.

"I wanted to. Don't ever think that I didn't. I don't regret one second with you... or mating you, even if I was too rough... but if you knew—"

"That wasn't rough." I've had worse, and I can handle it. "So give me another excuse."

His jaw tightens. "It's not an excuse."

I scoff. "Then it sure as hell is a world-class record. Most guys give me a least ten minutes to come down from my orgasm before they start the 'it's not you, it's me' bullshit."

His head snaps my way. Finally. "It's never been you that's the problem. It's always been me." Shifting his big body, he lays his palm against my cheek. I only just resist the urge to lean into it, though I don't jerk away from him like I probably should. "Damn it, Fallon. I don't want to take advantage of you."

If he didn't, then it's way too fucking late for that.

Good thing I'm not stuck in the 50s like Lucas obviously is.

"You didn't," I snort, stepping back and away from him after all. Hands on my hips, I tell him the truth. "I wanted sex. You gave it to me. There's nothing wrong with that. Just like there's nothing wrong with never wanting to do it with each other ever again. It's fine. You don't have to make a big deal out of it. Okay?"

Lucas opens his mouth. Closes it.

Without me there to caress, his hand drops.

"I have to go," he begins.

"Right." My hoarse voice sounds wicked when I adopt a wry tone like that. *Good.* "'Cause the big, bad Alpha has something to take care of now that I took care of him. That right?"

He winces. "It's not like that."

Whatever. "I told you. It's fine. Go."

Lucas does, though he pauses when his hand settles on the doorknob. With one searing look back at me, he rumbles, "This isn't done. Me and you... it's not over, either."

The sad part is I actually want to believe that.

FEELING REJECTED, EMBARRASSED, ANNOYED, AND stupidly hopeful all at the same time, I wait until I'm sure Lucas isn't anywhere in the hall before I get ready to escape to my room where, this time, a shower is definitely in order.

He already helped me arrange my clothing. Out of spite, I do it again, then tuck my opal beneath my tank top. I noticed him glancing at it a few times as he was pounding away inside of me, and while I'd like to think he was gazing at my tits instead, I know what I saw.

He stared at the opal necklace the night he saved me, too, I remember.

Maybe he wants it. Maybe I can offer it to him in exchange for everything he's done for me, then I can go on my merry way, he can pretend to stop being into me, and we can both chalk it up to amazing sex that helped us both get past the undeniable—yet inexplicable—pull we seem to be feeling toward each other.

I might not be able to leave yet, but that doesn't mean I *have* to stay with Lucas and the other wolves. There aren't just witches in Winter Creek. There are plenty of non-supes who have no idea that there's a curse going on around them. They probably just like the vintage feel of the town or something. Who knows? Maybe I can stick around some of them until the stupid train finally shows up and I can get the hell out of Dodge.

Seems like a good plan to me.

But, first, I need to get out of the piano room.

Once I'm sure I'm as decent as I'm going to get without a change of clothes or a hairbrush, I push open the door—

—just in time to nearly hit Tristan with it.

Fuck.

Because it would just have to be him that I run into as I start out on my walk of shame. Not that I'm ashamed of anything I did with Lucas—except for the way I almost pleaded with him to stay with me after he said he had to go—but *still.* I can't think of anything else to call it, especially when the first thing Tristan does is flare his nostrils.

In an instant, I'm thrown right back to earlier by the creek. When he gave me a crash course on shifters, and I learned just how good their senses are.

If he can tell when I'm getting aroused, there's no way he can't pick up on the scent of sex in the air, or Lucas's musk on my skin.

He would've found out anyway, I tell myself. One way or another, he would've known. It's like living in a dorm. You can't take a crap in a place like that without everyone knowing about it.

He would've found out anyway, but did it have to be like this?

"Tristan—"

He doesn't meet my eyes. Instead, gaze locking on a point just over my head, he says, "I was looking for Lucas. He was in here before."

I guess that confirms my suspicion in a way Lucas refused to. It wasn't Jade who snitched, but the Beta of the pack, Lucas's right-hand wolf who warned the Alpha before I stumbled upon him.

"He was, but he said he has something he has to take care of. He had to go."

He had to leave me behind.

Tristan clenches his teeth. From the way his cheeks hollow, his icy blue eyes gone dark, it's easy to see that he's as happy to hear Lucas's excuse as I was.

For totally different reasons, yeah. But the Beta is pissed—and I don't blame him one bit.

"I'm sorry—"

"You have nothing to be sorry for," he says firmly. "Nothing at all, Fallon."

"But—"

He bows his head, continuing to avoid my eyes. "I really have to talk to Lucas about something. I'll see you later, okay?"

I work up a grin that I wish like hell I could mean right now. "Yeah. Sure. Later."

Turning away from me, Tristan heads down the hall. He purposely keeps his head straight. I watch him go, wanting to call something after him, but having no idea what.

So I don't say anything. And when he's gone, I hurry to my room and try to figure out why the hell I felt compelled to apologize to Tristan like that—and why, for a split second there, I wanted to throw my arm around his neck, tug his head down to mine, and kiss that undeniably hurt expression right off of his pretty face.

CHAPTER 20
SECRETS

I really wanted to believe that Lucas was different.

Wolves mate for life, right? I remember reading that. Not that I expect a lifelong commitment after a little fucking, or even anything like what Eleanor and Kirk have with their partnership, but would seeing him at breakfast the next morning be too much to ask?

Apparently.

I'm no stranger to an awkward morning after. Usually, they're because I stayed over after sex, and I have to grab my crap and figure out a way home. You've never really done a walk of shame until you're heading on the E train with bedhead, I'll tell you that.

It should've been even easier for us. We might have fucked in the piano room, but with his post-nut clarity came Lucas realizing what we just did. He made his excuses and his escape, and once again I was left watching Tristan's heart break as he realizes that, for the second time, I chose Lucas.

It sucks. Blondie's the one who told me I had a choice in the first place, but I'd be lying if I said that, after getting past Lucas's grumpy facade, anyone else was a consideration.

I like Tristan. I do. He would've been a fun summer fling. But when I reach deep inside of myself, answering this whisper-thin tug I can't ignore, it always seems to lead me to Lucas.

And that's my problem. No matter how much he keeps on making me think he feels the same thing, the Alpha inevitably ends up rejecting anything that might be between us.

He did it after our kiss. Then he did it last night, making a quick appearance in the kitchen after I dragged myself downstairs. After announcing that it was his turn to go on patrol, he conveniently skipped dinner to disappear out the back door, only giving me a sidelong look that I refused to acknowledge.

At least I got off a lot luckier at dinner than I was expecting. Jade was missing, too, and Tristan went back to keeping his gaze on his plate as he ate his sausage and mashed potatoes with a single-minded devotion that left him no time to participate in the conversation that sprang up between Eleanor, Kirk, and me.

Well, mainly Kirk and Eleanor, but eager to show the rest of the house that I couldn't be fazed by their leader's obvious rejection—or, second to that, me learning their big honking secret—I tossed my opinion in here and there. Plus, because I no longer had to be kept in the dark about their being wolves, I take advantage of Eleanor's amiable nature to ask as many questions as I want to, daring any of the others there to stop me.

They don't, so I probably asked way too many questions between dinner and dessert. For some reason, I strayed away from the topic of their being supes. I'm far more interested in the curse—and what it's like to know it's well into the twenty-first century when each one of them was close to being born nearly a hundred years ago.

Even Eleanor, who despite being human like me, is a shifter's bonded mate. That, I discover, is the reason behind the bite on her neck, and the reason why she stays inside of the house with me instead of going on patrol. Shifters *do* mate for life, so long as they perform some supe ceremony I willfully refuse to ask about—at first. All I needed to hear was that, after tying herself to Kirk before the curse hit, when it *did*, it considered her as much a supe as the other wolves, keeping her frozen in time, too.

Kirk and Eleanor are bonded mates, but the other

human woman and me? We're a match made in heaven.

I love to ask questions. Eleanor loves to talk.

And now that Lucas isn't around to order anyone to stay quiet—and the whole house knows that Jade gave up their secret—she doesn't have any reason not to answer me.

It was easy to see that Tristan was listening to our chat, though he purposely kept quiet; he probably figured he's told me too much already. And Kirk... though he was as much a part of the conversation once I piped up, he was definitely careful to keep our chat focused on the differences between then and now.

It was pretty obvious. When I did decide to subtly —or not-so-subtly—bring up Lucas, this idea of mate bonds, my grandmother's role in the curse, or even the beast that haunts the woods, Kirk would immediately lead us right back to discussing the pack seventy years ago, and the pack now.

He was doing it on purpose, but Eleanor didn't seem to mind, so why should I?

Tucking aside everything I *did* learn, I was hoping to get the chance to talk to Lucas when he came back to the house—only he didn't. Finally admitting to myself that he was probably spending the night at his hunting cabin—something I learned he does pretty often when he needs some time away from the pressures of being in charge, though now I know it's because he's the Alpha—I didn't take it personally when he seemed to have fallen off the face of the earth.

But that was last night.

This morning, my outlook is far more bitter.

Oh, no, Fallon. Lucas didn't just ditch his friends and his house because he gave in to the sparks flying between you and decided to go down on you while you were sitting on top of a piano that probably cost a semester's worth of tuition at Rutgers. And then, when you whimpered that you needed him, he was just doing what a good host—a good *protector*—would do by fucking you senseless.

Right?

He has other things to do.

Better things to do, whispers the nasty voice in the back of my skull.

It sounds suspiciously like Jade.

And whatever those things might be, he's still doing them the next morning. Maybe he roped Jade and Tristan in on it, too, because for the first time since I've been staying at the house, only two people are sitting at the breakfast table when I pad into the room, holding my breath.

I exhale roughly, barely hiding my disappointment—and my frustration.

Great. I've been here for maybe two weeks and I screwed up a five-person pack that has been living together for more than seventy years.

Nice going, Fallon.

Bang-up job.

Ugh.

Kirk is leaning back in his seat, sipping his morning coffee when I make my way into the kitchen. Call me pathetic, but I stopped by both the library and the piano room before taking the stairs down to the ground floor. I shouldn't have bothered. This strange sixth sense I've developed that tells me when Lucas is around has been dull since he walked out the door.

He's gone, and I don't know when he'll be back.

I did, however, expect to see the other wolves. Nope. The only other person in the kitchen is Eleanor, grabbing a second helping of hashbrowns and eggs one of the two of them must have whipped up. Probably Eleanor. Whenever one of the others makes a meal, there's always a meat component to go with it. Eleanor, like me, can take it or leave it, but not the wolves.

And that, Fallon, should've been another clue. Another sign. Everybody else in the house is a ferocious eater and a carnivore, too.

Kirk's done eating. His dish is already cleared, leaving only his coffee in front of him.

One of these days I have to ask where they get all their food. There's gotta be a grocery store that's on neutral territory that I haven't had the chance to visit yet, but since the idea of any of the wolves doing something so mundane as grocery shopping doesn't compute—even before I knew they were wolves—I imagine a magic portal that they treat like it's an Alexa, requesting whatever they want and getting it.

I'd ask, but I already know that none of them have any clue what an 'Alexa' is.

One downfall to being stuck in time in a nearly hidden town means that they missed the tech explosion of the last couple of decades. They know about phones because they used to have landlines way back when, and there are a few unlucky non-supes—and some curious supes who risk getting trapped in the curse of Winter Creek—who find this place, bringing their worthless cell phones with them.

But more recent advances like Uber or Alexa or Doordash? All things I take for granted?

They look at me like I have three heads whenever I mention them... which, yeah, probably should've been *another* clue that this place is like nothing it should be.

They don't have tech, but they do have magic. Who knows? Except for their whole stance on being mortal enemies with the witches, they might very well have a portal that makes food appear out of thin air.

Hey. It could happen.

No portal today, I notice, glancing around. No Lucas, either.

Damn it.

I offer them a wave. "Mornin', everyone."

"What's with the long face, Fallon? You okay?" Plopping down in the seat next to Kirk, Eleanor scowls. Not gonna lie, but it's kind of adorable when you take in her bouncy curls and her slightly upturned nose. "Did Jade say something to you again?"

If only. "I can handle Jade."

Well, as a human, I can. If she goes furry on my ass, I'm toast, but since I'm using the fact that Lucas hasn't booted me from the house to mean he's still protecting me, I doubt she'll use her claws and fangs on me.

Fingers crossed.

Kirk gives me a small amused smile that makes me think he knows exactly where my thoughts have gone. "It's better if you don't listen to her. It's not your fault that she's wanted Lucas for years and the most he sees her as is a little sister."

"A bratty little sister," adds Eleanor. "I'm human, and even I know you don't go against the Luna no matter what."

Kirk doesn't argue—or, to my annoyance, explain. I'd always suspected that was the case, but to have confirmation...

Instead he just says, "She knows that, too. She'll get over it."

Eleanor shrugs, scooping some of her eggs into her mouth. "Been seventy years, honey. She hasn't yet."

"Then she'll just have to wait until the curse is

broken and the Luna speaks to her. Then she'll have her fated mate, and Lucas can work on claiming his."

My ears perk up.

Lucas can work on claiming his...

The memory of Lucas's rumbling voice echoes in my ear.

Say it again.

I'm yours.

You always have been...

My stomach goes tight. So Lucas doesn't have a mate—a... a *fated* mate—yet. Is that why I feel so drawn to him? Or why he took the chance to sleep with me?

Could it be me? Or did he think there was a chance, but then he came to his senses and that's why he made his escape as quickly as he did before disappearing?

I don't ask. For all the questions I peppered at them last night, those are a few I can't bring myself to say out loud.

Call me a coward, but I don't think I want to hear the answers.

Instead, I lock onto something else Kirk said and add it to Eleanor's quip about Jade.

The Luna again. Always the Luna...

I was going to go grab a plate and get my own breakfast. No longer as hungry, I hold off on that, sinking down into the seat opposite of Eleanor, facing both her and Kirk. It's not where I usually sit, but I want to be able to watch their faces.

"Funny that you say that. Lucas... he seems to mention the Luna a lot, too. For the longest time, I thought that was just a weird name for the moon, but you two made her seem like an actual person just now."

Eleanor swallows her mouthful, then sets down her fork. "That's because she's both."

Huh? "What?"

"The Luna is our goddess." Leaning over to his mate, Kirk nuzzles the mark on Eleanor's throat. "The moon represents her, but that doesn't mean she's not real. I mean, she brought me my Ellie. The Luna led her to me, showing me with one glance that she was the one female for me." Casting his eyes toward the ceiling, almost as though he's praying, he murmurs, "And, curse or no curse, I thank her for that daily."

"Ah, honey. I love you, too," Eleanor coos, leaning into him.

"Of course you do. We're fated."

"Fated?" I echo. "Like, there's no way around it? No way getting out of it?"

"Of course not," Kirk says, a sniff indicating that I might've offended the wolf. Whoops. "A mate gets to choose. But, in my experience, the Luna never gets it wrong." He pauses for a beat. "Almost never."

Before I can ask him what *that* means, Eleanor cuts in with an amused smile.

"I have to say, you're taking all this wolf stuff much better than I ever did, Fallon. When Kirk told me what he was, I was convinced he belonged in an asylum. If he didn't, then I sure did, since I was ready to hop into bed with him the moment we met. Which, you gotta know, that's not what too many folks did back then before we were married."

A twinkle in Eleanor's eye tells me that, while too many folks didn't, she wasn't one of them. I raise my eyebrow at her.

Her laugh is shameless as she lays her hand possessively on Kirk's upper arm. "I didn't need a wedding to know he was mine. I just... I *knew*, and he was worth jumping in with both feet, no marriage required. Besides, that's not really a thing shifters do. We're mated and, if you ask me, that's better."

"Really?" I wonder. I've never been one for the whole white dress, walking to the altar thing myself, but Eleanor seems so sure. "Why?"

"Humans have divorce, don't they?" Kirk says, bringing the topic back to mates. "Not shifters. When we mate, it's for life. A shifter's bite says 'I do' more than any silly human ceremony."

Eleanor pats Kirk's arm, still keeping the connection. "Not that I believed all that hooey when I first met my honey. Asylum, remember? He had to carry me kicking and screaming to this place to convince me that everything he was saying was real. Then he turned into a big brindled wolf in front of me and it was all I could do not to faint—"

"You did faint, Ellie."

She waves Kirk off with her other hand. "I might've dozed off for a second or two. Not all of us can be like Fallon who's just going along with it. I mean, handsome man turns into a handsome wolf? In one way, I was like you. I had no idea shifters were real, but you know what they say. Seeing is believing. When I saw Kirk's wolf the first time, damn right I believed."

I get that. And I don't correct Eleanor about me going along with everything so easily because, well, I did, didn't I? And then, on the heels of discovering that Lucas can turn into a huge black wolf, what did I do?

I banged him.

So, yeah... she isn't wrong, is she?

Trying to ignore how I can still feel the brand of his hands on me, I focus on the couple in front of me. "And then what? You two got mated?"

Because, if I learned anything last night, it's this: there is a difference between 'mating' and *mating*. One is straight-up, animalistic sex—like the kind I had with Lucas—and the other is the shifter ceremony of committing to each other.

Does Eleanor know which one I mean? From the way her eyes continue to twinkle mischievously, it's probably *both*.

"Oh, hell no. I made him work for it," she laughs, taking a sip of her mate's coffee. "But not that hard. We're fated, you know. Meant for each other. He always knew he'd get me in the end."

Using the side of his thumb, Kirk runs it over her mark. "And then I bit her so that everyone in town knew that she was mine."

And that, right there, is why I know that I was nothing more than a willing woman to Lucas.

Because even as he buried my face in his neck, he didn't try to bite mine. The little nip on my tongue had to be a fluke. Other than that, he didn't mark me in any way apart from his scent—and all that did was put me in an awkward situation with Tristan when I nearly collided with him.

Disappointment has me lost in my own thoughts when, suddenly, I hear Eleanor say, "Yeah, but not before Jade tried to run me out of Winter Creek."

My head snaps up. "She did?"

Eleanor gives me a confiding look. "Oh, yeah. She's always thought that being the only female wolf in the pack gives her pull around here. Just because she's one rank above Kirk in the hierarchy, and us humans don't count when it comes to ranking dominance, she thinks she's better than us."

Yeah. I don't have a hard time believing *that.*

"She didn't even stop when Kirk claimed me," Eleanor adds. "Jade gave me crap for a good decade after the curse started up and only finally gave it a rest when she realized she was stuck with me."

"I would've challenged her for you," Kirk tells his mate.

Another pat on his arm. "You silly wolves. You think you can settle everything with a challenge."

She's not wrong about that, either.

Another sly glance my way, making sure I'm paying attention. "When shifter challenges usually end in death, why let any of them risk it? I learned to handle Jade." She bobs her head toward me while addressing Kirk. "Fallon will, too, if she hasn't already."

I'm working on it. And now that I hear that shifter challenges can be deadly, I'll definitely have to stop baiting her.

I always knew she hated me. She didn't hide it. Hearing that she pulled the same shit with Eleanor has me curious.

"So... let me get this straight. Jade doesn't like me because I'm human?"

Please let it be a bigot thing. I can't do anything about being human, but I'd rather that than because she's got the hots for Lucas. I don't know why she still is holding out on him choosing her after seventy years plus they've been in this house together and he *hasn't*, but if she hasn't found out I screwed him yet, she will.

And then *I'll* be screwed...

Please let it be a bigot thing—

"Oh, no," Eleanor says, dashing my hopes, "it's definitely because you're the first woman Lucas has brought home since—" She stops short, leaving me to obsess over what she would've said long after this conversation is over. "Either way, she's also had a thing against humans for as long as I've known her. It's just how she is."

"Me, too," Kirk says, cutting in before I beg Eleanor to finish her earlier thought. "And I knew her for a couple of years before I even met my Ellie. If it wasn't for the fact that the only alpha she-wolf in our history there's ever been is the Luna herself, I'd think Jade was one. She can be nasty when she wants to be."

He can say that again.

"Maybe she's the beast," I mutter. "God knows she's a big, bad wolf in a tiny human package."

I don't know why I say that out loud. No denying I saw Jade in her wolf form, and now I know what Lucas looks like in his. Tristan helpfully described his wolf, too. So, unless it's *Kirk* who turns into that misshapen thing, it can't be anyone in the pack...

"It's not as simple as that," Kirk begins before his mate cheerfully interrupts him with an, "If only. It would explain so much."

"Ellie!"

"What?" she asks innocently. "It's not her, but it should've been."

"You know that's not true—"

"Wait." Forget everything else we were talking about. "You guys know about the beast?"

"The creature that haunts the woods is a sad story," Kirk says, more to his mate than to me. It's like I've suddenly vanished, and the whole world is made up of just the two of them. "Ellie... it's what could happen to me if anything ever happens to *you*."

Gripping his chin, Eleanor turns his face so that she can give him a quick kiss. "Never, honey. It's you and me 'til the end and you know it."

"Shifters very rarely survive losing their mates. You know *that*. When the Luna creates a bond between a pair, it really is for life. No straying. No cheating. And when one dies, the other usually follows."

I don't mean to interrupt this thing going on between them, but the words simply slip out on their own. "They die of a broken heart."

She squeezes his shoulder. "And that will never happen to you," she says firmly. "I promise."

Kirk's eyes darken as if remembering something terrible. "You don't know that. When the curse hit..."

His voice trails off, almost as if it suddenly dawns on him that I'm still sitting here. I get the feeling he had forgotten and probably said more than he would've if he hadn't.

But then he surprises me by shifting in his seat, purposely meeting my gaze as he says, "The big, bad wolf that haunts these woods isn't a beast, Fallon. Not really. He's a lost feral wolf who's as trapped in the witches' curse as the rest of us."

"Feral," I echo. "What's a feral?"

"It's a shifter thing. When the man and the wolf

break, that's what happens. He's out of his head, more beast than man. Ruled by his basest instincts. To feed..."

"To mate," supplies Eleanor.

A massive erection on a broken body flashes before my mind's eye. Yeah, mating was definitely on the table if I hadn't frightened him with my scream.

But, more than that, I think I understand. "So, if something calls to him, he'll just... he'll take it?"

"He won't even know he's doing it. Attacking an innocent, dragging one back to his lair, slashing them to ribbons... when a wolf goes feral, he's worse than even a wild animal. He's... he's—"

"Rabid."

That's the only word I can come up with to describe the monster they're talking about. And while the beast I met was a little different—he seemed more frightened of me at first, and he howled in pain when he scented my blood—I could easily see him using his massive claws and fangs to tear me to pieces... to use that huge cock of his to rip me apart... all if my piercing scream hadn't sent him running away.

"This feral... did you know him before he broke?"

It takes Kirk a few seconds to decide to answer me. When he does, he just nods his head once.

So it's a former packmate, I'm betting. No wonder they're so close-lipped when it comes to talking about him. Knowing he's out in the woods, broken and alone while they live in the pack house must be so hard on them.

Unless he's part of the reason the wolves of Winter Creek constantly keep up their patrols...

"Can't you save him?" I wonder. "Do something to help him?"

The mated couple exchanges a look.

"He knows he always has a place with the pack," Kirk says carefully. Gently. "And until the curse is broken, that's about as much as we can do for him."

I nod, and don't say anything in response to that.

But all I'm thinking is: I was brought here to break the curse. It might not have worked when Marie shed my blood to lure the feral closer, but if it's the last thing I do, I'm not leaving Winter Creek until I figure out why it was supposed to be me—and do whatever I can to finally break it.

After all the wolves have done to protect me, it's the least I can do.

Even if their Alpha is a jerk.

IT'S LATE, ABOUT AN HOUR AFTER A DINNER THAT WAS just the three of us again, when I hear the knock at my bedroom door.

For one hopeful moment, I think it might be Lucas. But then I realize that the doorknob didn't rattle, his constant reminder that he doesn't understand why I would lock him or any of the others out, so it can't be him.

It wouldn't be Eleanor, either. As close as we've gotten the last few days, she doesn't bother with a quaint knock anymore. She just bangs on the door with the flat of her palm, shouting my name until I answer her.

That really whittles down my options. Torn between ignoring the knock and seeing who could be out there, I sigh and climb out of my bed.

I'm still dressed. I hadn't bothered to get ready for bed yet, just in case Lucas decided to come home and I could have it out with him. It's been more than twenty-four hours since he disappeared on me. And, okay, I know he doesn't owe me anything just because we had sex, but I thought he was a much better guy than that.

I *needed* him to be a much better guy than that.

Padding in my bare feet across the floor, I flip the lock on the door, then grab the handle, opening it up.

When I see who's standing on the other side of the threshold, I have to resist the very powerful urge to slam it in her face.

It's tough, but I do it.

Purposefully meeting her eyes because I know it'll irk her, I ask, "Jade. Forgive me for being blunt, but what do you want?"

She gives a tiny jerk of her head. Woo hoo. I guess I'm forgiven. "I've been waiting to get you alone."

I can only imagine why. "Sorry, but I told you. I'm just not into you. Though," I add, because she deserves it, "you do have nice tits. Since you wanted to show them off and all."

To my surprise, instead of getting pissed, she actually preens, sticking out her chest just enough to be noticeable. "Thanks. That's the best thing about the modern age. Nudity isn't as big a deal as it used to be."

I highly doubt that's why she came to see me. As proud of her body as she has every right to be, we both know that she's not into me.

Oh, no. She wants Lucas, and unless she managed to miss out on the pack gossip—and I doubt it—she had to know that I had him for one night, then he ran off on me.

Which is why I should've been expecting it when she smirks at me. "It's not what I want. It's what you want." She pauses. "*Jolie.*"

I should've been expecting it—but I wasn't. The way she uses my pet name against me, either.

It's like a gut punch. With a soft *oof*, I take a step back.

How did Jade know that my grandmother called me that? And why do I get the feeling that there's more to it than her simply mocking what happened between me and Marie?

I swallow. "What did you say?"

She doesn't answer me. Instead, her smirk growing infinitesimally wider, she just asks, "You want to know where Lucas is, don't you?"

Desperately, but I don't want her to know that.

"He's on patrol," I tell her.

Jade shakes her head, long blonde hair swaying with the motion. "Lucas never patrols when the Luna goes dark."

Fully aware she's most likely lying to screw with me, I can't help but wonder where Lucas might be if he *isn't* on patrol...

Damn it. She knew exactly what bait to throw at me to get me hooked, and it *worked*.

"Fine," I say, giving in. "If he's not on patrol, then where is he?"

Her green gaze glitters like emeralds. "In the Alpha's cabin. That's where he goes when the Luna is in control." She lifts up her hand, ticking off her claw-tipped fingers—because those aren't nails, they're *claws*. "The full moon. The new moon. Whenever the Luna calls to him, Lucas exchanges pack land for his personal territory—and it's time someone told you."

Okay, then.

"If that's so, why is it you? Why are you telling me this?"

Why would she decide to be so very helpful to *me* of all people?

After she made it perfectly clear that she hated me for reasons completely out of my control—being human, being attracted to Lucas, having Lucas paying attention to me instead of her...—I can't imagine why she would want to do anything for my sake.

And then she says, "Because I don't like secrets," and it suddenly makes a little more sense.

Realization slams into me. "That's why you shifted in front of me. You did do it on purpose!"

"Of course I did," retorts Jade. "If it was up to the others, you'd never know. If I'm forced to deal with a human, it better at least be one who knows about supes. This curse is bad enough. I'm not about to hide what I am because Lucas is—"

She cuts herself off.

I jump on it. "Lucas is what?"

Jade grins. It's so predatory, I don't know how I never guessed before that she had a wolf inside of her.

"Here's an idea. Why don't you go to his cabin and find out?"

If it wasn't for Jade's detailed directions, I doubt I would've ever found my way back to Lucas's hunting cabin.

And if it wasn't for her picking a fight with Kirk, with Eleanor instinctively backing up her mate despite being the human of the pair, I probably wouldn't have been able to sneak out, either.

There was no sign of Tristan around when I started off toward the woods. Of course, I learned my lesson from the last time I went off on my own. Just because I don't see him, it doesn't mean that he isn't there.

Figuring he's the odd wolf out who's on patrol since Lucas isn't, I hope that he's closer to the witches' territory, keeping an eye on them instead of tracking my every move.

And, okay, I still feel kind of guilty. I don't even

know for sure *why* I do, but the pit in my stomach when I think about Tristan, his dazzling smile, and the dark look in his icy blue eyes when I left the piano room, has only gotten bigger since yesterday.

First things first... I want to confront Lucas. Not even confront him. *Talk* to him. As much as I'm dying to ask him about fated mates—and if I might be *his*—at the very least, I have to know if what happened between us was a one-time thing, a mistake, or something else entirely.

I blame it on the mated pair. The more I've learned about a shifter's mate, the more I have to ask myself: am I Lucas's? Is that why my feelings for him are more like a compulsion? I barely know the guy but, in the heat of the moment, I would've said or done anything to have that connection with him.

I'm yours...

Go back even further. I hardly knew his name and I was willing to follow him to his house in the woods.

Two weeks later, and I still don't even know his *last* name.

This is crazy. All of it. It's nuts, and if I'm going to entertain this insanity any further, I need to know exactly where his head is at. No more hot and cold. No more mixed signals. Either he wants to explore what we might have brewing between us, or he doesn't.

I can take being rejected. What I can't handle? Is being baited on his hook like prey and left dangling.

Should I have waited until he came back? Of course.

Is risking my ass by sneaking off into the woods when it's freaking *dark* out an incredibly stupid and impulsive idea? You betcha.

But I'm Fallon Witt. That's what I do, whether it's hopping on a train to meet a grandmother I've never known or following this tug deep inside of me that, for some inexplicable reason, is leading me right toward Lucas.

Because despite Jade's explicit instructions and my vague remembrance of how I got to the pack house the first time, my directional skills are so shitty that I probably would have accidentally ended up nearer to my grandmother's territory if it wasn't for something telling me which way to go. It's almost like I have an internal compass and Lucas is north.

I follow it, and after close to an hour's trek through the woods with nothing but a flashlight that Jade smuggled to me and the determination to find out what exactly Lucas is hiding in his cabin, I stumble upon it.

Immediately killing the flashlight so he doesn't get an advance warning that I'm out here, I have to peer through the dark night to make sure it's the right one.

I mean, it has to be his cabin, right? I can't imagine there is more than one in these woods.

Unless... does the beast have a cabin of his own? Is

that where he went when he left Lucas's pack? To a building in the woods where he could be alone?

Oh, boy. That's probably something I should have thought to ask before I started out on this trek. My genius ass didn't even think to grab a coat—or even Eleanor's red cape—so while today was unseasonably warm, with nothing but pitch black sky and a sprinkling of stars overhead, I'm close to freezing again.

My determination to see Lucas kept me warm for half my walk. The promise of getting him to light the fireplace inside his cabin did the trick for another quarter. At some point, nothing worked, and as I stand here in the dark, I wrap my arms around myself and shiver.

Then, I hear a muffled sound, almost like a snuffle, and the shivers become more like tremors.

My heart jumps straight into my throat.

That sound? Whatever made it, it isn't human.

Cool it, Fallon, I tell myself, forcing myself to calm. It's not like you don't know that he's a wolf. Maybe that's what he does. Goes for a run in his fur, gets some of his dominance out of his system, then crashes on the couch in the hunting cabin.

Alpha cabin.

Whatever.

I don't really know how a lot of this works. Does he sleep in his wolf shape? Jade was splashing around in the creek in her fur, so why wouldn't he curl up as a wolf and get a good night's sleep.

Maybe that's how wolves snore. How am I supposed to know? I've never been close enough to a sleeping wolf to hear what they sound like.

Shoot, if we're being fair, I banged the Alpha, and even then I have no idea what he looks like asleep in his skin, either.

It's not the beast. This is definitely Lucas's cabin. He's the one in there.

It's not the beast.

I swallow the lump lodged in my throat and nod to psych myself up.

It's not the beast, and the only way to prove that is to walk into the cabin and hope Lucas recognizes me when he's his wolf.

Blowing out a rush of air, I slip the flashlight into my back pocket and shake out my numb hands. If there's one thing I do know about Lucas, it's that he won't bother locking the door, and I'm right. When I grab it, twisting it under my hand, it turns easily.

Here goes nothing.

I push in the door—and like the night I slipped and fell face-first into my own blood, I nearly lose my fucking mind.

It's not even that the inside of the cabin is destroyed. It is. At least, *most* of it is. The only things that seem basically untouched in the entire mess are the couch I laid on all those nights ago and the afghan that Lucas tucked over me. The couch is on its side, the afghan strewn over it, but that's nothing compared to the rest of the place.

There are weapons everywhere. Scattered fluff. Broken pieces of wood that might have been the chair that Lucas sat on. The deer head is still mounted on the wall, but the wolf is on the ground, slashes ripping out the taxidermied fur. Sand is spilled everywhere.

There's blood, too, and that's not even what has me gagging in terror as I stare, frozen in place.

It's the beast.

He's in there.

The beast—

The feral—

The half-wolf, half-human abomination that circled me when I was tied to that tree and howled when he saw I was bleeding—

He's in there, and when his hunched body whips toward me, flexed claws out, his flaccid dick on display, fangs jutting past a muzzle more mangled than I remember, all I can really see are his eyes.

They're amber.

Not orange. Not brown. Not even a red to match the blood smeared over the human parts of his body— blood that has to belong to him because I see gaping wounds from where he must have clawed his flesh apart—but *amber*.

I… I know those eyes. I've been fantasizing about them for two weeks.

Screaming over the noiseless terror in my mind, I have to know: why does the beast have *Lucas's* eyes?

The answer is super fucking simple.

With a groan and a cracking sound that I'll hear in my nightmares for the rest of my life, the beast forces himself into an upright position. As he does, his body gives a violent shake, and as I watch in ill-disguised horror, that broken face becomes one I know intimately well.

Shaky fingers touch my bottom lip as I sob out his name.

"Lucas, no."

Anyone but him. The big, bad wolf in the woods could have been anyone but Lucas, and I would've dealt with it. But it's him, and I don't know what to do until he flings himself to the floor.

That's Lucas on the outside, but whatever made him that… that *thing* is still in control.

He knows it, too. And while his eyes look at me with desperation, he digs his claws into the floor so that he stays where he is.

"Run," he snarls in his own voice before his body lurches and, suddenly, Lucas is that *thing* again.

He rips his claws out of the floor, blood spraying from the force of it, and I know that if I don't do what he says, that thing is going to come after me.

Even if I run, he'll chase. As I slam the door closed, hoping that'll do something to stall him before I take off wildly, I know he'll be coming after me.

Why? Because he's the beast, and I've always been the prey.

Run.

When he doesn't come bursting through the door immediately after I closed it, I thought I might have a chance.

I might be able to get away.

Run.

I fucking run like my life depends on it.

He told me to go. Even if he hadn't given the order, I would have.

I escaped that beast once. The whole time, I thought it was because Lucas was my knight in shining armor, my savior, my *hero*—and, all along, he didn't save me from anything but himself. He must have gotten control over the other side of him the night of the full moon and used it to get close to me.

Well, he couldn't have gotten any closer, could he?

But why? To break the curse?

I have no idea, but I'm not sticking around to find out.

I take it back. I wouldn't mind helping the others,

but they had to know. When Kirk was telling me about the feral in the woods... was that a warning? Or was he trying to get me to feel sympathy knowing that this was inevitable?

And Jade... she fucking knew. She *sent* me to the beast. Secrets, right? It was a secret, sure, but one I would've preferred they took to the grave.

Instead, it's me who might be heading toward an early one.

I run. Keeping the hills at my back, following the Winter Creek when I find it, I run even after I feel like I'm about to drop from exhaustion. The adrenaline keeps me going, my opal slapping me in the chest when I run with a speed I'd never thought myself capable of before.

When the creek widens, I let out a whimper of relief. I'm heading the right way. Come hell or high water, I'm making it to the train platform. If I have to jog down the tracks itself to get out of here—to leave all this supernatural shit behind—I will.

I have to.

Someone's playing with me. Over my panicked breathing and the crunch of the dried-out, fallen foliage beneath my feet, I can hear someone closing in on my heels. I spare one terrified second to look behind me, only telling me something I already knew. Whoever it is, they're on two legs.

It could be that feral version of Lucas.

It could be one of the wolves in their human form. It could be two, if a four-legged wolf is tracking me from another direction.

It could be—

"Fallon! Come to me. I know you're out here. Return to the coven. Return to me. I will protect you!"

Fuck no.

Remy. Unless I'm wrong or my ears are playing a trick on me—*please, please, please let it be a trick*—that's Remy's voice echoing around me. I can't see him, and he could very easily be the man chasing after me, but when his pleas are drowned out by a ferocious howl, I know that there's definitely one of the wolves nearby.

Once upon a time, I would've gone to the protectors to save me from Remy. He was the threat. The danger. But now...

Who is going to protect me from the protectors?

I guess I have to.

It hits me right as I reach the steps that lead to the platform that Fate is a funny thing. It's almost like I was meant to end up in this place. As I'm frantically trying to flee it, at least one of the guys I met upon my arrival is chasing after me. Might even be both.

If that wasn't Lucas howling, it could've been Tristan. Maybe he's here to see me off, too.

And maybe I'm Marilyn freaking Monroe.

I thought I was still on wolf territory, but with Remy shouting for me, at least one wolf—though the frequency of the howls chasing me might mean there are two or three—drowning him out with their baying cries to the dark moon, I remember how they both regarded the train station as theirs.

Neutral territory like the town square, I guess, before forgetting all about it. It doesn't matter why they're here.

It only matters that I get away from all of them.

Flying up the stairs, I need every precious second to spur myself forward. I don't know where exactly the border of the curse is, but I'm willing to bet my life that none of these supes will risk themselves to follow me all the way out of Winter Creek.

I saw what happened to Armand when he left for a quick trip. Hopefully, leaving the cursed town wouldn't be worth it.

I've spent my whole life wanting to be special to someone and losing that when my mom died. I've been chasing that feeling ever since, but I'd gladly give that up forever if I can get free now.

Almost there, Fallon. Almost there...

I reach the rope bridge. The widest part of the Winter Creek rages below me, angry and violent. I can't see the black water beneath the slats under my feet, but I hear it slapping into rocks. Forget going for a swim. If I landed in that river, I don't know if I'd survive it.

I'll have to take the chance. Grabbing the knotted

rope railing with my hand, gripping it tightly as I start across the bridge, I move as quickly as I can.

I had a bit of a lead, but I knew it wouldn't last. I'm barely a third of the way across when the rope bridge bounces.

Another weight has been added to it. Terror flares up in me again.

I glance behind me, but it's still too dark. All I see is a silhouette stepping onto the rope bridge, obviously coming after me.

In my panicked brain, the train platform has been the end goal. If I can reach it, I'll be okay. I'll be safe.

If I don't, I can't imagine what's going to happen to me.

That seals it. It's worth risking a fall to my doom to possibly get across the bridge faster.

"Fallon, no!"

The voice is familiar enough, but the raging water below swallows it up before I can recognize it. Not like I would listen anyway. Whoever it is wants me to stop, and there's no way in hell I'm doing—

That.

I didn't want to stop. I had no intention of doing so, but in a cursed town full of magic users, shapeshifters, and who knows what else, sometimes being a willful human just isn't enough. Especially when there's so much I don't know about being around supes, or what they're capable of.

Like, say, an invisible wall that cuts me off from the rest of the bridge.

That's what it feels like. When I run headlong into an immovable force that crackles the same way it did when I had that momentary electric shock my first day in Winter Creek. Only while that was like touching a battery with a wet finger, slamming into the invisible forcefield now sends such a jolt through me, I go flying.

Falling backward, my back slams down on the bridge. I bounce, a scream tearing from my throat as I lose all sense of where I am in the dark. My entire body has gone numb from the jolt—and maybe the cold—and I can't even right myself.

It's only inevitable that the rope bridge sways and, suddenly, I'm falling.

Good thing that the power of that zap was strong enough that I'm already unconscious before I even hit the Winter Creek below me...

AND... THAT'S IT FOR THE FIRST BOOK IN THE **WOLVES OF WINTER CREEK** trilogy!

Pardon the cliffhanger—or, in this case, bridge*faller*, I guess—but this concludes the first arc in Fallon's journey and this is the perfect place to end it. It was one thing to learn witches and wolf shifters are real, but now she knows that Lucas is the feral beast who Marie tried to sacrifice her to… and the same zap that hit her when she first crossed the bridge into Winter Creek came back with a vengeance as she tried to leave.

Because she can't, and readers—as well as Fallon herself—will understand why in the next book in the series… as well as who jumped into the Winter Creek itself to save her (because I'm not that cruel, I'll tell you this: yes, the mysterious person chasing her might have been after her for his own reasons, but he immediately jumps into the river to pull her out almost as soon as she hits the water).

Of course, that means that Fallon's story is far from over. *Pack* is out now. If you want to continue along with Fallon and Lucas (and the rest of the wolves of Winter Creek), keep scrolling/reading/clicking for more information about this series—and the universe as a whole!

FALLON
AND
LUCAS

WOLVES OF WINTER CREEK

ONCE UPON A TIME... AGAIN.

Since my arrival in Winter Creek, I've learned that witches exist, that monsters lurk in the woods, that a small town can be cursed, and that wolf shifters aren't just real—I've been taken in by a pack of them.

Worse, thanks to the aforementioned curse, I'm stuck here. With a grandmother who tried to sacrifice me to break the curse on Winter Creek, and the realization that I might be one of the only non-supes in town.

And that's not all...

As if finding out that my hero-turned-crush... fling... *something* is actually the same beast that has been treating me like its prey all along isn't bad enough, I feel a bit like a chew toy between Alpha Lucas and the pack Beta, Tristan. Both guys seem to think that I'm meant for their wolf, and while I'm coming to grips with the idea of fated mates and their wolfish instincts, I'm not sure if it's a good idea to get involved with either of them.

Especially since Lucas still has secrets he's continuing to hide, Tristan's loyalty will always be to his pack first—and I'm still an outsider.

At least, I *was*. Now that I know the truth about the supes in Winter Creek—and that a blood ward is keeping me a prisoner here—I'm starting to become more comfortable in the pack house.

Sure, if my grandmother realizes I'm still alive, that'll be a problem. And continuing a relationship with Lucas as he tries to navigate the mating dance and his beast—plus a couple of jealous packmates—isn't the smartest idea, but I can't help myself.

I'm drawn to him, too... until I finally learn the biggest secret he has—and realize that he doesn't just need me to break the curse on him and his pack.

He needs me because, seventy years ago, he lost his mate the night the town was put into stasis—and nearly everyone in Winter Creek is convinced that's *me*.

NEVER HIS MATE

What the fuck is he doing here?

He... he's not supposed to be here. In Charlie's. In Muncie. Anywhere near I am. He's supposed to be in his cabin with his chosen mate, not staring at me as if he can't believe that I'm here, too.

That's all right. I'm probably pulling the same face.

Because I can't. I can't believe it.

Did I think that the whole bar watched when Aleks walked in earlier? That's nothing compared to the reception Ryker gets. Even non-supes can sense that there's something different about this male. Between his Alpha aura, his animal magnetism, and his looks... he's almost as dangerous a lure as Aleks, just not so pretty.

That's one thing I can say about the Mountainside

Alpha. He's not pretty, but hell if he's not still the most alluring male I've ever seen.

He's grown his hair out a little since I saw him last. Instead of being closely cropped against his skull, it's shaggier than I remember, though I haven't forgotten what a nice shade of chocolate-colored brown it is when he isn't chopping it all off. Like his lush lips, it's a small hint of softness on such a hard male.

His jaw. The sharp planes of his cheeks. A straight back that looks like it's made of steel.

And those eyes...

Even from across the bar, I can see the immovable force of his alpha wolf peering out from behind those angry eyes.

I'm not afraid. I'm *not*.

Well. Not of him, at least.

I'm afraid of the way my body immediately betrays me. One peek at him and, if only for a moment, I'm that fifteen-year-old girl again, the one who looked at Ryker and saw her forever. I take his scent into my lungs, my knees going weak, my panties going damp, my heart singing out for its mate.

Only he's not my mate. He can't be.

He rejected me.

So what the *fuck* is he doing here?

I've never heard Charlie's fall so quiet before. A hush, a murmur, a few shocked exhalations when the vampires realize that one of their enemy is walking so boldly among them. It doesn't take long for them to peg Ryker as a shifter, but they can also sense that he's not just *any* shifter. He's an alpha, and not someone to fuck with.

Me? I'm fair game, for the most part; at least in comparison, I am. When it becomes even more obvious that his complete focus is on me, the rest of the bar starts sneaking peeks my way. They're following my lead. And since I'm not about to sacrifice my new life in the vamp town for the sake of Ryker Wolfson, I bring the fakest grin to my face as I can, as if he's just another customer and not the bastard who broke my heart.

"Hi, there. Welcome to Charlie's."

The spell breaks. The humans who don't quite understand what's happening just shrug and go back to their drinks, their food, their company. The vampires watch Ryker from the corner of their eyes, but they leave him alone. They might not know that I'm a shifter, but it's obvious that the dark-haired alpha has come for me. Unless I give them some sign that I need help, they're going to let me take care of it.

Ryker makes a beeline straight for me. As if I expected anything less.

I reach for one of the spare waitress pads Charlie keeps under the bar. Always prepared, he has a bucket of pens and pencils down there, too.

"How're you doing?" After a year working the bar, I

don't need to take down a customer's order. With Ryker, though? I make an exception if only because, if I don't have something to do with my hands, I'm not so sure I can control my claws. "What can I get you?"

He's staring at me. I watch as his nostrils flare, trying to catch my scent, before his rugged features form a deep scowl when his nose fails him.

Thank you, Aleks. It's good to be reassured that his charm and his tea don't just fool vamps. Seems like even the Alpha can't pick up on my scent. Definitely good to know.

I poise the tip of my pencil to the pad. "Well?"

"Aren't you going to say anything?"

His voice is a deep rumble as he continues to stare as if he's thought I've lost my mind or something. Maybe I have. That's as good an explanation as any for how I feel drawn to the prick who cast me aside more than a year ago.

Keep smiling, Gem. "I did. I asked you what your order is."

"Gemma—"

I tap my name tag with the edge of my pencil. "Call me Gem."

He clenches his teeth so tightly, I can see a vein bulging in the side of his neck. It's so big, I decide to name it Duke.

Duke doesn't look happy. Come to think of it, neither does Ryker.

"What?"

His eyes flash. "Don't do this. Not here. Not now. I'm hanging onto my wolf by a thread, *Gemma*. A year. A whole fucking year I've been looking for you and you ask me what I'll have. You. I came here for *you*."

My heart lodges in my throat. Worse, my hand flexes and the pencil snaps into three distinct pieces.

Oh, *hell* no.

After my mate rejected me, I wanted to kill him. Instead, I ran away—which nearly killed *me...*

A year ago, everything was different. I had just left my home, joining the infamous Mountainside Pack. The daughter of an omega wolf, I've always been prized—but just not as prized as I would be if my new packmates found out my secret.

But then my fated mate—Mountainside's Alpha—rejects me in front of his whole pack council and my secret gets out, I realize I only have one option. Going lone wolf is the only choice I've got, and I take it.

Now I live in Muncie, hiding in plain sight. If the wolves ever left the mountains surrounding the city, I'd be in big trouble. Luckily, the truce between the vampires and my people is shaky at best and Muncie? It's total vamp territory. Thanks to my new vamp roomie, I get a pass, and I try to forget all about the call of the wolf. It's tough, though. I... I just can't forget my embarrassment—and my anger—from that night.

And then *he* shows up and my chance at forgetting flies out the damn wind.

Ryker Wolfson. He was supposed to be my fated mate, but he chose his pack over our bond. At least, he did—but now that he knows what I've been hiding, he wants me back.

But doesn't he remember?

I told him I'll never be his mate, and there isn't a single thing he can do to change my mind.

To Ryker, that sounds like a challenge. And if there's one thing I know about wolf shifters, it's that they can never resist a challenge.

Just like I'm finding it more difficult than I should to resist *him*.

---

* ***Never His Mate*** is the first novel in the *Claw and Fang* series. It's a steamy rejected mates shifter romance, and though the hero eventually realizes his mistake, the

fierce, independent heroine isn't the sweet wolf everyone thinks she's supposed to be...

Out now!
Or, if you want to get their whole story in one book?
Never Say Never is available, too.

KEEP IN TOUCH

Stay tuned for what's coming up next! Follow me at any of these places—or sign up for my newsletter—for news, promotions, upcoming releases, and more!

SarahSpadeBooks.com
Sarah's Newsletter
Sarah's Signed Book Store

facebook.com/sarahspadebooks
x.com/stressie
instagram.com/sarahspadebooks
amazon.com/author/sarahspade

ALSO BY SARAH SPADE

Holiday Hunk

Halloween Boo

This Christmas

Auld Lang Mine

I'm With Cupid

Getting Lucky

When Sparks Fly

Holiday Hunk: the Complete Series

Claws and Fangs

Leave Janelle

Never His Mate

Always Her Mate

Forever Mates

Hint of Her Blood

Taste of His Skin

Stay With Me

Never Say Never: Gem & Ryker

Bound by the Moon

Sombra Demons

Drawn to the Demon Duke*

Mated to the Monster

Stolen by the Shadows

Santa Claws

Bonded to the Beast

Fated to the Phantom

Claimed by the Creature

Stolen Mates

The Alpha's Heart*

The Feral's Captive

Chase and the Chains

The Beta's Bride

Wolves of Winter Creek

Prey

Pack

Predator

Protector

Claws Clause

(written as Jessica Lynch)

Mates *free*

Hungry Like a Wolf

Of Mistletoe and Mating

No Way

Season of the Witch

Rogue

Sunglasses at Night

Ain't No Angel

True Angel

Ghost of Jealousy

Night Angel

Broken Wings

Of Santa and Slaying

Lost Angel

Born to Run

Uptown Girl

A Pack of Lies

Here Kitty, Kitty

Ordinance 7304: the Bond Laws (Claws Clause Collection #1)

Living on a Prayer (Claws Clause Collection #2)

Diamonds are a Witch's Best Friend (Claws Clause Collection #3)

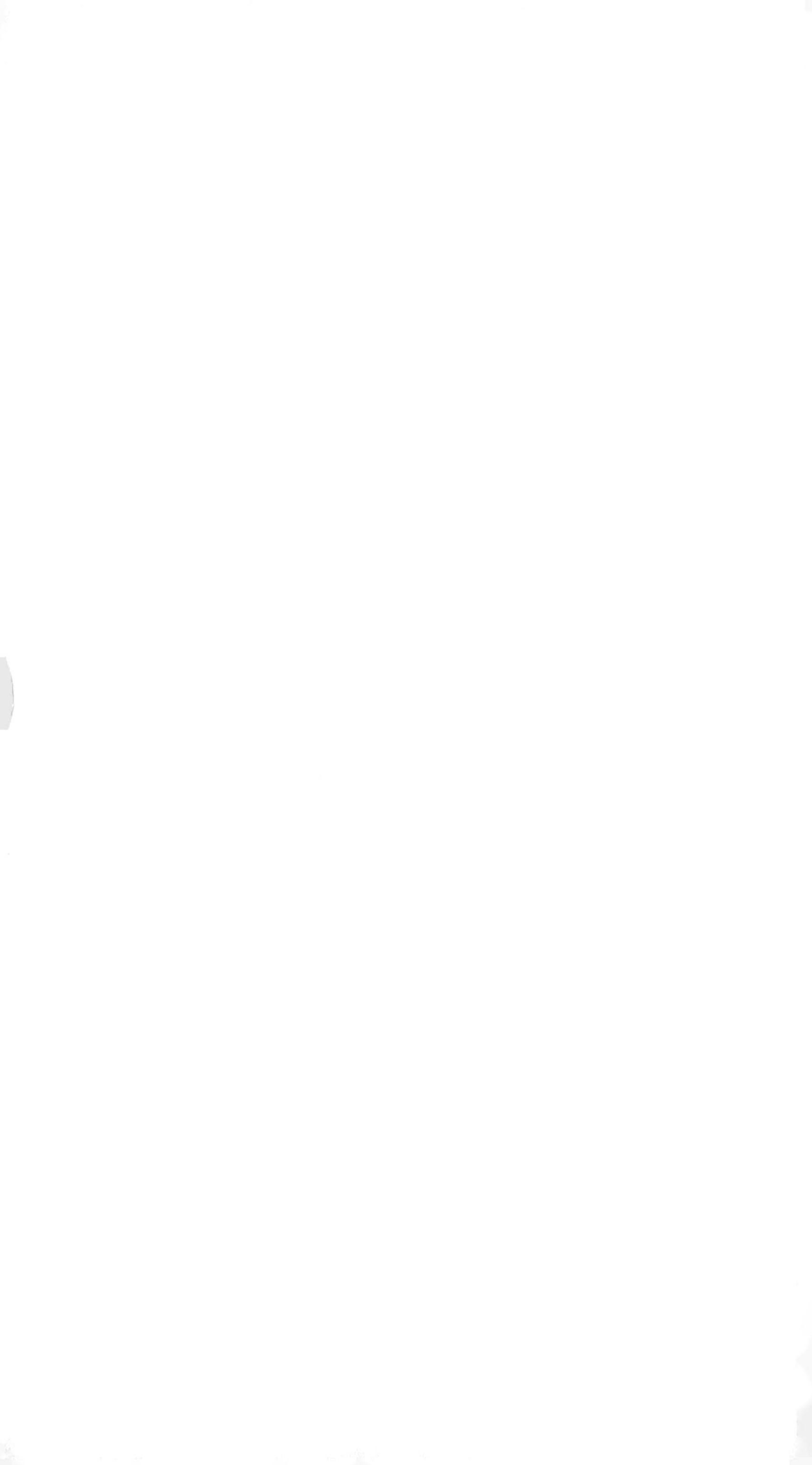